The Magic Lantern

Copyright

This paperback edition is self-published 2024
by Judith Bowers
Utilising an imprint of Jasami Publishing Ltd.
Glasgow, Scotland
https://jasamipublishingltd.com

ISBN 978-1-913798-86-4

Jasami Acknowledgements

The Jasami team is integral to the production of all of our titles. They are talented, creative, and hardworking. Thank you!

Cover Designers

Bebop Moon

Editors

Bailey Caughey

(Mal) Mary Alice Lange

Review Editors

Erin McEntegart

Claire Jack

Acknowledgements

The Magic Lantern, Part One, has been a long journey and I would like to thank all of the people who have supported, helped, and encouraged me on the way.

Especially:

Sylvia Smith at the Mitchell Library

Meredith Joy Robinson and Annie Sanderson for reading the first draft for me.

Bailey & Mal for editing the final draft for me.

Erin & Claire for proofreading the final draft for me.

Michèle Smith at Jasami Publishing & Productions CIC for the flavonoids and formatting.

Bebop Moon for their incredible cover artwork and creating my pre-launch videos.

And you for buying a Limited Edition copy.

Dedication

This book is dedicated to June Marion Bowers,
21/7/1934 - 16/8/2023
my mentor, my motivator, my mother.
Always and forever in my heart.

Table of Contents

Part One

Chapter One

Tam

It was the longest, darkest night of the year and much of the city had already closed doors, lit lamps, and stoked up fires to fend off the bleakness. Only a few brave souls were out wandering the streets. Wind-driven, icy sleet whipping their faces, the biting cold penetrating their clothes. Battling the elements in his third-hand woollen coat was seventeen-year-old Tam Murray and, although he didn't know it at that moment, tonight would be the most significant night of his life - for tonight, he would die.

A fresh blast of bitter wind brought with it what sounded like a woman's high, desperate scream. Tam shivered, his spine tingling. Was it a scream or the howling of the wind? He was just about ready to convince himself it was only the wind when he heard it again - a high, desperate shriek, then silence for a moment, then the scream again - louder, higher, more desperate. It sounded like she was screaming his name. Tam shouted back. "Nellie? NELLIE! Is that you?!"

Nellie was Tam's sweetheart. Every week he was sent to collect the films from St. George's Cross for his employer Mr. Pickard, and every week Tam and Nellie would meet briefly in the street. When they had met earlier that evening, they had kissed and arranged to meet the following night in town. Nellie had returned to her work while Tam continued on his errand. They had only parted a few minutes ago. What could have happened in a few short minutes?

“NELLIE!" he shouted again. On the wind, a man's voice carried back to him one single, terrifying word, "MURDER!"

Tam hefted the sack of film canisters he was carrying further up onto his shoulder, turned on his heel, and jogged in the direction of the cry. The film canisters clanked noisily as he ran.

As he turned up the dark lane, a cloaked figure came hurtling towards him. They collided, falling into a tangle, and in the moonlight glow Tam saw his assailant's blood smeared face - a face he recognised.

"You?" he uttered in surprise. This was the last person he expected to meet in a dark alley.

Tam struggled to his feet but the bloody, cloaked figure had already jumped up and now swung a stick at Tam, hitting him hard enough across the back of his shoulders to knock him down to the cold, wet cobbles.

A set of running footsteps approached, yet through his confusion and pain Tam heard an unfamiliar voice with a strange accent say, "Give me the brooch."

Tam's assailant seemed to freeze at the sound of the stranger's voice and turned to look at the speaker.

"What are you doing here? I told you I would come and see you later this evening. If someone sees us together-" Tam's attacker spat angrily.

The man with the accent laughed, "I have an airtight alibi. Take my word for it. Now give me the brooch." The man commanded and grabbed the cloaked figure's arm, holding it tight while he dipped inside their pocket and pulled out an enormous diamond brooch. Tam had seen it before. Miss Gilchrist always wore it. She said it was a family heirloom, a bit of Victorian paste of no real value. Why would anyone want to murder her for it?

Tam had, for a moment, been forgotten and, even though his shoulders were on fire with pain where the stick had hit him, his fear forced his body into action. He stretched out his arm, reached for his canvas sack, and swung it as he sprang to his feet, striking a lucky nose-breaking blow at one of them. Tam didn't wait to see which; he was already running.

He ran as fast as he could up the dark, narrow lane, burst out onto the gas-lit street beyond, and kept on running. He wasn't sure if he was being chased and didn't dare stop to check. He strained to hear their footsteps pounding the pavement. Instead, all he could hear was the clanking of film canisters in the sack slung over his shoulder. He ran towards the nearest subway station, clattered through the doors, threw a penny at the girl in the ticket office, and danced impatiently from foot to foot as he waited for her to pass him his ticket, which he grabbed, then dashed through the turnstile. He raced down the steps and onto the empty underground platform, panic tightening his chest. If they chased him down here there was no one to help him and nowhere else to run.

Then a sudden rush of stale air from the tunnel told Tam that the train was coming. He glanced back towards the steps. There was no sign of his pursuers. A moment later, the train noisily emerged. Out of breath, with his heart practically pounding out of his chest and looking like the devil was on his heel, he pushed open the first carriage's iron lattice gate and jumped on, pulling it closed behind him.

The electric-lit carriage was a bright contrast to the cold darkness of the gas-lit streets above. As the underground train slowly jerked into action and trundled into the tunnel, Tam slumped onto a bench, every muscle in his body quivering like jelly.

The train carriage was furnished with two long, wooden benches that ran the whole length on either side. Tam shared his bench with a young couple who sat cuddled together at the far end, too caught up in each other to notice the new passenger. An older couple sat primly in the middle of the bench opposite. The woman stared suspiciously at Tam, who was still clutching the sack of films as if his life depended on them. He realised he probably looked like a fleeing burglar gripping a bag full of stolen swag, or something equally suspicious. *Well,* Tam thought, *she can think what she likes.* He stared straight ahead at the window which reflected his own pale, dishevelled image; that of a wet, cold, bedraggled, and scared boy. He certainly wasn't the brave hero he had imagined himself to be, if ever he was tested. When his Nellie had needed him most, he had turned and run. But it couldn't have been

Nellie they had murdered. They had old Miss Gilchrist's brooch.

Nellie was Miss Gilchrist's maid. She had been out buying the old lady's evening paper when they had met barely fifteen minutes earlier. Had Nellie returned from her errand to discover the old lady's murdered body? Is that why she had screamed? He silently prayed that she was alright. When he got back to work, he would go to Mr Pickard's office and ask him to telephone the police.

Tam worked at the Panopticon, a music hall and funhouse on the Trongate in Glasgow, which boasted everything from variety acts and the latest moving pictures, to an attic carnival and basement zoo. He didn't have any specific duties. He had only started working there a few months earlier, but it was his dream to become a moving picture projectionist. Tam loved the flickers and Mr Pickard, the manager, had promised him that he would eventually be trained to use the cinematograph projector. First, however, he had to serve his time as a general hand, doing whatever needed to be done, from picking up the films from St George's Cross to sweeping up manure in the basement zoo. But tonight, Mr. Pickard was putting him in charge of the magic lantern; an old-fashioned glass-slide projector which old Mr. Hill, the Panopticon handyman, had recently converted to electricity.

It was a metal box with a brass-encased lens jutting out from the front. It looked like the ancestor of the modern cinematograph, and tonight Tam's job would be to use the magic lantern to project advertising slides between the variety acts. It was up to Tam to make sure that each slide was clearly in focus on the screen and that they were shown the right way round. It wasn't exactly the flickers, but it was a damn sight closer than mucking out the monkey house.

By the time he got back to the Trongate, the front doors of the Panopticon were already open and the crowd was pouring in for the 7:30 p.m. show. Tam could see a small gang of boys pushing their way through, his wee brother Bobby carried along in the torrent with them, but he couldn't see his other brother Jamie, though he surely wouldn't be far behind.

The force of the crowd was too strong a tide for Tam to fight through, especially with the bulky sack of film canisters, so he made his way up a dirty, manure-strewn alley to the stage door. He thumped at the door with his fist and a grumbling man in a flat cap with the stub of a cigarette poking through his ginger moustache opened it.

"You're late," he growled.

Tam ignored him and sprinted up the back stairs, the canisters clanging and battering against his back, shoved open the heavy door at the top and entered the clamour beyond.

The stalls were a riot of noise as people battled for a space on the hard wooden benches or fought for a spot to stand at the sides or the back. Tam forced his way through the throng to the doors at the back of the stalls which people were still flooding through. He pushed his way against the tide and out into the foyer, turned right, and slowly made his way through the jostling crowd up the stairs to the balcony. There he slipped into the projection room, where he dropped off the sack of films with the projectionist Mr. Richards, then he pushed his way back down through the stall's foyer to Mr. Pickard's office. He knocked on the door and waited, listening for signs of life. No one answered. He knocked again.

"He's gone out," said a voice at his shoulder. It was George Saprini, the stage manager.

"What happened to you?" he asked as he eyed the boy's dishevelled appearance.

"I've just…I've been…look; I think there's been a murder. I need to telephone the police. Mr. Saprini, please let me into Mr. Pickard's office."

"Not a chance of it."

"But it's important! I think there really has been a murder, Mr Saprini - old Miss..."

"Did you see a body?"

"No, but there was a scream and..."

"So you didn't see a body?"

"No sir, but..."

"So you haven't actually seen a murder, lad?"

"No, but..."

"No but, nothing," Mr. Saprini interrupted impatiently as he glimpsed at the time on his pocket watch. Everything was running late tonight and he didn't have time to listen to this lad's fanciful excuses.

"Get to your job, lad, or you'll be seeing Mr. Pickard to get the sack."

"But, Mr. Saprini..." Tam began.

But Mr. Saprini had no time to listen to another word and was already gone, swallowed by the crowd.

"Mr. Saprini, I think an old lady's been murdered! I saw the murderer covered in blood..." Tam called after him, but his voice was lost in the melee.

Tam forced his way through the excited crowd to where the magic lantern stood. It was on a slightly raised platform at the back of the stalls. A group of men in cloth caps and woollen jackets already crammed the platform, puffing away on Woodbine cigarettes.

"Gonnae move!" he shouted at them above the sound of the band, which had suddenly begun playing a rousing and very loud overture. The men moved enough to allow Tam to squeeze past. He got into position behind the magic lantern and began readying it for the first advertisement of the evening.

He barely noticed the first two acts as he fiddled with the newly installed electric light bulb, making sure it was securely in place and checking the wires were nice and tightly screwed in, desperately trying to focus on his job whilst his mind raced with worry about Nellie and his own terrifying escape from his would-be murderers.

The third act, a group of high-kicking dancing girls, were just finishing their routine to rousing approval from the audience when Tam finally looked up from his task. As the dancers left the stage in a flurry of colourful petticoats, a screen tumbled into place and Tam switched on the magic lantern. The electric bulb flared brightly into life, cutting a brilliant tunnel of light through the thick, tarry darkness of the smoky auditorium. He peered through the smoke at the screen to make sure the image was in focus. Tam knew it showed an advertisement for the next week's shows but he didn't really see it. No matter how hard he tried to concentrate, all he could see was the blood-smeared face, bloody hands, and murderous looks of his attackers in the lane. His head pulsated painfully with the memory as he fumbled in the dimness to change the glass slide. His palms were sweating and he nearly dropped the fragile square. *I should just go to the police now*, he thought. *I should've run straight to them instead of coming back here.*

He slid the next advertisement into place, a colourful picture of a lady in an apron pointing to a blackboard with the words: Go early to bed, drink Camp when you rise, and you will be Healthy, Wealthy, and Wise. After staring at it for a few seconds he pulled out the advertisement and turned the magic lantern off. As the screen rolled back up and disappeared above the proscenium arch, the next act was introduced. The audience roared their approval as a funny little chap with rosy nose and cheeks, wearing a ridiculously long kilt and over-sized sporran, stepped onto the stage and began a comic routine.

Tam scanned the packed music hall, watching the people laughing and shouting at the comic. Old men bared toothless gums as they cackled; mothers rocked with laughter, their babies wrapped in woollen shawls; young men guffawed, and their young ladies giggled. His eyes wandered up to the balcony above where he could see the gang of boys he had watched enter the Panopticon earlier that evening. They were leaning over the front of the balcony, which swept around the edge of the music hall. Tam peered through the smoky tendrils that hung low like a cloud. He could see his brother Jamie had joined them.

A few short years ago, he himself had been up in the balcony enjoying the freedom of naughty boyhood. Other things occupied him now, though. His gaze returned to the stage then out of the corner of his eye, he saw them; his attacker from the lane and the man with the accent.

The feeling of panic which he had been trying to suppress began to rise again as he saw their faces bobbing amongst the throng. There was menace in their eyes which cut through the dimness, hitting Tam square in the chest. Surely, he was safe here among all these people? He reasoned with himself; but as the crowd seemed to part for them, Tam felt his panic become pure terror. Within moments, his attackers stepped up onto his little platform at the back of the stalls and flanked him. Nothing was said as Tam looked from one to the other, the fear shining in his eyes. Heckling and laughter filled his ears. He cried out for help, but the yell was drowned in the joyous shouts and cheers of the crowd. Then he felt a sudden pain in his left side as if someone had punched him.

Tam looked down and saw a sharp blade glint and drip with blood. His blood? It must be. His hand found the wound and came up wet. He looked into the faces of his murderers, for he was sure now that he was dying. They were laughing heartily with the rest of the crowd, the cloaked figure casually wiping Tam's blood off the knife with a delicate handkerchief on which Tam could see the embroidered initials A.B. He still could not believe that this person, whom he had thought to be good and kind, could in fact be so deadly. The tears wet his pale cheeks as he felt his life ebb away. Then the world went black.

Chapter Two

A Strange Boy Appears

Jamie Murray - newsboy, messenger, and scourge of all truancy officers - was running late. The music hall show had already begun, but he had been held up in Noah's Ark, the Panopticon's basement zoo, where, whilst looking for his brother, Tam (who also seemed to be running late), had become the latest victim of the Panopticon's Phantom Pickpocket.

The pickpocket had for several weeks avoided capture and dozens of visitors had lost their wallets, watches and all manner of other objects. Jamie and his gang had been trying to catch the thief. He hadn't expected to be the next target, and a whole penny bag of sweets stolen at that! It was a most heinous crime. He retraced his steps in his mind. He had bought the sweets from the shop on the corner just before coming in. He had pushed his way through the crowd in the lane and down the spiral stairs that led to the zoo. Then he made his way through the Aviary, the hall of mirrors, and past the bear and baboon cages, before heading to Tam's room behind the monkey house. When he realised his brother wasn't in, he had reached into his pocket for his sweets and that's when he had made his horrifying discovery - they were gone! He could have only lost them either when he was making his way through the queue to Noah's Ark or in the zoo itself.

For half an hour he scoured the basement looking for suspicious characters, but all he could see were giggling girls, babbling boys, and courting couples, gawping and gasping at the exhibits, and now he was late for the music hall show.

He gave up his hunt, conceding to the fact that he would never see his precious sweets again. Jamie despondently climbed the three flights of stairs that led to the balcony, half-heartedly hailing Flora, the usherette, on his way past. He battered his way through the balcony doors and pushed through the jostle of men who crammed the back of the balcony, smoking and laughing with over-rouged ladies in large, feathered hats. He squeezed past the seated rows of courting couples and gallus gangs of other boys, then finally made his way down six wooden steps to join his friends at the very front, which slightly over-hung the stage.

This was a favourite spot coveted by all the regular boys at the Panopticon. From here they had a bird's eye view of the stage, which allowed them to see the trick behind most magicians' illusions, and to look down the tops of the dancing girls. But best of all, they could wee over the edge onto any act on the stage below that didn't meet with their approval. Jamie and his gang were the current, undefeated rulers of this prized corner, their subordinates consigned to less advantageous viewpoints, from which they resorted to throwing horse manure instead. The act on stage just now was a troupe of dancing girls and therefore safe from any kind of deluge.

After the dancing girls had whirled and cartwheeled off the stage, a screen came down and an advert for next week's shows appeared. Jamie glanced down to the stalls beneath and along to the back where he could see his big brother, Tam, standing next to the magic lantern on a platform which elevated him enough for his head to be above the rest of the crowd. The noise of the rowdy audience lowered to a steady hum of chatter for a few moments, then Tam turned the projector off and a comedian, who was introduced as "Jack McCormick, the Funny Chap" bounced onto the stage.

Comedians were the favourite sport of the boys in the balcony. Rotten jokes were regarded as fair game, and it wasn't just the boys who would physically demonstrate their disapproval. Everyone joined in for a good pelting, throwing all sorts of rubbish, from whelk shells to solid steel shipyard rivets. Comics had to learn to move fast on the stage. Jack McCormick, the Funny Chap, however, lived up to his introduction and the hall rang with raucous laughter. His routine ended without a single projectile being thrown.

As he stepped off the stage, the music hall chairman announced the next act.

"And now, for a very late edition to the bill, we have a debut performance from our youngest turn tonight. The boy comic, Mack Millan."

No one stepped onto the stage for a moment, leaving the audience to stare expectantly at the empty boards. Then suddenly, a ragged lad was shoved on. He looked younger than Jamie and as the boy comic stood trembling in the spotlight, it quickly became apparent to all assembled that this timid, young comedian was likely to receive the first pelting of the night. In fact, the audience seemed to be limbering up as they began a slow, rhythmic stamping of impatience.

"Go on," someone shouted from the side of the stage. "Before they turn against you."

Thump-thump-thump-thump - went the feet of the audience on the wooden floor, and the boy just looked more terrified. Thump-thump-thump-thump. The boy, sensing that the audience was about to turn nasty, suddenly puffed out his chest and, taking a deep breath, bellowed as loud as he could, "What did the stamp say to the envelope?"

The thumping stopped and a cavernous silence replaced it as the audience waited for the punch line. "Stick with me and we'll go places."

It wasn't worth waiting for, and a cacophony of boos and jeers rang around the music hall as the audience voiced its displeasure. Jamie in the balcony above decided that the time had come to use his position at the front to its best advantage. He unbuttoned his fly and made ready to urinate over the edge and onto the young comedian below, but at that exact moment a very strange thing happened. The magic lantern suddenly switched back on, the beam's sudden appearance made the boy comic vanish from the stage and as one boy disappeared, another boy mysteriously appeared, as if projected there by the magic lantern. However, it was not a picture, it was an actual, real, live, flesh-and-blood boy who had fallen flat on his face in the barrage of muck and rubbish intended for Mack Millan. Everyone stared at the boy; the over-rouged ladies in huge, feathered hats; the cloth-capped, Woodbine-smoking men; the courting couples and gallus gangs; the nursing mothers and toothless old folk. From stalls to balcony, all were stunned by the sudden appearance of an odd-looking boy with huge, hairy feet and peculiar costume, who struggled to stand up and for a moment looked around, bewildered, as if he had no idea what he was doing on the stage, before being simultaneously splashed by Jamie's wee and hit by a metal screw square on the forehead.

Chapter Three

A 21st-Century Ghost Hunt

It was the 2nd of November, and an early snow had left a thin carpet of white that sparkled in the light of the street lamps and crunched crisply under Sandy's furry snow boots. She trudged down the road, bundled up against the cold in a woolly bobble hat, scarf and gloves (all knitted by her gran), snow boots and a puffer coat that was so big it practically drowned her. A short distance behind her, Sandy's mother cautiously picked her way along the slippery pavement in high heels - her mother always wore high heels.

"Come on, Mum, I don't want to be late," Sandy called over her shoulder.

"I'm going as fast as I can, sweetie. I don't want to slip and break something, do I? They'll wait for you," her mother called back.

It was 10:00 p.m. and usually Sandy would be going to bed at this time; but tonight she was going to join some of her classmates for a sponsored ghost hunt in an old theatre in the city centre - that's if they make it to school before the bus leaves.

A little thrill of excitement flooded through her as she thought about the night ahead. She and her friends had been planning ways to scare some of the other kids in their class, so her school bag had been emptied of books and pens and filled with snacks and a gruesome collection of grizzly Halloween jokes that they had bought from Tam Shepherd's Magic and Joke Shop. She couldn't help but have a little giggle to herself as she thought about the plastic spiders, severed fingers, glow-in-the-dark skull and eyeballs they had bought. They would certainly get that snotty cow, Charmaine, screaming the place down.

She looked back over her shoulder. Her mum was getting farther behind, hanging on to railings, hedges, and lampposts. They were never going to get there at this rate. If only her mum hadn't dumped Mike, he could have driven them there.

"Mum, for God's sakes hurry up, I'm not going to miss this just 'cos you won't wear proper boots!"

"You're not going to miss the bus, darling. They've got to come past this way anyhow, so even if we're late I'm sure they'll pick us up on the way by."

Sandy's mum had taken time off work so she could be a chaperone on the ghost hunt. She worked night shifts and was used to being nocturnal, but that was not the reason she had decided to join Sandy that evening. Nor was it to keep her daughter company. Sandy had no illusions about that. Her mum seldom chose to hang out with her if there was another option available. No, Sandy's mum offered to be a chaperone because she had found out that Sandy's history teacher Mr Oakley was going and her mum had a big crush on him - hence the ridiculous high heels. There was no way her mother was going to let a man she fancied see her in a pair of clunky, dirty snow boots.

The school was only a few minutes' walk away and they were supposed to be there at 10:00 p.m. It was now five minutes past, so Sandy decided to leave her mother behind. She marched on through the snow, breathing out thick plumes of steam as she muttered impatiently under her breath.

Five minutes later, she walked through the school gates, her mother slipping and sliding along soon after. Sandy thought her mum looked ridiculous in her fake leopard fur coat, short skirt, and high heels, but judging by the expression on her history teacher's face, he didn't agree. Great, Sandy thought to herself, *now she's going to start going out with one of my teachers. Awkward!*

Her mother was great at getting boyfriends but rubbish at keeping them. It always started off well and then her mum would begin to find faults with them. Larry was too clingy. John worked too much. James smoked too much. Harry moaned too much. Gordon smelt funny. Jamie didn't dress in the right clothes. Gary volunteered for a charity and was too poor. Steve couldn't drive. And now there was Mike, the latest in this long list. But he lived too far away, and her mum complained that she needed somebody every day, not just two weekends a month. Sandy wondered what fault her mother would eventually dump Mr Oakley for. It would probably be because he wore glasses, was too intelligent, or smelt of books.

Mr Oakley walked towards Sandy. "Hi, Sandy," then looked past her towards her mother in the distance who was struggling up the path towards them. Mr Oakley quickly dashed to her aid. "Ah, so glad you could make it, Mrs McMillan," offering Sandy's mum a strong arm to lean on.

Sandy winced as she realised she wasn't the only one witnessing the mortifying display her mother and history teacher were making. As her mum clung on to his arm and every word he uttered, the two girls Sandy hated most in school, Chelsea and Charmaine, were holding on to each other's arms, looking into each other's eyes and mimicking the scene. It was embarrassing.

"Oh, Mrs McMillan, you look so lovely in your little booties," Charmaine simpered.

"Oh, Mr Oakley, you're so big and strong," cooed Chelsea, in what Sandy thought was an impressive imitation of her mother.

Yeah, laugh it up, girls. I'll get my revenge later, she thought.

Sandy stepped onto the bus and made her way past the already-seated rabble. Chelsea stuck her foot out and Sandy tripped but didn't fall.

"Oh sorry, Ant. I didn't see you there," she said with mock sympathy before she and Charmaine erupted with laughter.

Ant was what most of her schoolmates called her. She was the smallest in her class, even smaller than the smallest first year. It was infuriating, people treating her like a six-year-old when she was thirteen and probably the smartest in her whole year. Small was a family trait. Her mum was only 4' 11" and always wore heels - even her slippers had three-inch heels.

Finally, Sandy made it to the back where her best friends, Lucy and Michelle, sat. Once everyone was settled and Mr Oakley had read the riot act (don't touch anything, don't steal anything, don't set fire to anything, don't be cheeky...remember you are representing the school. Blah, blah, blah), the bus pulled away, drove out of the school gates, and began the twenty-minute journey to the city centre where the old, haunted theatre waited with the promise of a terrifying night.

Just after 10:30 p.m., the bus pulled up and parked in front of a four-storey Victorian building which glowed in the light of two large lamps that flanked either side of the enormous front doors. Above the doors, a sign in gold letters read Britannia. Sixteen school children, two teachers and four parent chaperones stepped off the bus and stood huddled together in the bitter November evening.

"I don't see any kind of doorbell. How are we supposed to let anyone know we're here?" Mrs Ridgley, the drama teacher, questioned.

"Mr Oakley, sir, I don't think it's open," one of the boys from Sandy's class piped up.

"That's because we're not entering this way. Follow me," Mr Oakley, tried his best to sound mysterious. Sandy just felt more embarrassed, watching her mum cling to his arm as he trudged to the corner of the building and disappeared into an alleyway.

The children followed their teacher up the alley to a set of open fire doors which spilled golden light onto the white snow. A night watchman sat just inside the doors watching Coronation Street on a laptop. He didn't look up.

"Ahem." Mr Oakley cleared his throat in an effort to get the guard's attention. It worked. The night watchman pressed pause.

"You must be the school party," he uttered, almost accusingly, and plucked a clipboard from a hook on the wall behind him. "Thornliebank High School. Mr Oakley, Miss Ridgely..."

"Mrs Ridgley," the drama teacher corrected. The guard drew her a look.

"Mrs Ridgley," he corrected, "four adult chaperones and sixteen children."

"Yep, that's us." Mr Oakley cheerfully responded to the grumpy night watchman's roll call.

"Go on up," the night watchman said as he placed the clipboard back on its hook and resumed watching his programme. "And don't touch anything!" he snapped, as they traipsed noisily in, stamping the snow from their boots.

Chattering excitedly, they followed each other, one by one, up the ancient spiral stone staircase. When they reached the top, the excited babble suddenly stopped. It was as if a cold hand had grasped the spine of every child, parent, and teacher. The hairs stood up on the back of every scarf-wrapped neck and they held their breaths in anticipation. What lay beyond the set of modern fire doors?

Mr Oakley pulled open the double doors, slowly and dramatically. They creaked eerily, and Sandy heard one of the girls squeal a little. She couldn't tell but she hoped it was Charmaine. Hanging on to each other in pairs, the boys, girls, teachers, and parents cautiously entered the old music hall. Once inside, they gasped in astonishment - it was as if they had literally stepped back in time.

The empty auditorium looked like it had been abandoned years ago and left to decay. Dirty, stained yellow and brown paint was peeling in one corner of the high half-vaulted ceiling, revealing another layer of decoration beneath; one of dark blue, speckled with gold stars like the night sky. Plaster had crumbled away in parts and exposed lathe bones beneath. The floorboards creaked with every step and, above them, a balcony curved in a horseshoe shape around three sides of the auditorium, with the ends of the horseshoe touching either side of the old proscenium arch that had once framed the acts on the stage below. The edge of the auditorium was lined with glass cabinets full of artefacts and, in headless lines, stood various mannequins in different styles of Victorian and Edwardian costume.

It smelt of ancient dust, was freezing cold, and was full of dark corners and gloomy shadows. To add to the atmosphere, as if it needed to be added to, the wind had suddenly picked up outside and now howled around the high arched windows, rattling the windowpanes, and echoing through the hall like a moaning phantom. It was certainly fulfilling its spooky reputation.

As they all filed through the doors, they were too busy looking around in bewilderment to notice the figure leaning against a piano in front of the stage, watching the group through round wire-framed spectacles. He was a very old-fashioned looking gentleman in a tweed three-piece suit with a waxed moustache twisted into upturned points at the end, and he wore a bowler hat. Mr Oakley was the first to see him and nearly jumped out of his skin when the man moved. He had thought it was just another costumed dummy. The squealing girl squealed again, obviously having thought the same as her teacher. This time, Sandy saw with some satisfaction that it was Charmaine. The costumed man chuckled, took off his bowler hat - which he placed on top of the piano - and stepped towards the startled teacher.

"You must be Mr Oakley," said the man, grabbing the teacher's right hand and shaking it vigorously with both of his. "I'm Albert, the night curator."

"Oh, h-hello, you t-took me a bit by surprise. I thought you w-were a g-g-ghost there for a moment," he stuttered nervously. "Thanks for letting us c-c-come in like th-this."

"Not at all, Mr Oakley, not at all. Visitors are always welcome and the ghosts here like a bit of fun. Though I warn you now, they never do quite as you expect them to," said Albert with a slightly devious smile. "Come in, come in..." he said, beckoning the group who had stopped at the door. "Take a seat, make yourselves comfortable, and I'll tell you a little bit about them."

The sound of creaking chairs filled the old auditorium as the party of ghost hunters settled themselves into the hard, plastic seats and politely focused their attention on Albert, who now stood on the stage.

"Originally, this old theatre was called The Britannia Music Hall when it first opened in the late 1850s, but in the early 20th century it was renamed The Panopticon," he began, "and it is the oldest surviving music hall in the world. It entertained the poorest people of Glasgow for nearly eighty years before the doors were finally closed in 1938 and the auditorium left empty - save for the ghosts."

One of the boys at the back of the group made a "Woooooooh!" noise, imitating the sound of a ghost.

"Shut up, Sanj." Mr Oakley snapped over his shoulder.

The class settled back down and continued to listen, trying to ignore the cold as Albert described what the music hall was like in the Victorian days. How boys used to wee over the front of the balcony onto the act on stage below, how people would throw all sorts of rubbish including horse manure and fish heads at acts they didn't like. He told them about some of the different acts that had performed there - actors, singers, comedians, magicians, athletes, acrobats, contortionists, ventriloquists, and animal acts. There had even been a Flatulist, who played tunes with his bottom. The whole class had laughed at this, except Charmaine who proclaimed it "Gross."

Albert described the entertainments as a "veritable cornucopia of the most popular acts of the time." He told them that in the Victorian Days, the music hall had even more entertainments in other parts of the building.

"In the early twentieth century, Mr Pickard, who was a showman, converted the attic above us into a rooftop carnival with all the latest amusements of the day - aunt sallies, coconut shies, rifle ranges and automatons. Wax work figures of the most famous people of the time were dotted around the place. But, most popular of all, the attic also accommodated a freak show. All sorts of strange wonders were exhibited upstairs, including the world's tallest man and shortest man, the world's fattest woman, a leprechaun and even a human spider." Albert paused and looked up at the ceiling above him. "And Mr Pickard didn't stop at the attic. He also converted the basement into a zoo, with twenty-nine cages of birds, monkeys, bears, reptiles and all manner of exotic beasts..."

Sandy couldn't help but feel sorry for the poor animals. She hated zoos and the thought of keeping a bear in a basement was just horrible.

"It was because of all of these entertainments that Mr Pickard renamed the building the Panopticon. It comes from the Greek Pan, meaning everything, and Opti, meaning to see - and you could see everything from the attic to the basement for just one ticket price. It was the amusement park of its day."

Then he started talking about the ghosts. The sixteen children, two teachers, and four parents suddenly leaned forward in their creaky seats, hanging on to every Albert's every word.

"There are many ghosts in this old theatre. I certainly never feel alone..." he quipped, and lowering his voice, he continued, "when it's quiet, that's when this building really seems to come to life. The piano plays itself, the keys pressed by invisible fingers. Sometimes the sound of children laughing, or of a man whistling, drifts across the auditorium. Occasionally, I see the figure of a lady in a long, black Victorian dress walking past the doors up there…" Albert pointed up to the balcony and all eyes followed.

"We think it's the ghost of Mrs Rossborough, who ran the Britannia after her husband died." Albert peered into the gloom above. "I feel her watching me as if she is still inspecting that all is in order and to her satisfaction. I would hate to think what would happen if it wasn't to her satisfaction," he declared ominously, pausing for dramatic effect. Then, in a more cheerful tone he continued. "A soldier is often seen sitting in the balcony, especially when a beautiful young lady is on the stage. But the most frequently encountered ghost is a Chimpanzee called Solomon. He likes to move things around, especially props and clothing. One minute it's there and the next moment it's vanished. He has been heard in the basement chattering away and has even been recorded by a TV crew when they were filming a documentary about haunted buildings a few years ago. Back in his day, Solomon, known as Darwin's Missing Link, was the most popular attraction in the basement zoo where he shared a cage with his wife, Betsy." The school party chuckled at the thought of a chimp being married. "Yes, he was married, and he and Betsy both seemed to think they were human. They would only be seen in public if they were fully dressed and Betsy, apparently, was very flirtatious with men."

The group laughed a little at this before Albert continued in a more serious tone. "But today has seen the most unusual and inexplicable event of all, as it seems we have truly received a message from beyond the grave."

Albert stepped down off the stage and walked briskly up the aisle that ran through the middle of the chairs to the back of the music hall where a cloth-covered object stood on a table. With a dramatic flourish, he pulled off the cloth and revealed what looked like an oversized, old-fashioned camera.

"This is a magic lantern," Albert explained. "Before the cinema experience that we know today, people watched magic lantern shows where stories were related through pictures painted or printed onto glass slides and then projected onto screens. This magic lantern belonged to none other than the famous author of Sherlock Holmes, Sir Arthur Conan Doyle. Not only that, but Sir Arthur Conan Doyle left it to the Britannia Panopticon in his will. "The little audience didn't seem at all amazed by this revelation. Albert, perhaps reading their minds or perhaps discouraged by their tepid response, continued, "so you're thinking, ok, great, you've got Conan Doyle's magic lantern, what's so spooky about that? Well, consider this; Sir Arthur Conan Doyle died in 1930. However, this magic lantern was only delivered here today by a firm of solicitors, only an hour or so before you arrived. With it was this note." Albert pulled an age-yellowed envelope from the interior pocket of his jacket, pushed his spectacles up his nose, unfolded the letter and read:

July 7th, 1916

Dear Sir,

You will think this an odd sort of bequest, but I can assure you that this is no ordinary projector. It is imperative that this magic lantern be used on the night of the 2nd of

November 2016, when children from Thornliebank High School will be carrying out a ghost hunt in the Panopticon music hall. I cannot explain why, but it is vital that this wish be fulfilled. The future of us all depends upon it. I beg you not to take this request as a hoax, and leave it in your trust to ensure that my final wish is granted.

Yours Sincerely,
Arthur Conan Doyle

Albert pulled off his glasses and looked at the group of bewildered faces in front of him.

"What's he talking about?" whispered Sandy, who had been updating her status as 'Ghost hunting in an old theatre' and hadn't been listening.

"Arthur Conan Doyle left the magic lantern thing in his will; and it has to be used tonight or the world will end or something. Now put your phone away," her mother whispered back.

The old man raised an eyebrow in the direction of Sandy and her mother before continuing. "Well, I suggest we carry out his last wishes. What do you say?"

A wave of noisy chatter rippled amongst the children and adults.

Sandy, who was sitting in front of her mother and teacher, overheard Mr Oakley whispering. "Clever, a message from beyond the grave - nice way to set the tone for our ghost hunt. Great way to engage the children."

"Oh yes, great idea," she heard her mother reply in her 'I have-no-idea-what-you-are-talking-about' voice.

"Perhaps before I switch the magic lantern on," Albert paused, "I should tell you that these projectors were originally used to project ghosts to terrify the audience. They were known as Lanterns of Terror." He paused again. "Well, shall we see if it works?" The children and adults nodded in unison.

He switched on the magic lantern and a beam of light hit the screen. Albert slid a wooden frame out from behind the lens and slotted in a square of painted glass.

"This selection of magic lantern slides is called 'The Haunted House.' A suitable subject, I think, for tonight's entertainment." A picture of an old mansion at night appeared. He showed slide after slide of the inside of the old, haunted house, with ghostly figures standing on stairs, peeking through curtains, staring out from behind windows and appearing in the face of a large mantle clock. It wasn't the thrillingly spooktacular show they were expecting after the strange and intriguing way the magic lantern had been introduced; in fact, Sandy thought it was rather dull and had found herself nodding off a couple of times.

"Lantern of Terror? More like Lantern of Snorer," Sandy muttered to Michelle. *Perhaps people had been more easily frightened in the olden days,* Sandy thought.

When the magic lantern show was finished, the children split into small, jabbering groups which disappeared into different spaces around the building, eager to explore every dark nook and cranny for ghosts.

Sandy, Lucy, and Michelle climbed the stairs to the attic to seek out the best places to hide their gruesome collection of pocket money surprises.

They spent the next hour hiding their spiders, glowing eyeballs, and severed fingers before deciding to find a space to sit and wait for the screaming to begin. They went back down to the auditorium and, after selecting a spot in front of the stage, near the old allegedly haunted piano, they crawled into their sleeping bags. Still dressed in their coats, boots and hats for warmth, they began their ghost vigil.

For a while they entertained themselves by making up their own ghost stories and trying to make each other jump. When they had run out of ghost stories they began to tell bad jokes instead and, when the jokes were exhausted and still no ghosts had appeared, they just talked, scrolled through their phones, and ate their snacks. Then one by one they nodded off to sleep. Throughout the building, the giggling and whispered conversations were gradually replaced by snoring. There had been no screaming from anywhere. It seemed nobody had been surprised by their hidden horrors and no ghosts had appeared to frighten them.

Sandy was in the middle of a rather satisfying dream in which Charmaine was being chased by an army of glowing plastic skeletons when something woke her up. She opened her eyes and instantly closed them again against an intensely bright white glare which seemed to envelop her. Shielding her eyes with her hand she squinted into the light. What is that? Where is it coming from? Is it coming from that old magic lantern? Had one of her classmates switched it back on for a laugh?

"Turn it off!" she yelled as she struggled out of her sleeping bag.

She stood up and instantly felt dizzy. The music hall began to wobble, bend, and distort, as if she were looking at it through a heat haze. The blood rushed through her ears. Everything was muffled except for the sound of her own breathing, which seemed very loud. It was like her head was under water. All the strength left her. Her legs buckled and she felt herself fall with a sickening jolt as though a trap door had suddenly opened beneath her. Had she fallen through a hole in the old theatre's floor? She seemed to plummet through what felt like an endless pit filled with the magic lantern's blinding white light. Sandy flailed her arms as she desperately reached out, grasping at the air, trying to find something to grab and hold on to; but there was nothing.

This is how Alice must have felt when she fell down the rabbit hole, she thought as she kept on falling, on and on through the light, wondering when she would hit the ground. Then suddenly her face abruptly, and quite painfully, found the floor as she landed with a thud.

Something warm and wet splashed her left cheek, while her right cheek was pressed into something squidgy, slightly sticky, and indescribably smelly - in fact, her nostrils were suddenly assaulted by a rush of smells. Stench would be a better way to describe it. She had never smelt anything as horrible as this - the stink of dirt, pungent body odour, a pong like rotting fish, the reek of wee, the unmistakable tang of farmyard manure, and an undertone of stale beer mingled with thick, tarry tobacco smoke, which was so dense it hung in the air like a curtain of foul, stinking blue fog.

Whilst her nose was filled with smells so disgusting they made her gag, her ears were deafened by the roar of a thousand voices yelling and laughing, and the thunderous sound of applause and stamping feet. She struggled to get up, still shielding her eyes from the bright light. Was it still the glare of the magic lantern? Then a hard object hit her squarely in the middle of her forehead and knocked her out.

Chapter Four

21st December 1908

Sandy came around slowly and, without opening her eyes, her fingers searched the contours of her forehead, wincing when she found a tender lump where something had quite definitely hit her. Her fingers travelled to her right cheek, which felt bruised. What had just happened? One minute she had been in an old music hall and the next minute she had been falling as if the floor had quite literally disappeared from underneath her and she had landed in...well, that was the thing, where had she landed? All she could remember was a blinding light, terrible cacophony of smells, thick, eye-watering smoke and a roaring sound like hundreds of people yelling, cheering and stamping. She must have dreamt it - though her bruised face and bump on her forehead told her differently. Had she actually fallen through a hole in the floor and bumped it?

Tentatively, she opened her eyes. She was in a gloomy office lit by flickering lights with an old-fashioned, leather-topped, wooden desk and an old-fashioned wooden chair. The desk was very neatly laid out with a wire tray full of letters, a bottle of ink, a fountain pen lying in a black oblong tray, an antique candlestick telephone, and a wooden box with numbers on it - which, on closer inspection, Sandy realised was a calendar displaying the date 21 Dec 1908.

She could hear the constant clip-clop of horses' hooves from outside, the occasional parp-parp of a vintage car horn, and the sound of voices shouting and cheering. The latter seemed to be coming from somewhere on the other side of the office door. What she didn't hear were the sounds she was familiar with - the buses, cars, and sirens which you always heard in the city centre.

She got shakily to her feet, walked the couple of steps to the window and gazed out onto an unbelievable scene below. The street was, without doubt, the Trongate, but there was no sign of the minibus that she had travelled there in, or the modern street lamps which had washed the pavements with their bluish white glow. Instead, pools of pale amber light flickered here and there, cast by the sort of lamps which lit the way in *The Lion the Witch and the Wardrobe.*

Wires stretched across the street from building to building in zigzagging lines and old-fashioned trams trundled along beneath them. A constant stream of horse-drawn carts and carriages, and the occasional vintage car - their small headlamps like pale yellow smudges in the thick fog filled night - replaced the usual flow of motorised traffic.

It had been cold and clear when they had arrived earlier that night. Earlier tonight? She thought to herself, *I only got here earlier tonight, how can the whole street have changed so much in just a few hours? Am I still dreaming?* She pinched herself to check, the sharp pain confirming that she wasn't.

The street below was fascinating, like the set of a costume drama.

That must be it, she thought, *they're making a film.*

Last year, Sandy had seen a film being made in George Square. They had blocked off the whole area to modern traffic and made it look like it had done in the Victorian days, with horse-drawn carriages and people in fancy costumes. That must be what she was now seeing out of the window, the Trongate of the twenty-first century made up to look like it would have done a hundred years ago. It was the only logical reason for the radical change outside. But it looked so real, right down to the thick fog.

The door to the small, old-fashioned office opened and in walked a red-faced little man with a moustache twisted into neat points that turned up at the ends. He wore round glasses, a bowler hat and tweed three-piece suit.

“Albert?" she tentatively asked. He looked like a much younger version of the man who had told them all about the music hall. In fact, apart from the lack of grey hair and wrinkles they were identical.

The man flashed her an angry look.

"That's Mr Pickard to you boy!” He barked, as he stood with his arms folded and glared at her. "Who in blazes do you think you are?"

Sandy was stunned. Boy! He had called her boy. So she had short hair, but so did a lot of girls. She had never been called a boy before. She was obviously a girl.

"Well, boy?!"

Sandy felt a little prickle of annoyance and was going to correct him for his mistake, but her mouth didn't follow her brain. Instead she found herself apologising.

"Um, oh, um - sorry sir, I just woke up here a moment ago and, I-I think I must have fainted or something," she answered honestly, rubbing the lump on her forehead. "I think I hit my head."

How could she have thought that this man was old Albert? Albert had seemed nice and gentle. Maybe he was Albert's son or something.

The man looked her up and down with a puzzled, slightly repulsed expression on his face, as if he had never seen anything quite like her before. Sandy felt uncomfortable and squirmed under his scrutiny.

"Judging by the strange costume and the way you arrived on stage, I take it you're a young magician that decided he was going to make his debut today unannounced and disrupt my show. Now, young man, that isn't the way you go about things, though I hear from my staff that it was quite a spectacular entrance and scared off the useless act that was on before you."

Costume? Stage debut? Sandy thought. *What's he on about?*

"I-I'm not a magician sir. I'm with the school party doing the ghost hunt," she explained, a little uncertainly.

"What are you talking about, lad? School party? Ghost hunt? Is this some new thing, some new act? Do you perform some kind of ghost show? If you want me to book you, lad, then you can go through the usual procedures and audition like everyone else," he growled, still eyeing Sandy sceptically. "Come back tomorrow morning at eleven and don't be late. I want to see your ghost show. You impressed my stage manager and that's no easy task."

The man stepped over to the door and held it open. "What's your name, boy?" he asked.

"Sandy," she muttered as she approached the open door. She was going to add "and I'm a girl," but once again her mouth did not agree with her brain and she ran through the open door instead, desperate to get away from the weird, rude man and find her classmates.

Outside the small office was a short corridor which led back to the music hall. However, as she entered the music hall, nothing was quite how she remembered it. The crumbling old auditorium, which had been empty except for sleeping classmates, teachers, and parents, was now completely crammed with costumed people both standing and sitting, intently watching a black and white silent film. The décor was renewed - not a peeling layer or hole in the plaster to be seen, and the dirty yellow and brown ceiling was now a midnight blue sky, scattered with hundreds of gold stars and lit by large circular lights that hung from the centre of the high ceiling.

Sandy wove her way through the dense crowd, sure that her friends would be somewhere in the middle. Mr Oakley must have organised for her class to be extras in the film as a surprise. They had only just finished studying the Victorians and Edwardians and he had gone on constantly about the smell and how people today wouldn't be able to stand the pong. Well, whoever the film's director was, they were certainly going for realism - the smell was rotten, really stinking and full of tobacco smoke that stung her eyes. It was too realistic, it was making Sandy feel sick. All thoughts of her classmates were instantly forgotten and replaced with a sudden desperate need to find a way out into the fresh air before she threw up everywhere.

She turned around and pushed her way back through the noisy, packed, stinking music hall with both her hands firmly clamped over her mouth. Finally, she found her way to a staircase and made her way down to a small foyer and ticket office. She dashed across to a set of large wooden doors which she pushed open and then stepped out onto the street beyond. She took her hands away from her mouth and, with the prospect of fresh air, took a deep breath in and instantly regretted it. Outside smelled almost as bad as inside. The air was so strong she could almost taste it - horse manure and something pungent like rotten eggs mixed with rotting fish. The fog was so thick she could feel it on her skin.

The street was bustling with people dressed in old-fashioned clothes. Some of them looked ragged and half-starved. All of them cast Sandy a look of utter surprise, staring at her - particularly at her puffer coat, her jeans, and most of all, her furry snow boots. This was all wrong. This couldn't be a film set. It was too real. Her stomach clenched and fear crept up her spine as she finally realised the impossible truth. If it wasn't a movie set, and it wasn't a dream - she wasn't capable of dreaming this - somehow, as unbelievable and impossible as it seemed, she had travelled back in time.

Giving into the stench-fuelled nausea, she threw up on the pavement. A woman who was passing at the time cursed at her as some of the vomit spattered the ragged hem of her long skirt. As Sandy straightened back up and tried her best not to cry, a grubby-faced boy appeared at her side.

"Looks like you had a good-sized dinner. Shame it's on the pavement now though," he greeted her with a wide, friendly smile.

Chapter Five

A Basement Zoo

Sandy had never felt as lost and helpless as she did in that moment of nausea, and the realisation that her comfortable modern world had suddenly been replaced by this dark, noisy, and smelly place. The scruffy, dirty boy who had appeared at her side looked at her as if she were some kind of freak. Sandy bent over, clutching her stomach, and threw up again. The boy patted her comfortingly on the back as she did so.

"Thanks," Sandy managed to mutter as she wiped her mouth with the back of her hand and stood shivering in the freezing, drizzly night, tears streaming down her cheeks.

"Come on, we should get you out of the cold," the boy's voice was kind as he motioned for Sandy to follow him.

The boy scampered up a lane to the left of the music hall entrance and disappeared through a door halfway up. It was the same door Sandy had remembered entering the previous night when she had arrived with her school friends, only then the lane had been empty and now it was crowded with men smoking and laughing. They glared at her as she passed.

"Looks like Pickard's got himself a new freak," one of the smoking men joked.

"Och, just ignore them," the boy declared, and Sandy followed him through the door. There was no security guard watching Coronation Street on a laptop; instead, there was a constant stream of people going up and down the spiral staircase. Sandy expected to go up as she had before, but the boy led Sandy down. When they reached the bottom, new and even more pungent smells greeted them. *The smelliness of this place just seems to escalate,* she thought.

As they entered the basement a look of stunned disbelief froze itself on Sandy's face. The boy grinned at her. Albert, the twenty-first century Panopticon curator, had told them about the basement zoo, but she had never expected it to be quite like this.

A large bird cage covered the wall to the left from floor to ceiling and corner to corner. All the residents - a collection of macaws, mynah birds, and lovebirds - were singing, squawking, and twittering as if vying for the attention of the dozen or so people crowded round them. The people were equally noisy, whistling and calling "Pretty Polly.", "Polly want a cracker?", "Who's a pretty boy then?", whilst poking their fingers or boiled sweets through the bars.

On the opposite side of the room, a group of girls were giggling at their reflections which were warped and misshapen on a wall of distorting mirrors. Some of the girls' reflections made them tall and skinny, others short and round. A couple of girls laughed hysterically at their reflections which showed them with tiny little heads, long necks, and short fat bodies. When they squatted down, their reflections became round and fat, which provoked fresh gales of high-pitched tittering.

This first room led through an opening into another with a motley collection of animals; a small bear-like creature which cowered in the corner of its cage, a wild cat which hissed at anyone who went close, a couple of lemurs who clung to a bare branch, and stared at everyone with wide, terrified eyes. In the middle of it all was the star attraction; a huge Russian brown bear and a battle-scarred baboon, both of which squatted miserably in cages barely big enough for them to lie down in. Sandy instantly felt heartbroken, fresh tears welling in her eyes. This was awful, and so cruel. How could anyone think this was right? How could anyone want to see this? Yet so many people did, and a young man with the beginnings of a fuzzy moustache wearing a peeked cap - Sandy assumed he was the zookeeper - fought to keep the crowds of gawping people from getting too close to the more dangerous animals' cages.

"Amazing, ain't they?" the boy expressed with a great deal of pride.

"Yeah, amazing," Sandy replied flatly. "I love seeing animals in small cages," she added sarcastically. The boy didn't seem to notice her scornful tone.

"The bear and the baboon got into each other's cage a few nights ago and nearly tore each other apart," the boy continued enthusiastically. "Tam said they had quite a job splitting them up. Mr Pickard's having new cages built for them through there."

The boy pointed ahead to a room which was blocked off from view by a curtain and a sign which read:

After their epic battle earlier this month which destroyed their cages, Bruin the Russian bear and the dog-faced baboon will soon be on view in their new accommodation.

"Old Mr Hill's workshop is through there an' all, so it's strictly out of bounds," the boy announced.

Sandy wasn't interested in Old Mr Hill's workshop. She was too busy being horrified and desperately hoped that the new cages would be a lot bigger than the temporary ones.

When the boy had finished showing Sandy the bear and baboon, he led her through an archway and into the largest room yet, which contained a bizarre collection of exhibits. Paintings covered the walls. Some were colourful depictions of rosy, plump men and women laughing and drinking, whilst, in bleak contrast, others were black and white drawings of people being tortured. Sandy shook her head. This was hell, and it was a hell crammed with happy, chattering people that seemed to flow like a human river past the various exhibits on display. Beneath the dubious artworks the crowd gathered around various tanks containing snapping alligators, turtles which poked their heads tentatively from their shells, and languishing pythons. Most of the mob, however, were at the far end of the room. This last exhibit was so crowded by people guffawing and shouting that Sandy couldn't see what poor creature they were all so amused by. The boy pushed his way through the crowd and joined a gang at the front. Sandy squeezed through behind him and was amazed to discover the object of this last and most popular of the exhibits was a pair of chimpanzees, both dressed in smart outfits. One in a shirt, bowtie, waistcoat, tailcoat, spats, and top hat, the other in a frilly, pale blue dress, blue lace gloves, and an unfeasibly large, frilly, blue hat that wobbled on her head as she chattered back at the audience. A sign on the front of the cage announced the pair as Solomon - Darwin's Missing Link - and his wife Betsy. *These must be the chimps that Albert had told them about,* she thought. Solomon was one of the resident ghosts in 2016. She stared at him in awe. However, it seemed that the scruffy boy had not dragged her here to see Solomon and Betsy, but to meet the group of raggle-taggle, grubby-faced urchins who crowded the front of the cage teasing the chimps.

"Come on, lads, I've got him," the boy announced.

As the others turned and stared at Sandy, she gave a small wave and a weary smile. They didn't smile back. Instead they shoved their way along the front of the cage. The boy from the pavement grabbed her wrist and dragged her behind him, following the others to a door at the back of the monkey house.

They entered a small room lit by oil lamps and candles. The room contained a couple of large and rather worn-out old wing chairs which sat on either side of a small round stove. At the far side of the room, a bench covered with tools and bits of broken machinery extended the length of the wall. It was stuffy in this room, but mercifully not as smelly as the zoo.

"Take a seat," offered the boy.

The gang of boys all turned at once and focused their attention on Sandy as she lowered herself cautiously into one of the chairs. A spring dug into her bottom. The boys all stared at her in awed silence. She could imagine what they must have been thinking. She realised she must look very strange to them in her modern clothing and, judging by the way the boys all seemed to be fixated by her furry snow boots, she guessed they had never seen anything quite like her before. How could they have? She was now starting to feel embarrassed under the intensity of their curious gaze.

"You should've taken him up to the attic to join the other freaks. Look at his feet. That's no right," said the tallest and skinniest of the boys with a look of disgust on his face.

Sandy was mortified. He actually thought her furry boots were her feet! What an idiot. She would have laughed if she hadn't felt so hopelessly lost.

"They're not my feet," she said, a little sulkily. "They're boots."

The boys all "Ah'd," nodding in unison, then continued to glare at her silently. Sandy felt uncomfortable. It was as if they were waiting for her to do something, so she did. She jumped up so suddenly she even surprised herself and, thrusting her hand forward towards the boy she had met outside, she introduced herself.

"My name's Sandy McMillan."

There was a moment's pause, then the boy took her hand and shook it.

"I'm Jamie Murray. This is ma wee brother, Robert, but we call him Wee Bobby." A small, grubby, snot-faced boy, about the same size as Sandy, with a face full of freckles and tousled brown hair, stepped forward and shook Sandy's hand. His hand was sticky. Sandy didn't want to imagine why.

"Andrew here's the oldest, he's thirteen." Jamie introduced her to the one who had thought her boots were her feet. He nodded but did not shake Sandy's hand. His dark eyes scowled at her suspiciously from beneath a thick mop of tangled dark hair. "This here's Sam," Jamie continued. Sam was so different to look at than the others, he was neat and looked relatively clean. His hair was cut very short at the sides with the hair on the top of his head a little longer and combed down flat on his head. His clothes looked clean; short trousers, a shirt, a jumper and a little jacket. He had polished boots, and his socks were neatly pulled up to his knees. His eyes, however, sparkled with mischief.

"Hullo," he said, briefly squeezing Sandy's hand before putting his hand firmly in his pocket.

"Charlie," Jamie continued, pointing to another boy.

"Wotcha," the boy standing to Sam's right answered; offering a small wave instead of a handshake. He was about the same size as Sam and something about the way they stood together made Sandy think they were best friends. They looked very different from each other. Sam was neat, Charlie was scruffy. He reminded her of the Artful Dodger in the musical Oliver. Her gran loved that film.

"This is Jimmy." A boy with a shock of red hair and face full of freckles glanced at Sandy and muttered, "Hello," then stepped further back as if she was going to bite him.

"Welcome tae the gang," Jamie said with a wide smile once the introductions were finished.

"Thanks," Sandy tried her best to return the smile.

"Say, that trick you did was quite something," Jamie said amongst a sea of enthusiastic nods.

"Trick?" Sandy asked, puzzled.

"Aye, the way you appeared out of the magic lantern beam - very clever. We've never seen that one before, have we, boys?" Jamie looked around the group.

There was a general mutter of agreement in the assembled group.

"How did you do it? Cos ye didnae use the trap, an' ye didnae use smoke. Are you a real magician?" Bobby asked, with such awe in his eyes that Sandy felt terrible that she wasn't.

"No, I am not a magician. My magical appearance was not a trick. In fact, I don't know what happened. All I know is that one minute I was in an old theatre with my pals on a ghost hunt and the next I'm here with you guys," Sandy blurted, once again on the threshold of tears. It was all so confusing. She was a huge fan of science fiction and loved films and programmes about time travel. She had thought it would be the most exciting thing ever to be able to travel through time, but that was when it was fiction when she had believed that it wasn't physically possible. Yet here she was. It wasn't exciting, it was awful.

Very tentatively, and trying not to sound completely crazy, she added, "I appear to have travelled back in time - to your time." In the absence of any other explanation, she decided to just go for the truth.

For a moment, the boys just stood staring at her as if she had spoken in some foreign language which they didn't understand. Then they all burst out laughing.

"Oh, that's a good one," said Jamie. "Come oan, we're no daft, and we wullnae tell anyone your secret. We just want to know how you did that trick."

"But that's the point," Sandy insisted. "It wasn't a magic trick. I really have travelled from the future - 2016, to be exact. I mean, look at my clothing. When have you ever seen clothing like this before?"

"You see all sorts in here - 'specially in the music hall and freak show. It could just be a costume," said Bobby.

"I saw a turn once who wore really long boots. They woz longer than he woz tall and he walked on 'em like they woz stilts," Andrew stated.

"Aye, I remember him. He was funny," added Sam.

"Look, I promise you this isn't a costume. These are my clothes and I'm not a magician. I really am from the future! I live in a tower block in Thornliebank with my mum who works night shift packing shelves in the supermarket."

The boys looked sceptical.

Charlie broke the silence. "What's 'packing shelves'?"

"What's a 'supermarket'?" asked Sam.

"Aye, and what's a 'tower block'?" added Andrew.

Sandy sighed. This was a nightmare and she needed to get out of it and back to her comfortable world in the future. Then a horrible thought occurred to her; what if she couldn't get back home?

"A supermarket is a big shop where you can buy food and stuff and a tower block is a really tall building with hundreds of flats."

"How tall?" asked Sam

"Twenty-two floors," answered Sandy.

"Sounds made up to me," declared Andrew. "I ain't never heard of no supermarket and there is no such thing as a building which is twenty-two floors high. Why, that's even taller than the tollbooth tower."

"Well, in the future, where I come from, buildings are really tall and supermarkets are everywhere," Sandy replied defensively.

"It's a pretty far-fetched story. Your clothes are strange, though. I ain't never seen anything quite like 'em. But that don't mean you're from the future," remarked Jimmy from the back of the gang.

The threatening tears were hot at the back of her eyes now, but she wasn't going to give in to them. She wasn't going to let this bunch of ruffians see her bawling. She certainly didn't want them to know she was a girl. She had no idea how they would take that little snippet of information. Sandy suspected being a boy was far safer than being a girl in 1908. She'd seen enough costume dramas, courtesy of her gran, to understand that.

Getting back home was her only priority right now and she would probably need help from these boys. They're all she had, which meant she needed to convince them that she was telling the truth. The only proof she had were her clothes and the couple of items in her pockets. Items that she knew from her TV-science-fiction-diet could change the course of history and re-write time completely, but she had to show these boys some sort of proof.

Sandy slumped back down into the tattered armchair, shifting her bottom to avoid the spring poking through the stuffing. She looked at the curious, grubby faces that gazed down at her.

"You all have to swear the most awesome swear ever that you will never tell another living soul about the stuff I am about to show you. If you tell anyone, you might change the whole course of history and I kinda like the world - my world - the way it is. Do you all swear?" she entreated.

Each boy looked at the others and all nodded in agreement.

"On my mither's grave," promised Jamie.

"Oan my ain life," agreed Charlie.

"Oan my marble collection," added Bobby.

"Aye," agreed Jimmy.

When all the boys had sworn to keep the secret, Sandy pulled from her puffer coat pocket an item that she knew they would understand; sweets and, in this case, popping candy. As she pulled the pink and yellow paper packet from her pocket, the boys watched in silence, anticipating the wondrous item from the future.

"This," Sandy said, holding up the packet, "is a sweet from my time. It's called exploding candy." She emphasised the word exploding and with a flourish tore open a corner of the paper packet. The boys gingerly stepped back, perhaps expecting the packet to bang. "It's alright. Look, it's just candy."

"What's it going to do?" asked Jamie, eyeing the packet suspiciously.

Sandy couldn't help but chuckle when she saw the look of fear on the boys' faces.

"It's ok, it's perfectly safe. It's a sweet that explodes in your mouth. Listen." Standing up, she poured some of the candy on to her own tongue, moving closer to the boys so they could hear the crescendo of hollow popping sounds. The boys fear immediately evaporated and was replaced with wide smiles and curious chatter.

Bobby jumped in front of Sandy with his mouth open, ready to receive a mouthful, which Sandy duly poured. His eyes lit up with pure delight at the popping eruptions on his tongue. Seconds later all the boys were standing in a huddle, their mouths open as they listened to the crackling in each other's mouths.

Sandy searched her pockets again, discarding a dirty tissue in her left pocket. Her fingers closed around her phone in her right pocket. Was this a bit too advanced for them, her mobile phone? She knew that the telephone had been invented. She had seen one in the small office in the music hall, but she knew they certainly wouldn't have anything like her touch screen smart phone. She wondered what they would make of the videos on her phone.

"You've all seen films, yeah?" she inquired.

The boys looked at her blankly. Sandy had seen a film playing in the music hall earlier, so she knew they had. "You know, movies? Moving pictures?"

"The flickers? Aye," confirmed Charlie.

"Well, in the future we carry the flickers in our pockets," she said pulling out her mobile phone. The boys gasped when they saw the small, smooth, black, rectangular piece of plastic. When Sandy unlocked it, the black rectangle came into glorious full-colour life, with a picture of her white poodle, Casper. The boys gathered closer, each dirty, reverential face illuminated in the glow of the small screen.

After a moment of astounded silence, Sandy slid Casper up revealing her icon filled home screen and tapped the film icon and pulled up her video menu. She ran her index finger up the screen, scrolling quickly through colourful little thumbnail pictures until she came to the picture she wanted. She tapped on her selection and Christina Aguilera's 'Candyman' video burst into life. It was the most vintage tune she could think of. It was like a vibrant, technicolour window into the 21st century. Sandy turned the volume up and gathered the boys closer. They looked either ready to faint in their amazement or run in fear, but they were all frozen to the spot. Every jaw dropped and every pair of eyes popped. They were mesmerised and half terrified of the saucy, fast-moving music video. When it finished, they stood soundlessly stunned, staring at the screen until Sandy locked the phone and it went black. It was as if she were a hypnotist clicking her fingers and bringing the boys out of a trance.

"You must really be from the future all right," Jamie's voice was full of awe. "I could never...I mean, how can that be? How can you have people and music in that little black slate thing? Where's the projector? Where's the band?"

"What are they wearing?" asked Sam and Charlie in unison.

Sandy laughed. "Fashion and technology are way more advanced in my time. We have our own screens in our houses that we watch thousands of different films and programmes on. This," she indicated her phone, "isn't even really for watching films, it's really a phone."

"A what?" asked Andrew.

"A phone. You know, a telephone. You use it to call people," explained Sandy.

The boys looked totally bemused.

"You do know what a telephone is, right?"

"A telephone, aye. We call it a 'bell.' Mr Pickard has one in his office, but I've never used one," answered Jamie.

"Well, this is the 'bell' of the future. It's just a telephone, but we call them mobiles 'cos you can walk around with them. We use them for loads of stuff, like texting, chatting, surfing the net, downloading films and music, taking pictures and videos. Look, I'll show you," as she started to corral the confused gang into one group.

She unlocked her phone. "Say cheese," she commanded and tapped the screen. The phone flashed, and the boys shielded their eyes against the sudden bright light as if it had burned them. She called the boys over to look at the snapshot she had taken. Still blinded by the flash, they timidly peeked at the picture of themselves.

"See, it's you all." And she showed them the picture of their white, surprised faces.

The boys looked at her with fearful eyes.

"It's okay," she laughed. "It's not going to hurt you. Look, let's make a video. Line up and show me your best cancan." Sandy moved the boys into line and told them to dance. They started kicking their legs up in the air like the Panopticon dancing girls and Sandy filmed them. When she played the footage back, the boys gathered around silently, still unsure. Sandy played it again. The boys began to chatter, then laugh, and suddenly the fear of the unknown melted away and they were so excited they started talking about who they had to show this to.

"You all swore you wouldn't tell anyone. You can't, you mustn't. If adults heard about this, it really would change the course of history and that probably wouldn't be a good thing. In fact, I know it wouldn't. I've seen it on TV."

The boys all protested a bit, but Jamie said that if Sandy had seen it on something called TV - which he assumed was some kind of wisdom machine in the future, like the fortune-telling machines in the attic carnival - then they had all better shut up and swear again that they wouldn't tell another living soul about what they had seen and where Sandy was really from.

The boys took it in turns to swear again. Sam was in the middle of saying "...and I promise I won't tell another living soul outside this room..." when the door burst open and a harassed looking young man in a peaked cap stormed in yelling, "Where the bloody hell is he, Jamie? Where's Tam?"

This angry invader didn't even notice Sandy.

"I've nae idea, he was about earlier. I saw him working the magic lantern," Jamie replied.

"Aye, well he's no at the magic lantern now, and he left his post before the show ended. Mr P is on the warpath. They're letting in for the next show already and Tam's nowhere to be seen," the vexed man said as he impatiently turned and stormed back out, slamming the door behind him.

"That was Harry. He's the zookeeper. His dad's the handyman here," Jamie explained to Sandy. "Tam's my brother and I guess he's done one of his famous vanishing acts."

"Aye, he's good at them," added Bobby.

Jimmy, who was still staring at Sandy as if she were from another planet, piped up. "If you're from the future, how did you get here?"

"I don't know," she said. "I think the magic lantern brought me back here."

"But I thought you said it wasn't a trick," said Sam.

"It wasn't a trick," Sandy replied. "All I can tell you is there was a magic lantern where I was before I came here. We were having a ghost hunt in this old theatre and I guess I dozed off. Something woke me up. I'm not sure what it was, but I woke up and, when I stepped out of my sleeping bag, I was suddenly staring into this bright light which I think was from the magic lantern. Then I was falling. I thought I must have fallen through a hole in the floor, but I must have been falling through time. How it works though, I have no idea."

"Do you sleep in bags in the future?" asked Bobby.

"Sometimes," she replied. "Usually when we go camping."

"Camping?" asked Charlie.

"Yeah, you know, when you go to the countryside and build a tent and sleep in it?" Sandy explained.

"Like explorers?" Sam asked.

Sandy guessed they didn't go camping for fun much in 1908.

"Yeah," she agreed. "Like explorers."

"If you stare at the magic lantern beam again, will you go back to your own time?" Andrew asked.

She shrugged. She certainly hoped so. Surely it had to be the way back. She couldn't bear thinking about the rest of her life spent here, in the early 20th century. TV, computers, mobile phones, and the internet wouldn't be invented for decades yet.

"I saw a magician use one once to make a picture of a butterfly turn into a living, moving lady," announced Charlie.

Sam rolled his eyes and looked at his friend. "Och Charlie, you didnae fall for that old gag, did ya? The lady just hid behind the screen and steps through a hole in it when the magician makes a puff of smoke. I've seen it loads of times."

"Oh, aye, where?" Charlie quizzed.

"Roon the corner in the Metropole music hall," Sam answered, quick as a whip.

"Mr Pickard only got that magic lantern recently," said Jamie thoughtfully.

"Do you know where he got it from?" asked Sandy.

Jamie shrugged. "Aye. Tam says he got it from an auction. Mr P's always buying stuff from auctions."

"Maybe it used to belong to a really powerful magician, and it has a time travelling spell on it," Bobby suggested enthusiastically. "I want to have a go. Let's see if we can travel through time too."

"Aye, that's a great idea. Let's all have a go," agreed Charlie, grinning eagerly at Sandy.

Sandy thought it was a very bad idea. She had travelled through the beam and ended up here. Where would the boys end up? Where would she end up? "I don't think any of you should try it and I don't think it's magic. Real magic doesn't exist. Everything has a logical explanation."

"So, what's the logical explanation then?" asked a puzzled Andrew.

That was a very good question.

"Maybe it's a ghost," suggested Sam. "You did say you were on a ghost hunt."

"Well, when the music hall closes, why don't we go and find out," proposed Jamie.

Chapter Six

Back to the Magic Lantern

After the last show had finished at 11:00 p.m., the public poured out onto the street and the building became quiet. Even the animals in the zoo ceased their screeching and squawking. Sandy and the boys made their way out past the cages and up the stairs to the music hall.

As they entered the empty auditorium Sandy felt, for a moment, the same atmosphere she had experienced in her own time; that feeling of abandonment and emptiness waiting to be filled. Sandy used her phone to light the way. Her new friends gasped at the bright light.

"Your future bell is like some kind of miracle," Sam said, squinting into the bright LED.

The little gang picked a path through the auditorium to where the magic lantern stood on its platform at the back of the hall.

"The magic lantern was on when I woke up," said Sandy.

"Well, that's easy enough." Jamie walked over to the magic lantern and, after a moment searching, found a switch at the back and flicked it down. The electric bulb behind the lens glowed. The gradually brightening light cut an ever-widening path across the empty music hall and washed over the stage and painted backcloth depicting a Scottish Highland scene. Jimmy, Sam, and Charlie made a dash for the beam, but Andrew pulled them back.

"Go and stand in the light, over on the stage where you appeared earlier," Jamie instructed as he fiddled with the lens at the front, trying to look as if he knew what he was doing. Sandy made her way through the music hall towards the stage.

"I think I was standing around about here, but I don't know," Sandy said as she stepped onto the front of the stage, trying to figure out the exact spot she had landed on. "It's hard to tell. I mean, I was standing in front of the stage in my own time and it was nothing like this one…and the seating had been further back, the floor had a carpet and..." She looked over to the boys. They weren't listening; they were staring straight past her, wide-eyed and open-mouthed. She turned slowly with some trepidation, expecting to find a giant spider or something creeping towards her. "Oh," she sighed in relief as she saw what the boys were gawping at.

The words 'Count back with A.B. Get diamond. S.' had suddenly appeared on the backcloth behind her.

"What does that mean?" asked Andrew.

"Who's A.B?" Jimmy questioned.

"A diamond?!" Charlie exclaimed.

"Treasure!" Sam gleefully shouted.

Jamie was fiddling with the slide carriers behind the lens. "They're empty. There's no slide to project," he announced. "How's that possible?"

"I've no idea, but I would say that it's confirmation of one thing," pronounced Sam, "there definitely appears to be a ghost in the magic lantern - and I think it's trying to tell us something."

After what had happened and what they had all seen that night, none of them argued the existence of ghosts - in fact, it seemed the only plausible, logical explanation.

"Who dae ya think the ghost is? Do you think we know them?" Andrew asked, staring at the words that were beginning to fade.

"I don't know any dead people," Jimmy commented.

"My granddad died; do you think it's him?" asked Charlie.

"Did he have any treasure?" Sam enquired.

"No, definitely not," Charlie answered sadly.

"Then it's probably no your grandda," stated Sam, slapping his pal on the back.

"Has anyone got something to write the message on before it disappears completely?" Sandy requested. The boys all shrugged. None of them had ever needed to write anything down before.

"Och, it's no difficult. I can remember it. 'count back with A.B,' whoever A.B. is, and, 'get a diamond. S.' Do you think S is the person who wrote the message?" Jamie asked. "Or do you think that S is who the message is for?"

The boys looked at Sandy.

"Why are you looking at me like that?" she asked.

"S, as in, Sandy. That message must be for you," declared Jimmy.

"Not necessarily. It could be from someone whose name begins with an S," Sandy replied.

"It has to be you. Of course it does. You came here through the magic lantern from the future," remarked Charlie. "Stands to reason, doesn't it? S is for Sandy."

The word Sandy very faintly travelled through the air, hissing like the ghost of an echo.

"Did you hear that?" she asked.

The boys looked at her with slightly terrified expressions and nodded.

Sandy looked at the magic lantern. "Who's there?"

There was no response. They all looked at the back cloth, where the words still faintly lingered.

" 'Count back with A.B. Get the diamond. S,' " Sandy recited again. "What do you mean? Who is A.B? What do you want us to count with them? Where is the diamond you want us to get?"

They all stared back at the wall, at the patch of painted sky where the last trace of the words faded then vanished. They waited for new words, some sort of explanation, to appear. Nothing did.

Sam shivered. "This is giving me the creeps."

"Me too," agreed Charlie.

"Do any of you have any clue who A.B. is?" Sandy asked.

None of the boys knew. The message was a complete mystery. It didn't make any sense.

"Are you going to go back through the beam?" Bobby suddenly asked.

That was a good question. The message was intriguing, and she loved a mystery. Part of her wanted to stay and solve it, but really all she wanted to do was go home. She was tired and stinking. She missed her own clean, comfortable, technologically advanced world, and her mum and gran. She looked at the beam that still washed the backdrop. It seemed duller now that the message was gone. It certainly wasn't the incredibly intense light that had brought her to this era.

The boys looked at her expectantly.

"I have to try." Sandy answered as she stepped into the amber light and waited. Her arms at her sides, fists clenched, rocking forward slightly on the balls of her feet and head thrust upwards, she willed herself to travel back to the future. Nothing happened.

"I don't think I can." Her voice was filled with defeat, and she felt a lump in her throat, the tears threatening again. What if she was stuck here? She desperately wanted to wake up from this nightmare. She closed her eyes as tight as she could and muttered to herself over and over again. "Send me home, send me home, send me home…"

Still, nothing happened. She screwed her eyes closed even tighter and, remembering the words from *The Wizard of Oz* (one of her favourite films), began chanting, "There's no place like home. There's no place like home. There's no place like home." There was no sense of falling or movement through time.

She opened her eyes again and looked at the boys, hastily wiping away the few tears that had begun to trickle down her cheeks.

"Nope. I'm still here," Sandy mumbled miserably and gave into the flood of emotions.

Sam and Charlie stepped up to either side of her and patted her on the back.

"Och, yer fine with us, aren't you?" Sam said consolingly.

"Aye, you're 'mong pals," agreed Charlie.

"I don't recon that thing is gonny let you go back to your ain time until you've solved that riddle," stated Jimmy.

The other boys nodded in agreement.

Sandy wiped her nose on the back of her coat sleeve and sniffed. Perhaps Jimmy was right, maybe she had been sent here to solve a mystery. Why else would she be here? And when it's solved, then, maybe, she would be sent back to her own time.

"Yes," she agreed wearily. "I must have been sent here for a reason and that message must be meant for me. Or us," she added as she looked at the boys.

"Does any part of the message mean anything to you?" asked Andrew.

"Not a clue," replied Sandy with a sorrowful tone.

"Well, what do you think we should do?" Sam wondered aloud.

"I've no idea," answered Sandy as she slumped onto one of the benches and folded her arms.

"Well, I guess we could go and find Tam," suggested Jamie. "He might know what to do."

"Your brother? The one who the zookeeper was looking for?" Sandy enquired.

"Aye, he was operating the magic lantern earlier when you came through it. He lives in the basement," replied Jamie.

"What, in that little room behind the monkey cage?"

"Mr Pickard lets him live there free and all by himself." Jamie answered proudly, as if the stuffy, smelly little room was a luxury flat.

* * *

Back in the room behind the monkey house, Andrew and Jimmy relit the lamps. A few embers still glowed in the stove. Jamie grabbed the iron poker that rested against the stove door and rattled them back into flame, adding some small chunks of coal. The fire roared back to life.

"Where dae ya s'pose Tam is?" Bobby asked his older brother.

"He must be off seeing Nellie or something," Jamie replied, "I'm sure he'll turn up soon though."

"Aye, an' we have a lot to tell him." Bobby announced gleefully. "Don't worry, I won't mention your future bell," the small boy hastily added, in response to a scowl from Sandy.

The gang of friends sat around and discussed the strange message, their various theories about ghosts and time travel while they waited for Tam to return. At 1:00 a.m., when he still hadn't come home, the boys decided it was time for bed and that they would come back and see Tam in the morning. Sandy could stay there for the night. Jamie would stay too, so that he could explain who the stranger was when Tam finally got back. Sandy was glad of the company. She didn't fancy being on her own. The two new friends made themselves as comfortable as they could on the old chairs and, with the cosy glow from the stove warming their faces, they drifted off to sleep.

Chapter Seven

22nd December 1908
A Brutal Crime is Discovered

The next morning, Sandy was awoken by Jamie and Bobby, who came running into the little room waving a Daily Record newspaper in the air. They caused such a commotion, the zookeeper appeared at the door to see what the matter was.

"What're you lot doin' in here then, eh?" he demanded, eyeing Sandy dubiously.

"It's all right, Harry. Tam said Sandy could stay here the night," Jamie lied in response to the zookeeper's scrutiny.

Harry grunted, "Well I s'pose if Tam said it's all right, it's all right, but don't let Mr P catch him at it. You know he don't take kindly to vagrants in his building," he directed his comment at the strangely dressed boy who was stiffly uncurling from the armchair, yawning and stretching. "Anyways, where is Tam? He didn't turn up at all for the nine o'clock. Mr P was raging, I can tell you. Had to get the old man up to work the magic lantern."

"I haven't seen him since last night either," said Jamie, a little wistfully. "Not since he said Sandy could stay here," he quickly added, wondering where was his big brother?

"Well, when you do see him, you tell him Mr P's looking for him." He paused and looked at Jamie's strange new friend again. "Don't suppose you'd know anything about a pickpocket, do you, boy?"

"A pickpocket? No, I don't," Sandy replied.

"Damn thief got another two last night."

"Make that three! He stole my sweets, the rotten villain," Jamie asserted, recalling with a shudder the horrible moment when he'd discovered his devastating loss.

Harry laughed. "Well, maybe we should be looking for a fat man with rotten teeth, eh, Jamie?"

At that moment, Andrew came crashing into the room with another boy - a small, frail-looking lad with dark, scruffy hair just like Andrew's, but unlike Andrew in every other way. He wore glasses that were far too big for him and made his brown eyes look huge on his tiny face and his legs were so withered and bent he had to walk with two sticks. They didn't seem to hamper him though; he was just as quick as the other boy.

"Well, if it isn't wee George!" exclaimed Harry, as he ruffled the small boy's hair. "Why are you not at your schooling today? Not like you to play truant. Thought mischief was your brother's department," he said, motioning to Andrew.

"I'm working for Mr MacBrayne today, sir. My mam says that me sitting in school all day isn't gonny bring in any food," George lied. He was playing truant, though it was true that his parents would prefer it if he earned a wage. There weren't many opportunities for crippled boys and Mr MacBrayne was willing to give him a chance. He couldn't do the normal work of a delivery boy, but he was good with numbers and Mr MacBrayne had him do the bookkeeping along with writing up the receipts for the customers. Normally, school was where George preferred to be, or stowed away in a quiet corner with his nose in a book, but when his brother Andy had told him about the time-travelling visitor from the future, he had to come and meet them for himself.

"You're smart, George. You could be a clerk or a banker or something. You're meant for more than us, so don't be hanging around with these louts too long. Right, boys, I've got work to do, so don't be getting into any mischief, you hear?" Harry ordered.

"We won't," replied Jamie, flashing Harry a bright smile, beaming with innocence.

Harry wasn't convinced. He harrumphed and then sauntered off.

Sandy stared at George. "Who's this guy?" she asked, nodding her head towards George.

"Och, he's just ma wee brother, George. He had to come and meet you after I told him what happened last night," said Andrew.

George nodded his head enthusiastically, his glasses almost flying off. He had barely slept at the prospect of meeting a real time traveller. The Time Machine was one of his favourite books. "Can I see your future bell that makes pictures?"

"My what?" she asked.

"Your telephone that makes pictures," said the boy, pushing his glasses up his nose.

"You told him? You swore twice that you wouldn't tell another living soul," stated Sandy furiously.

"I didn't think that meant George. He's one of us and he's got more brains than the rest of us put together. He might be able to help." Andrew defended himself.

"Help with what?" Sandy tartly replied.

"Well, you know, the magic lantern and the clue and how to get you back to your time," Andrew replied.

Sandy regarded the small boy who stared back at her with magnified brown eyes full of hope and excitement. He was really cute, and Sandy melted.

"Well, I guess it's too late now anyway. He already knows. But no one else, ok?" She clarified.

"No one else, I swear," Andrew promised, crossing his heart.

Sandy pulled her mobile phone out of her pocket and the boy watched with eager interest as she switched it on. She watched as George stared gormlessly at the screensaver of her dog. He didn't look that bright to her. She played the video of the boys she had made the previous day, and the young lad instantly became mesmerised. When the short video finished and Sandy turned the phone off the boy looked at her, his magnified eyes wide with wonder. "Jings! Where's the projector? Howzit work? I mean, I mean, I could never imagine… It's, well, it's impossible."

"No, it's just from the future. Believe me, the future is very different from this place."

George wiped his glasses on his ragged jumper. "I must know more," he stated as he popped them back on his face and stared earnestly at Sandy.

Sandy sighed. "I can't tell you more. I probably shouldn't have even let you see my phone."

The little boy looked at Sandy and nodded. "Yes, I suppose you are right. We shouldn't know what's ahead of us or we are in danger of changing our own futures."

Sandy was stunned by the small boy. "Wow, how old are you?"

"He's eight, going on eighty." Andrew answered for him, "Pa says George is an old head on young shoulders. He seems to know everything, even stuff we don't learn at school. It's like he was born knowing it."

"Is Tam back yet?" he asked, changing the subject.

"No, and this is in the papers today," Jamie said, waggling the newspaper he was holding in the air.

"Listen, this is important. 'Brutal Crime in Glasgow. De-fence-less old lady mur-dered. A girl's g-hast-ly dis-covery.' "

Sandy looked at Jamie puzzled. "What's that got to do with the magic lantern?"

"Didn't say it did. Listen."

Jamie continued reading, struggling over some of the words, spelling out each syllable until George impatiently snatched the paper out of his hands.

"Maybe if you actually went to school once in a while, you might learn something. Like how to read," George sarcastically sniped, pushed his glasses up his nose and continued reading the article out loud.

Fluently gliding through the paragraphs of tiny newsprint, George recited how an eighty-two-year-old lady, Miss Marion Gilchrist, from a respectable part of Glasgow, had been brutally murdered at about 6:30 p.m. the previous evening.

"Just over an hour before I arrived," Sandy announced.

George scrutinised Sandy for a moment over the top of his glasses, then continued his recitation. " 'Miss Gilchrist's maid, Nellie, had returned from an errand to find the downstairs neighbour, Mr Adams, waiting at her mistress' front door. He had heard a banging from the apartment above and was concerned that the old lady had fallen. Hastening to open the door,' " George read dramatically, " 'the maid and Mr. Adams entered the hallway as a stranger came with nonchalance from the lighted interior of one of the back rooms, passed the couple with the greatest coolness and walked swiftly downstairs. His lack of concern was astounding. He impressed Adams and the girl with the air of an ordinary visitor. A few minutes more and the servant maid became hysterical at the awful result of the visit. The spectacle was full of frights and contrast of the dead and the living, and repeated itself for those whose courage or official duty prompted them to regard it.' "

George kept reading. " 'The blaze of gaslight in the old fashioned dining room was vivid. Nearly everything was undisturbed and spoke of the taste of a lady of refined and careful habits. The body, as it had fallen under the blows of the murderer, lay rigid before a living fire, whose light kept the death pallor out of the lined and worn old face. The black dress was scarcely ruffled. The head alone indicated the brutality of the assault. The skull was battered in,' "the listening boys gasped, then George continued, " 'the cheeks hacked and an eye dislodged…' "

"Cor, gruesome!" exclaimed Bobby with fascinated glee.

George read on. " 'Spots of blood darkened the steel of the grate and pieces of brain tissue were scattered about. An open coal box by the fireplace was the only object broken. It was splashed with blood and torn at the hinges, as if the body in falling had crashed against it.' "

Sandy felt sick. She was pretty sure newspapers didn't write stuff that graphic in the twenty-first century.

"'As he left the house,' " continued George, 'Adams, with the maid's horrified screams ringing in his ears, rushed down the stairs but immediately lost sight of the man. The glimpse that he had received was that of a man, dressed in a pale-coloured overcoat and cloth cap, beneath which he was gaunt like a skeleton. A true spectre of death.' "

"That's a horrible story - poor old lady! But what's it got to do with anything?" Sandy asked when George had finished reading.

"Tam," replied George, and Jamie nodded in agreement. "His girlfriend is Miss Gilchrist's maid, Nellie."

"Oh!" Sandy understood.

"Aye, and Tam was up at St George's Cross last night picking up this week's moving pictures. He could have been in the West End at the time of the murder," Jamie added.

"He was. I saw him when I was delivering a bill with Mr MacBrayne to a house on St George's Road. He and Nellie were kissing outside the newsagents at St George's Cross." George's eyes suddenly widened. "You don't think he saw the murderer and the murderer..." George paused and looked at Jamie and Bobby, who stared back at him with expressions of mounting horror. George continued as tactfully as he could, "...done him in?"

Jamie's face suddenly brightened. "He couldn't have been murdered. He was back here for the half-seven show. We saw him at the magic lantern and he seemed fine, didn't he?" Jamie looked at his brother Bobby for confirmation.

"Aye," Bobby agreed.

"Then Tam is probably fine." George paused before he continued. "Maybe he went back to the West End to look after Nellie after the shock of finding the old lady dead."

"Aye," said Jamie, "That must be where he is."

"It could be Miss Gilchrist's ghost haunting the magic lantern," Andrew suddenly suggested.

Sandy and the boys looked at him, puzzled.

"Well, I was just thinking that Tam knew old Miss Gilchrist, and he was working the magic lantern last night. It's funny how Sandy appeared in the beam not long after the old lady was murdered, and what the magic lantern projected last night could be a clue to the identity of her murderer."

They all thought about this for a minute. In the ensuing silence, Sandy's stomach rumbled loudly. She hadn't eaten since she had left the twenty-first century. Jamie, prompted by the hungry rumble, pulled a paper package out of his bag and handed it to her. "Thought you might appreciate a bit of breakfast. I went out early to collect the papers and got this from my mam on the way back."

Sandy opened the packet, which contained a thickly cut piece of bread smeared with something thick, grey, and greasy. She took the piece with a screwed-up nose and eyed it suspiciously. It didn't look anything like the pre-packed supermarket best-of-both loaves she was used to, and the grey smearing didn't look like sunflower spread. "What is it?"

"Don't tell me you dinnae ha' bread and dripping where you come from?" Bobby asked, dismayed at the thought of a future without bread and dripping.

"Dripping?" she repeated.

"Dripping, aye, you know - the fat that drips off cooking meat. That's goose dripping, my favourite. Mam got it from the cook at Sloan's Restaurant. It's good," Jamie encouraged.

Sandy tentatively touched the greasy smear with her tongue. It was salty, but delicious and she ate it hungrily whilst George brought the conversation back to the brutal murder of Marion Gilchrist.

"You know, I think Andrew's right. Maybe Miss Gilchrist was using the magic lantern to tell Tam who her murderer was, and you appearing in the beam last night like that surely means that somehow you are connected with it too," he said, looking at Sandy.

"How can I possibly be connected with something that happened over a hundred years in my past?" asked Sandy.

"I don't know," replied George. "Perhaps you're here to solve the murder."

"But why me? I don't know anything about solving murders, except what I've seen on TV. Why would the ghost of a murdered old lady pick on me?"

George thought about this for a moment. "Well, there must be some reason you've been sent through time, and it surely can't be a coincidence that you appeared soon after she was murdered. Maybe we should try and solve the murder, and we should start by..."

"Start what?" interrupted Sam as he entered the room with Charlie.

"Old Miss Gilchrist was murdered, Nellie found her deid body, an' Andrew and George think that Sandy's here 'cos he has to solve the murder," summarised Jamie.

"I know about the murder," said Sam, patting the bag full of newspapers slung over his shoulder. "Gruesome, eh? Is Tam back?"

"No," replied Jamie. "We reckon he's gone to look after Nellie. She must have been pretty upset after finding the old lady like that."

"So, are we going to investigate the murder then?" asked Charlie.

"Yes," affirmed George. "But first I want to see the magic lantern working and see if it has any more messages or clues."

* * *

It was 9:00 a.m. and, although the basement zoo and attic carnival had been open since 6:00 a.m. the music hall wouldn't open until 11:00 a.m. - when Mr Pickard would be holding auditions. Sandy and the boys snuck into the stalls and over to the haunted projector that sat on a table on a platform at the back.

George inspected it, walking around it with his crutches, looking into the lens, pulling out the frames and pushing them back in again, one by one. He opened a door in the side and inspected the interior. which was empty except for the electric light fitting. He pushed his glasses up his nose.

"It seems like a perfectly ordinary magic lantern to me." The small boy spoke with the voice of a knowledgeable adult. He turned to Sandy and instructed her to stand on the stage where she had arrived the previous evening.

"I think we need to recreate exactly what happened last night," he expressed in the same sagely tone.

She walked over to the spot where she had been standing when she'd arrived, remembering with disgust the warm trickle of wee that had run down her cheek from above. She automatically touched her cheek (which still hadn't been properly washed) and looked up to the balcony above. "If I ever get the dirty wee muppet that pee'd on me I'll…"

"Sorry about that." As Jamie apologised he reddened slightly. "I wasn't aiming for you. I was aiming at the comic, but he disappeared just as you arrived and by then it was too late. I couldn't stop it."

Sandy glared at him.

"Are you ready?" shouted George from where he stood at the back of the auditorium, ready to switch on the magic lantern.

“Very!" Sandy responded, while still glowering at Jamie for his disgusting behaviour.

George flicked the switch and the lamp behind the lens cast its light onto Sandy, who stood on the stage with her eyes shut tight, bracing herself for the sudden jolting drop again. Nothing happened. Her feet remained firmly planted on the sticky, wooden floor. She opened her eyes and looked behind her. She couldn't see a message either.

"Is anything happening?" she called across to the others who were all crowded around the magic lantern.

"No, I don't think so…not yet anyway. Do you think we have to do something else? What did you do to make the magic lantern send you back here?" George shouted as he hovered over the magic lantern, looking for some kind of hidden lever or switch.

"I didn't do anything. I woke up and the magic lantern was on so when I stood up, it zapped me back here," she answered.

"And when you all saw the message, what did you do then?" George asked the boys.

"Nothing, other than turn it on. Well, I did wiggle this bit on the end." Jamie replied, pointing to the thick brass cylinder that pulled the lens into focus.

George began to twist it. "Like this?"

"That's right." Jamie sauntered round to the front of the magic lantern and peered through the beam and into the lens.

"Don't get sucked into the beam," Sandy shouted across from the stage. "I don't want you disappearing and getting lost in some other time."

Jamie pulled his face away from the lens. They all stared at the back cloth, but the blue sky of the highland scene remained just that, a clear blue sky. No letters appeared.

"Maybe the ghost is sleeping," suggested Andrew.

Chapter Eight

Tam's Body is Discovered

It was 9:30 a.m. and with nothing mysterious occurring with the magic lantern, the boys all agreed that the best course of action was to go about their usual business of selling newspapers and running messages, and talking to the other messenger boys and newsboys across the city. If anyone knew anything about the murder or had seen Tam, it was this ragtag fraternity. Between them, they knew everything that was going on in the city. They had eyes and ears on every street corner.

Sandy went with Jamie and Bobby. They would meet back with the others later. Sandy and the two brothers spoke to every newsboy between Trongate and the top of Buchanan Street, but none of them had anything to tell. Then Jamie picked up a bundle of newspapers for his afternoon shift and they headed back to the Trongate and the corner of King Street so that he could sell them. It was lunch time when they got there and the street was a sea of people. There was a particularly large crowd outside the Panopticon. At first they thought nothing of it, crowds were usually seen cramming forward to get in to see the various entertainments on view. But when Jamie was suddenly flooded with a rush of customers clamouring for newspapers and jabbering about another body being found, his heart stopped.

"Body? What body? Where?" Jamie asked as he handed out newspapers and pocketed pennies.

"In there!" the man said as he snatched a paper and pointed at the Panopticon. "They found a body in the zoo, and it looks like it could be the same murderer as killed that old woman in the west end."

Jamie, Bobby, and Sandy gawped at each other, Sandy grabbed a paper and started scanning the pages. None of the headlines mentioned another body being found.

The children made their way up the lane and entered the Panopticon through the side door, instantly caught in the crowd of paying customers who were on their way down to the basement zoo for a gawp at the corpse. They were carried along with the mob through to where the new bear cage was being built. Harry the zookeeper stepped out of the crowd and grabbed Jamie and Bobby, pulling them to the side and away from the fray. Sandy was left standing on her own, jostled by the press of people around her. A few moments later she heard Bobby cry out. She pushed her way through the crowd towards the monkey house and the little back room. The door was open and both boys were sobbing while Harry tried to comfort them. Mr Pickard, the man she had thought was Albert the curator, was there too. He looked at Sandy as she entered the room.

"What the devil are you doing here, boy?" Mr Pickard snapped.

"It's ok, Mr Pickard," sniffed Jamie. "Sandy's oor pal."

"Well, that would explain last night's mischief, I suppose." He said rather harshly, glowering at Sandy. He looked back at the two sobbing boys and softened his tone. "But, given the circumstances, I suppose we can forget the matter."

"What's happened?" Sandy asked.

"It seems that young Tam was murdered. Workmen discovered his body this morning."

On hearing these words both brothers wailed and buried their faces and their sobs in the young zookeeper's chest. Harry consoled them as best he could.

"I think you best take the boys home to their mother," Mr Pickard said softly. "She'll no doubt want her sons with her at this terrible time. And you, boy, you can wait here I suppose, unless you have elsewhere to go." He added as he passed Sandy on the way out of the door.

Sandy didn't know what to say to her two new friends as they were led away by Harry. She sat on her own in the little room staring at the flames of the oil lamps as they flickered behind soot blackened funnels. She didn't have long to wait before the other boys returned and she explained what had happened. They already knew about Tam's murder - word had already spread via the newsboys of the dreadful discovery in the Panopticon Zoo. No one had found out anything useful.

Chapter Nine

The Detective

The gang sat glumly until George broke the silence. "I'm sure it's all connected. The message from the magic lantern, old Miss Gilchrist's murder, and…" he paused, staring sadly at the small stove, "…and Tam's," he added softly.

The boys seemed to think about this for a while, then Sandy piped up. "Maybe we should go to Miss Gilchrist's, then?" she suggested.

The others looked at her, puzzled. Then Jimmy's eyes lit up.

"Aye, Nellie will be there," he said.

The boys nodded.

"An' we can tell her about Tam. She probably doesn't know about his…" Andrew said, his voice trailing away, unable say murder.

"Why would Nellie be there?" Sandy said.

"She lived there with Miss Gilchrist. She's been with the old lady since she was a wean. Where else would she go?" Jimmy replied.

Sandy felt a little disturbed at the thought of spending the night in a house where there had recently been a murder and couldn't believe that anyone would be allowed to.

"I was actually thinking we could go up and investigate the crime scene, you know, like CSIs?" The boys looked at her blankly. "Don't you have CSIs?"

"See ess whit now?" Charlie asked in a confused tone.

"CSI stands for Crime Scene Investigators." Sandy explained, answering their vacant expressions. "They go into crime scenes and find all the forensic evidence which tells them who did the crime." Sandy was a big fan of detective programmes and CSI was her favourite. She watched it with her gran.

George stared at Sandy with a look of pure astonishment on his face. "What's frenzic evidence?" he asked.

"All sorts of stuff - hair, blood, fingernails. They find little bits of stuff lying around and collect it and then analyse it. You know, like if Miss Gilchrist's murderer cut himself and they found his blood at the scene of the crime, then they could match the blood to the suspect. I don't know exactly how, I'm not a CSI, but that's what they do." Sandy continued her explanation.

George and the others continued to look at her blankly. How could hair, blood and fingernails tell the police who the murderer was?

"Do you mean, like fingerprints?" asked George. He had read about fingerprints in a paper. He learned that everyone's fingerprints were different and detectives could use them to identify suspects.

"Exactly like fingerprints," answered Sandy.

"Do you think we will find stuff like that where they found Tam?" asked Andrew.

"Maybe..." Sandy was thoughtful. "I guess there's no harm in looking, but we're not going to get near it while that crowd's out there. We might find something at Miss Gilchrist's, though."

"Dae ya really think that whoever done in the old lady done in Tam too?" Sam proposed.

"Stands to reason," answered George, taking off his glasses and cleaning the lenses on the frayed edge of his ragged coat. "He must have seen the murderer when he was in the west end, and they followed him back here. Sandy's right, we might find some frenzicks at the old lady's house."

"We're going to Miss Gilchrist's now, then?" Andrew asked.

"Aye." They all agreed and, save for George who knew he would not manage the long walk to the west end, Sandy and the boys left the music hall and headed to Miss Gilchrist's. George ventured to the music hall to wait and see if the magic lantern would project another message. Maybe the ghost was Tam.

* * *

An hour later, Sandy, Andrew, Jimmy, Sam, and Charlie were standing at the bottom of the tenement steps outside Miss Gilchrist's building. They were frozen to the bone after their trek through howling wind and freezing sleet.

They looked up to the first-floor windows which glowed with amber light. Someone was inside. Hopefully, it was

Nellie, with the promise of a warm fire and a hot drink, but in the brief moment that they stood watching, the lights went out. An instant later, a door opened and a gentleman in a bowler hat and black woollen overcoat, carrying a black umbrella, came down the front steps towards them.

He stared at them and as he reached the last step, he queried. "Looking for something, boys?"

"What's it tae youse?" Sam queried back.

The man regarded Sam and smiled "Well, young man, as you probably know, this house here," he indicated the building behind him with his umbrella, "is the site of a rather gruesome murder, and I am the detective in charge of the investigation. So, boys, what is your reason for being here on this cold night?"

"We're looking for oor friend Nellie, " mumbled Jimmy, looking down at his feet.

"Speak up, boy," commanded the man. "I can't hear you over the wind."

"We're looking for Nellie," supplied Charlie, somewhat louder than his quiet friend.

"Nellie? The maid? She's not here, son. She's with Miss Gilchrist's niece in Hill Street. What business is she of yours?" The detective's tone was filled with curiosity.

"She's stepping out with our friend's brother, sir. We've come to tell her that he has…that he's been…well…he's been found deid, sir," Sam paused briefly then awkwardly added. "Murdered." As he stared up at the man in the bowler hat and black wool coat.

"Ah, I am very sorry to hear that. But, as I said, Nellie is not here." He pushed up his umbrella against the sleet and wind. "So I suggest you all go home."

The boys didn't move, continuing to block his path. They stared up at him mournfully. He felt sorry for the poor little wretches out here in the cold night. The least he could do was listen to their story.

"How was your friend murdered?" he enquired.

"Tam. His name was Tam," Andrew bitterly replied.

"Yes, sorry. How was Tam murdered?" the detective enquired again.

"He was stabbed," answered Sam.

"In the Panopticon," chimed Charlie.

"Oh, I see. And when was this?" the detective asked sceptically.

"Workmen discovered his body in the zoo earlier today," Sandy answered. The detective looked at the small boy who emerged from behind his taller compatriots in such strange attire he was quite taken aback. For a moment he just stared at the strange-looking child.

"We think his murder is connected to the old lady's," Sandy continued, ignoring the detective's astonished gaze.

"I think it is highly unlikely," the detective replied. "Two different ends of the town, two different ends of society. Why would the murderer of a wealthy west end lady be interested in a lad from the east end? And did you say he was stabbed? The old lady was bludgeoned. No, no, lad. I am very sorry for your loss, and I will see how we can help but…"

"Are you a Seeing Eye?" Charlie asked, interrupting the police man. The man in the bowler-hat looked at him as if he had spoken in another language.

"He means CSI, as in Crime Scene Investigator," explained Sandy, answering the man's quizzical look.

"Yes, I suppose you could call me that," the man said with a raised eyebrow. "Most people just call us the police." He pulled his collar up against the bitter wind as it suddenly gusted.

"Do you know who the old lady's murderer is?" asked Charlie.

"Ah, the favourite question of the day," the policeman cheerily replied. "And one that I am not at liberty to answer, lad. I suggest you get along now."

The group of boys did not move. Instead, they stood staring at the inspector as he pushed up his umbrella against the sleet.

"Sir, could you tell me where Miss Gilchrist's niece lives? We really should tell Nellie about Tam," asked Sam his tone determined.

"9 Hill Street," the inspector answered. The boys still did not move out of his way.

"Tam was here last night. He was up seeing Nellie," Sandy added. It was her last attempt to try and convince the detective to let them inside, or at least provide some sort of useful information that they could connect to the riddle from the magic lantern or the death of Tam.

The detective looked at the boy in the strange outfit. *Could he be right? Could there be a connection between the two murders?*

"Do you think it is possible that your friend saw something? Is that it?" he asked the boys, who nodded in unison. They now looked dismally cold and damp, shivering so hard he could hear their teeth chatter. "Well, perhaps we should get out of this weather and talk about this a bit further," he suggested.

The boys followed the detective up the steps and into the tenement building. The detective lit the gas jets in the hallway with a long match, echoing this action as they entered the dining room. The gas jets cast a lively light in the room but without a fire in the hearth the apartment was cold. Blessedly out of the wind and sleet, but chilly, nonetheless.

The room was exactly as the newspapers had described. It was grandly furnished and decorated with expensive ornaments and paintings. The body of Miss Gilchrist had been removed, however, her blood was still vivid on the hearth rug and up the wall next to the fireplace. Sandy couldn't help but stare at the stains that were less than twenty-four hours old.

"Alright." The policeman pulled a small notebook and pencil out of his coat pocket and commanded. "Tell me about Tam."

"George saw him with Nellie outside the newsagents around the corner last night at about half-six," answered Andrew, speaking on behalf of his brother.

"Which one of you is George?"

"Oh, he's no here. We left him back at the Panopticon. He's ma wee brother," Andrew replied.

"And the last time we saw Tam was in the Panopticon. He was working the magic lantern at the half-seven show but after that no one saw him. He just disappeared," Sam explained. "And that's all we know. He wasn't there for the half-nine show, so when Tam didn't turn up to work today and we saw that old Miss Gilchrist had been done away with, well, we just thought that maybe he was here with Nellie. Then we found out he had been murdered too," Sam finished, sadly.

"Do you think that Tam could have had something to do with the murder of Miss Gilchrist?" The detective continued his questioning.

The boys shrugged.

"I don't know, sir," replied Sam. "I know he didn't murder the old lady. Tam ain't that kind of person, but maybe he saw something after he left Nellie last night."

"Did any of you speak to Tam last night?"

The boys all shook their heads, all except the strangely dressed boy who stared at the blood stains as if transfixed by them.

"Can I ask a question?" Sandy inquired tentatively.

"Aye, son. I don't know if I will be allowed to answer it, but there's no harm in asking," the detective replied.

"In the newspaper today it said that Nellie and the man who lives downstairs saw a man in a pale-coloured overcoat," Sandy began.

"Yes, and?"

"The article didn't mention a blood-splattered overcoat," continued Sandy. "All that blood on the wall and rug - surely if the man in the overcoat was the murderer, wouldn't he have been covered in blood? How could the blood have splashed up the wall and fireplace and not covered him?"

The detective was taken aback at the boy's comment. This lad was extremely bright - strangely dressed, but bright.

"You, young man, would make an excellent detective." He paused, not quite knowing what to say next. Should he bait these boys with some information in case they knew something? "We think that two men were involved. The man Nellie and Mr. Adams encountered in the hallway had come from Miss Gilchrist's bedroom, not this room. We believe the murderer climbed out of the window over there and lowered himself into the back court, before making his escape via the back lane."

"But the papers only mention one man," said Jamie. The other boys nodded in agreement.

"Well, we aren't obliged to tell the papers everything. We keep certain information away from the public, especially in cases like these when there is a reward for information, and we have to rely on reports from members of the public - we want to make sure that what people tell us isn't just what they've read in the papers."

"So does that mean that you know a lot more than the papers are saying?" Sam asked.

"Possibly, and, no, I am not going to tell you anything else that isn't already reported in the press, or about to be," intoned the Detective. He decided to swing the subject back to what they knew - if anything. He turned his attention to Jimmy. "Did you ever meet Miss Gilchrist?"

"No, but they did." Jimmy quietly replied, pointing at Andrew, Sam, and Charlie.

"Aye. Sometimes I delivered her paper." Andrew answered.

"We ran messages for her." Sam added, and Charlie nodded in agreement.

"When was the last time you saw Miss Gilchrist?" the detective licked the end of his pencil and made ready to write a note of anything the boys said.

Andrew thought for a moment, then answered, "Must've been last Thursday. Nellie had the afternoon off, and Miss Gilchrist likes her paper by seven - she likes to read it after dinner."

"Did you speak to Miss Gilchrist?"

"No, sir."

"Then who let you in to deliver the newspaper?"

"Miss Gilchrist, sir, but she just lets me into the close. She has a special button that opens the door from her flat. I left the paper outside her door," replied Andrew, watching the pencil suspiciously and feeling a little bit uncomfortable that his words were being written down.

"Have any of you seen Nellie recently?"

"Yes, sir. Last Thursday when she came into the Panopticon to see Tam," answered Charlie. "She always comes to see Tam on her day off."

"Has Nellie said anything to you at all about any strangers watching the house or anything suspicious at any time?"

The boys thought hard for a minute, trying to remember any recent conversations any of them had with Nellie. Last time she had been in the Panopticon, Jamie had been telling her all about the phantom pickpocket. They hadn't really talked about anything else, though Nellie had mentioned that her knees and back were sore from having to crawl under Miss Gilchrist's bed.

"Come to think of it, she did say that Miss Gilchrist had made her check under the bed because she thought someone was hiding under it," Sam supplied.

The detective raised an eyebrow and jotted a note. "Can you think of anything else suspicious?"

None of the boys responded.

"I see. Well, I will call the Calton office and ask them to send an officer to talk to you in case you remember something else that might be relevant. I assume you all have addresses?"

"Aye, sir," answered Andrew. "Most of us are at the Goosedubs and Back Wynd. Sam lives on the Trongate - but most times you can find us at the Panopticon."

The detective grunted and was about to close his book when he asked, "Did Nellie say why Miss Gilchrist thought someone was hiding under her bed?"

Sam thought for a moment. He couldn't really remember. "No," he answered with a little uncertainty. "She was a wee bit batty though."

The detective sat back in his seat and reviewed his notes, then sat forward again and asked, "Where did Tam live?"

The boys replied in unison. "Panopticon."

The detective closed his book, put it and his pencil back in his coat pocket and stood up. "Well, lads, if that's all the information you have for me just now I suggest you go home for your tea and I'll go home for mine. Here's my card. Contact me at the west end police office and ask for Detective Lieutenant Trench if you think of anything else." He handed his card to Sandy. "And here's half a crown to share, for your trouble," he added, dropping the coin into Charlie's upturned palm.

Sam suddenly thrust his hand in the air.

"Yes, lad?" the detective enquired of the eager, small boy, who was obviously desperate to tell him something.

"Do you know who A.B. is?"

How do they know about A.B.? Detective Trench thought, as the other boys glowered angrily at Sam.

"No, I don't know who A.B. is." It wasn't a lie; he didn't know exactly who A.B. was - but the initials were believed to be connected to the murderer. "Why do you ask?"

"He just saw it written somewhere, that's all," Jimmy answered, then started to shove his small friend with the big mouth out of the door before he said something else that would be difficult to explain to an adult, especially a policeman.

Detective Trench watched the small raggle-taggle gang of newsboys and urchins as they wandered off down the street, huddled together against the bitter wind. The sleet had become soft flakes of wet snow that settled on their thin shoulders. The detective felt a pang of pity for them.

How did they know about A.B? How could they know? What were these boys hiding? And there was something else - the boy in the strange coat and furry boots. He couldn't quite put his finger on it, but there was definitely something not quite right with him. He would have to keep an eye on them, just in case.

Chapter Ten

The Man in the Pale-Coloured Overcoat

The walk to the tram stop was gruelling. The wind had become a gale, driving the thickening snow into their faces. They stopped to buy hot pies with the half-crown Detective Trench had given them before jumping on a tram to the Trongate with the leftover change.

When they got back to the room in the basement zoo, a fire was blazing in the little stove. It gave the windowless room a cheery glow and made their frozen cheeks tingle with warmth. They sat in front of the stove to thaw out and told George about their conversation with Detective Trench.

"Well that was a waste of time," commented Jimmy flatly. "We didn't exactly learn much about Tam's murderer or A.B."

"I wouldn't say it was a waste of time. We got half a crown and a hot pie out of it." Charlie countered.

"And I wouldn't say we didn't learn anything," Sandy added. "We learned that there are two suspects, not just the man in the pale-coloured overcoat the newspapers described. And I don't believe he's never heard of A.B., did you see the expression on his face when Sam mentioned him?"

Sam grinned and nodded.

As the warmth of the cosy stove thawed their frozen bones, they all began to drift into a doze, which was abruptly broken when Harry's voice, just outside the door, shouted, "Oi you! That's staff only in there!"

"I am a police detective, sir." They heard a man's deep voice answer in a strange accent.

Jimmy jumped up from the chair he was sharing with Sam and George, nearly throwing them to the floor.

"Shhh," he hissed. "Help me put out the lamps."

"Why?" Charlie whispered back. "It's another detective. Maybe he's from the Calton office. Detective Trench said he would send one round."

"Jimmy's right. That doesn't sound like a Glasgow Bobby," declared George. "He sounds foreign."

"He sounds German to me," said Sandy

"German!" exclaimed Sam in a quiet voice full of fear.

Sandy and the boys quickly extinguished the lamps and squeezed together under one corner of the workbench where they were hidden by one of the large, worn-out chairs. They stayed glued to the spot, holding their breath and straining to hear the conversation beyond the door. From this side of the room they could only hear voices, not words, as the talkers seemed to have moved away from the door.

"What do you think they're talking about?" Charlie whispered.

"Shhhh, I'm trying to listen," Jimmy whispered back.

The voices became more muffled and indistinct as they moved further away and merged with the general cacophony of the zoo outside. Sandy began to feel stiff from crouching and being squashed together with the boys, so started to crawl out of their hiding place.

"No!" George hissed, grabbing her by the ankle before she crawled out. "He might be waiting for Harry to go and then come back."

Sandy retreated to the shadows of the work bench, and they waited, squatting in the gloom. The minutes passed and then, just as the gang thought it must be safe to leave their cramped corner, they heard the door creak slowly open. A man entered and peered into the darkness. The boys and Sandy froze, not even daring to breathe.

The fraudulent detective in a pale-coloured overcoat struck a match and, using its brief bright flame, scanned the small room. The gang were so deeply hidden, crammed together in the shadows behind the chair, that the small match flame couldn't find them. But he knew they were there, he could sense their eyes watching him and smell the recently extinguished lamp and candle wicks. The match flame licked at his fingers. He shook it out, lit another, and searched the workbench. There was nothing - just bits of junk - but he did catch a glimpse of a shoe, which gave away their hiding place. He made no move to catch them. They would panic and scream, bringing that nosey zookeeper running, and he didn't want that. He went back to the door, glanced one more time behind him, blew the match out and left.

"Who do you think that was?" Sandy whispered.

"It was the man in the pale-coloured overcoat," stated Andrew.

"What? The man Nellie saw in the hallway?" asked Sam.

"Well, he fits the description in the papers," said Andrew.

"But what has a German man got to do with all of this?" asked George, who really was puzzled.

"Why do you think he's come here?" asked Sandy.

"I don't know," replied George, looking more than a little concerned. "But whatever it is, I don't think it's good."

"Do you think we should go to the police?" Charlie asked.

"Perhaps," replied George. "Maybe we should go and see that detective again. But it's too late to do anything tonight."

Chapter Eleven

23rd December
The Pocket Watch

Sandy woke up the next morning with something itchy and heavy pulled tightly around her. She was praying that, when she opened her eyes, she would find herself in her own bedroom, wrapped up in her woollen rug. Why she would be wrapped in her rug she didn't know, but she just prayed that she was, and that the boys, the murders, and the magic lantern were just part of a very detailed and incredibly real dream. The jungle sounds of the zoo outside brought her back to her new reality. She slowly opened her eyes and pushed off the heavy woollen blanket, then tried to uncurl her legs from the position they had been in all night and found that they had gone to sleep. Pins and needles prickled the soles of her feet and she winced as she tried to stand.

She desperately needed the loo, but the white-enamelled tin potty that Tam had kept under the workbench already had a wee in it, which meant she had to take it through the zoo, past the distorting mirrors, up the stairs, and out the doors into the lane where she could throw the contents down the drain. Oh, what she would give for a nice clean loo and real toilet paper - here they used cut-up squares of newspaper.

As soon as she stepped outside the little room, carefully carrying the tin chamber pot, Harry collared her.

"You, lad. Still here, I see?"

"Yes, sir," Sandy answered.

"Well, if you're going to stay in Tam's old room, you might as well take up his job. Here." Harry handed Sandy a broom. "Get Solomon and Betsy's cage swept and then I'll see if I can rustle us up some breakfast."

Sandy was stunned by the callousness. Tam had only been discovered murdered the previous day and his job was already being given to someone else. It seemed so heartless.

"You needn't look so injured. It's not like we don't care about Tam. What happened to him is nothing less than tragic, but the animals don't give a fig for who cleans an' feeds 'em, so long as they're seen to."

Sandy stood with the broom in one hand and her pot of pee in the other and looked at the pair of well-dressed apes. Solomon met her stare and made a noise that Sandy assumed was laughter. Harry laughed heartily too.

"Go get rid of that first. Chuck it down the drain in the Back Wynd." He took the broom back off her, propping it against the monkey house.

She began to slowly make her way to the exit door, careful not to slop any wee over herself.

"Come on, boy. Run, don't dander. I haven't got all day!" Harry barked at her and she began to trot, instantly spilling half of the contents of the pot down her jeans. Oh great, she thought to herself as the chimp and young man fell into gales of fresh laughter.

When she got back, Harry opened the door to the monkey house and Sandy entered, ready to clean up their mess. Solomon, who was dressed in a green velvet suit that made him look like a hairy leprechaun, tugged and pulled at Sandy's jeans. She tried to push him off but he was persistent.

"What is it, monkey man?" Sandy asked the chimp, who responded by baring his teeth as if smiling at her and making funny little whooping noises. Sandy made whooping noises back, then Solomon did a very strange thing. He reached into a small hole in the wall at the back of the monkey house, pulled something out and put it in Sandy's back jean pocket. Sandy tentatively put her hand in the pocket, expecting to find a bit of half rotten banana or a chunk of chimp poo, and was very surprised when her fingers closed around something hard and smooth. She pulled it out. It was an old-fashioned pocket watch with the name Thomas Murray engraved on the back. Wasn't Murray the last name of Jamie and Bobby? And wasn't Tam short for Thomas?

"Where did you get this?" Sandy asked. The ape responded by pursing his lips together as if he was blowing a kiss, blew a raspberry instead, then shook his head.

"Not telling, eh?" Sandy put the watch back in her pocket before Harry, who was sitting on a chair reading a newspaper outside the cage, could see it.

She tried to glance over his shoulder to see if she could catch a glimpse of any progress on the murder case, but the print was too small to read from this distance, so she hurriedly finished sweeping the muck into a neat pile and then scraped it up with a shovel. Harry let her out of the cage when she was done and told her where to put the muck. When she returned he was standing at the door of the small room that Sandy had called home for the last two nights.

Harry had relit the stove and a whistling kettle sat on the hot plate alongside a frying pan which was just beginning to sizzle. Harry added two bits of bacon and two eggs which jumped and sputtered in the hot fat. The aroma of the cooking meat and eggs was the most wonderful smell in the world. Sandy's stomach gurgled.

"You hungry?" asked Harry. "I bet you are. Go wash your hands. Breakfast will be ready in a minute."

Sandy showed the young zookeeper her hands, which she had washed at the pump in the Back Wynd after she had dumped the chimp manure. She had found a bar of disinfectant-smelling soap with the word 'carbolic' stamped on it in one of the store cupboards. It didn't smell particularly pleasant, but it did the job, and its medical scent was reassuringly clean.

"You are unnaturally clean for a boy," Harry commented and plated up the delicious smelling breakfast. "Get that down you." He handed her a plate of bacon and eggs and a cup of black tea. "Put hairs on your chest, that will."

After chewing for a moment on his breakfast, Harry asked, "So, where do you come from?"

"I'm from the North Pole," she lied, mumbling through a mouthful of succulent, sizzling hot bacon.

Harry nodded. "Of course, that would explain your clothes." He wasn't daft - he knew the strange boy was lying - but eventually he would get to the bottom of it. "And why exactly are you here?"

"I want to be a performer." It was the most obvious answer Sandy could think of and it was what she had told the detective the previous day.

"So, you knew Tam then, eh?"

"No. Not really. I know Jamie and he asked Tam if I could stay here. Just until I can get my own place." Sandy waited for him to ask her where her parents were, but the question didn't come, instead Harry just started talking about Tam and 'poor Nellie'.

"Such a shame. I wouldn't want to have been the person that found that old lady with her brains all smashed-in like that - horrible. And then what happened to Tam. Well, it just seems wrong." He eyed Sandy for a moment, waiting for her to answer.

"Yes, it's tragic." Was all Sandy could think of as a response.

"Well, finish up, lad. You've work to do. You'll be paid as well, don't worry, I shall speak to Mr Pickard. He's a fair man, if not the most generous. Do a good day's work and you'll get a bawbee or two for your trouble," he stated as he stood up. "Go and get these washed up then come back to me and I'll show you how to feed the animals," handing her his plate.

"Harry, can I ask a question, please?" Sandy appealed, as politely as she knew how.

"Well, lad, I suppose that would depend on the question."

"Well, it was just about the magic lantern. I've never seen one before and I wondered where Mr. Pickard got it from."

"Are you thinking of saving your money to buy one of your own? It'll cost you more than you'd earn here in a year." Harry looked at the strange boy's earnest little face. This lad looked and talked odd, but he was a well brought-up youngster, no doubt about it. "But, since you ask, he bought it at some auction a few weeks ago with some other bits and pieces. It's a bit old fashioned if you ask me. People want to see moving pictures these days, but Mr. Pickard thought we could use it to show advertisements between acts, so he got Tam and the old man to fix it up for the electric."

"But where did it come from?" Sandy pressed.

"I don't know. He doesn't exactly tell me his business. Probably some old music hall that was closing down. I do know he bought it in London, and he got it cheap," answering impatiently. "Now get on with your chores," he ordered in the most authoritative voice he could muster.

Sandy picked up the dirty plates and left. Harry's answers had left her with more questions. Where in London was this auction? Who had owned it? Why did it have such special powers? Did anyone else know about it?

* * *

By the time Sandy got back from washing the dishes, Harry had gone. His newspaper was left neatly folded on the chair outside the monkey house. Sandy took the opportunity to flick through it and see if anything else had been written about the murder of the old woman, which might give her a clue as to why she was here.

Solomon was reaching for her through the bars again and tugging at her jeans. Sandy handed him a banana and continued to read through the paper until she came across something on page four with the headline 'Revolting Murder in Glasgow' and Sandy realised that Harry had been reading yesterday's Evening Times. She was about to put the paper away, thinking there was no point in reading the same news twice, when she noticed that The Evening Times reported a slightly different version of events than the Daily Record article George had read out. This article suggested a motive - burglary - not by a 'Bill Sykes' type thug, but by someone known to the victim.

" 'The burglar had time, in the 10 minutes that Nellie was out, to light the gas in the bedroom and rifle through the papers in a workbox which were left strewn around the room. A number of valuable items - gold rings, bangles, chains and watches - had been left by the burglar. Only a valuable diamond brooch was missing,' " she read quietly to herself.

That's interesting. The message projected by the magic lantern had mentioned a diamond. Was it referring to the missing diamond brooch? She wondered.

Chapter Twelve

An Anonymous Note

Sir Arthur Conan Doyle was visiting his sister Connie for Christmas in Edinburgh. It had been his wife Jean's idea. He had been so engrossed that year in writing his latest book, *Round the Fire Stories*, a new collection of diabolical and thrilling tales, that Jean felt he had neglected his family. Now that the collection was published, she wanted them to spend some time together.

"Christmas is, after all, a time for family, my dearest," Jean said in that sweet and charming manner which always warmed his heart, making him agree to anything she wanted.

They had arrived in Edinburgh only two days ago and already he was bored. But that was about to change when the Sir Arthur was sorting a pile of unopened Christmas cards and discovered a mysterious anonymous note which read, *Come to the Panopticon in Glasgow and seek out a gang of boys in the basement zoo. The game's afoot!*

What did it mean? What could a gang of boys in Glasgow possibly possess that would be of interest to him? And how had the sender known he would be in Edinburgh? These were all intriguing thoughts, but what fascinated him most was the handwriting. The slope of the letters, the shape and flow of them. It seemed impossible, was impossible, but the letter was written in a hand identical to his own.

Arthur could never resist a mystery, especially when he was bored. He simply had to discover the meaning of this puzzling letter. He pleaded with his wife and sister to let him go. He showed them the letter and they agreed that the hand was indeed identical to his own, though this seemed to worry Jean more than intrigue her.

"Whoever wrote this has obviously studied you closely, or at least your handwriting. Honestly, Arthur, I'm not sure it's the wisest idea to go racing off to Glasgow to meet a gang of total strangers," she entreated.

His sister agreed. "You could be racing to your doom when you should be racing to tell the police."

"Oh, for goodness sakes you two! You're like a pair of old ladies jumping at shadows. It's probably just a bit of harmless fun. I have no doubt I'll be back again tomorrow, and I will be sure to notify the police the instant I think something is amiss," Arthur assured them both.

In the end, they knew they couldn't refuse him. In part because he would do what he wanted, as he always did. They did, however, insist that he have lunch first. He couldn't go running off after an adventure on an empty stomach.

With lunch delaying his departure, it was just past 3 p.m. by the time he arrived at Waverley Station. He paced the station forecourt, bought a newspaper from a news stand which he folded and placed under his arm, as it would give him something to read on the journey. Finally, he boarded the 3:30 p.m. service to Glasgow and spent the journey reading every article and advert the afternoon edition of The Scotsman newspaper had to offer. It was full of the usual claptrap - nothing really of interest at all except for one small snippet which filled one column of the huge broadsheet. It was a report about the ongoing investigation of the brutal murder of an old lady in Glasgow and the subsequent search for her missing diamond brooch. Pawn brokers and jewellers were asked to be on their guard and contact the Glasgow police immediately if such an item came into one of their shops. The old lady's murder was no mystery; it seemed obvious to him that the motive was the valuable item of jewellery. He thought for the briefest moment that the murder and the missing jewel might be connected to the mysterious letter, but it couldn't have been. The letter was dated and postmarked the afternoon of the 21st of December, and the murder had not occurred until that evening.

An hour or so later, he arrived in Glasgow and began heading for the Panopticon. As he marched along Argyle Street, he suddenly felt a creeping sense of apprehension. Were his wife and sister right to be concerned? Was he indeed marching towards his doom? Was his love of intrigue about to bring his end? He shook his head as if to shake off his anxiety, straightened his back, lengthened his stride, and continued to his destination. A few minutes later, he was at the front doors of the Panopticon. He bought a tuppence ticket from the lady in the ticket booth and followed the signs that directed him to 'Noah's Ark Zoo.' Here he would either find a gang of boys or confirmation of his wife and sister's fears. Either way, he would find some kind to answer as to the origin of the intriguing letter.

Chapter Thirteen

Sir Arthur Meets Sandy and the Boys

It was 4:00 p.m. and all the boys had gathered in the little basement room. Even Jamie and Bobby, who were determined to find their brother's murderer and exact vengeance.

"The police never even came to see maw. I had to tell her myself. I ain't never seen her so heartbroken." Jamie was looking sulkily down at his feet.

"They don't care. They just don't care and it's no fair!" blurted Bobby, sniffing back a fresh set of tears.

"Och, they're only interested in the rich old woman's murder," added Jimmy bitterly. "They'll no waste their time on one of us. We don't matter."

"There wasn't a single mention o' Tam's murder in the papers," Sam agreed. Sandy's fingers closed around the pocket watch that Solomon had given her that morning. She pulled it out and showed it to the boys.

"I found this when I was mucking out the monkey house. Well, actually, Solomon gave it to me," she said as she dangled the watch.

"That's Tam's!" exclaimed Jamie as he reached out to pluck it from Sandy's fingers. "It was our Grandda's."

"Aye, it's a family hair-loom," Bobby added proudly.

"Heirloom," corrected George.

"Air-loom, then," Bobby retorted.

"P'raps he dropped it when he was mucking out the monkey house on Monday morning?" suggested Jimmy.

"Tam wouldn't have dropped it, he was too careful of it. He loved that watch more than anything," said Jamie mournfully, staring at the silver timepiece.

"And he couldn't have lost it before Monday night. He was looking at it when I passed him and Nellie outside the newsagents," George declared.

"It's got to be a clue," said Jamie, looking up, his eyes glistening in the lamplight.

"Aye, maybe the murderer stole it," suggested Sam.

"Like he stole the brooch from Miss Gilchrist's?" added Sandy. The boys glared at her. "I read it in the paper."

"I read that, too," said George. "The article said that a valuable diamond brooch was all that was stolen and that rings, bracelets, and other jewels were just left lying around."

"Eh!? What kind of burglar would leave all those jewels?" Charlie asked, his eyes wide in disbelief. "I would ha'e taken the lot!" Sam nodded in agreement beside him.

"Dae ya think it was that huge brooch she always wore? You know, the one with the diamond as big as a glass eye?" asked Sam.

"Naw, Miss Gilchrist said it was just paste and not worth anything much at all," Andrew replied. "But maybe the murderer didn't know that."

"Or maybe she was lying and it was a real diamond. I mean, it really sparkled. It certainly looked real," commented Charlie.

"Well, onyways, how did Solomon end up with Tam's watch?" asked Jamie, trying to bring the focus back onto his brother's murder. He didn't care nearly as much about the old woman and her missing brooch.

"It must have been the phantom pickpocket. He was definitely down here on Monday night. He stole your sweets, didn't he?" Andrew said, looking at Jamie, who nodded in confirmation. "He must've stole the watch aff the murderer."

"Aye, an' then he dropped it and it got kicked into the monkey house," added Charlie.

Jamie turned the little silver pocket watch over and over in his fingers. "Then we find the phantom pickpocket," he announced with resolve. "An' he might lead us to the murderer."

"And how are we supposed to find him?" asked Jimmy. "He's called the 'Phantom' pickpocket for a reason. No one has seen him. He's like a ghost."

"Then it's about time someone caught him," Jamie spat.

"But why would the murderer steal your brother's watch?" Jimmy asked. Jamie gave him a treacherous look. "Well, a diamond brooch I can unner-staun being stolen, but your gran-da's old pocket watch? I mean…"

"I ken fine what ya mean," Jamie snapped.

"Hey, do you think the brooch is the diamond?" Sandy suddenly suggested.

The boys looked at her quizzically.

"You know, the one in the magic lantern message?"

"Oh, aye."

"I 'spect so."

"Must be."

"Aye," the boys all muttered at once in agreement.

"What time's it?" Andrew suddenly asked.

Jamie looked at the pocket watch, but it had stopped.

"Well, it was nearly four on the tollbooth clock when we came in, so it must be gone half past by now," said George.

"Jings, we're gonny be late!" said Andrew.

"What for?" asked Sandy.

"Och, some do-gooder women in the west-end are raising money to buy warm clathes for us poor newsboys," he said, putting on a pathetic expression.

"I'm not going anywhere," said Jamie firmly. "I'm gonna search this place for clues to my brother's murder."

"Aye, but Miss Gilchrist wiz one o' they do-gooder ladies and her friends will be there. We might find out some information," suggested Sam.

Jamie reluctantly agreed to go, but only so he could try and find out more about the old lady's murder and prove that her death and Tam's were connected. Jamie, Andrew, Sam, and Charlie left, while George, Sandy, Bobby, and Jimmy stayed behind in the basement zoo.

The remaining friends were discussing what they should do next when Harry appeared at the door looking very pleased with himself.

"Just as I thought. They're in here, sir," he said as he peered in.

The boys and Sandy looked up. A slightly plump middle-aged man in a heavy overcoat, sporting a bushy moustache, was standing in the doorway with Harry.

It was a good thing that George was sitting down because he would have definitely fallen if he hadn't been. He looked absolutely stunned at the sight of the stranger. The colour drained from his face - as if he had seen a ghost - but his expression was of awe, not horror.

"Arthur Conan Doyle..." he announced with mounting excitement. "It's Sir Arthur Conan Doyle!"

The name tickled at something in Sandy's memory.

"Hello there," the man jovially hailed. "I received a letter instructing me to look for a gang of boys in the Panopticon Zoo. Would that happen to be you by any chance?"

"This gang of ruffians is the only one that congregates here, sir," answered Harry.

The boys looked puzzled, none of them had sent any letters. Arthur Conan Doyle read them the note and held it up for them all to see. The boys were no less perplexed.

"Now, this gentleman," Sir Arthur indicated Harry, who was still standing in the doorway just behind him, "is sure that you are the gang of boys in question. Do you have any idea why I was sent this letter and who might have sent it?"

"No, sir," said George. "Not a clue."

"I know you. You write the Sherlock Holmes books!" Jimmy exclaimed.

"Yes, I do," answered the respectable gentleman. "Though I do write other things as well."

That was it. Sandy remembered why this man's name had tickled at her memory. In the 21st century Panopticon, the curator Albert had told them that the magic lantern had been gifted to the theatre by Sir Arthur Conan Doyle, the famous author of Sherlock Holmes. Sandy had seen the movies at least three times - she loved them. Sir Arthur Conan Doyle had instructed that the magic lantern be delivered on the very night her school would be at the old music hall. She had thought it was just a story, but now he was standing there in front of her. He really must have sent the magic lantern after all, which meant he was the very reason she was there.

"This is all very odd," Sir Arthur said. "Someone obviously wants us to get together. The question is, why? What mystery awaits us?"

Sir Arthur stepped over to the stove and the worn-out chairs. Jimmy, who had been sitting in one of them, jumped up and offered his seat to the legendary author. Sir Arthur reviewed the proffered seat and declined, he would prefer, he explained, to stand at the stove and warm his frozen, old bones. Harry, the boys, and Sandy stood around him, gawping at their famous guest.

"Well, do any of you have the slightest idea why I might be here? Have I met any of you before?" He scanned their faces one by one. "I don't recognise any of you and I never forget a face." His gaze lingered on Sandy longest as he took in the strange attire. "Is that outfit some sort of costume?" Sir Arthur asked.

Sandy couldn't speak. Her head was spinning. She wanted to ask him why he had sent the magic lantern to the Panopticon in 2016 and why he had sent her back in time, but how do you ask a man about something he is yet to do?

It was the Conan Doyle of 1916 that had bequeathed the magic lantern - wasn't it? She was sure Albert had said the letter was dated 1916, and this was 1908. Whatever the date, she felt compelled to tell him the truth about where she was from, but Harry was still lurking in the doorway.

Arthur Conan Doyle noticed her glance towards the zookeeper. Whatever this lad had to say, it was obvious he wasn't going to say it in front of him.

"Thank you for your help, Mr...?"

"Hill, sir. Harry Hill," Harry answered as he stuck out his hand and Sir Arthur Conan Doyle shook it. "Happy to be of service, sir."

"Well, thank you, Harry, but do you mind if I have a word with these boys alone?" Sir Arthur requested.

The young man looked a little disappointed at being asked to leave, but he did his best to hide it. "Of course, sir. I was just about to leave anyway - it's time to feed the animals." He left, pulling the door closed behind him.

When Harry had gone, Sir Arthur turned his attention back to Sandy. "Well?"

"It's not a costume, sir, and, well, I'm not sure why you are here. But…" she paused.

"But, what? What do you know, child? Are you behind the letter?" asked Sir Arthur.

"I don't know who wrote the letter, and I don't have a clue why you were told to come here and, well, it's really hard to explain and you'll probably think that this is a wind-up, but, well..." she paused to consider how she was going to phrase her next line, and finally blurted. "I'm here because of you!"

The boys each let out a small gasp and stared at their new friend in disbelief.

"You never mentioned Sir Arthur Conan Doyle before!" exclaimed George.

Sir Arthur Conan Doyle looked puzzled. "Explain yourself, boy."

Again, Sandy paused as she considered the best way to explain all that had happened before deciding to just come right out with it.

"I'm from the year 2016."

"Now, really..." Sir Arthur began indignantly. He had feared that this trip was a hoax and now his fears seemed to be confirmed.

"But it's true!" exclaimed Bobby.

"And I travelled here through the beam of a magic lantern which once belonged to you," Sandy continued. "You left it to the Panopticon in 1916."

Sandy turned to her friends to explain. "I had forgotten all about what had happened earlier that night, you know, before I came through the magic lantern's beam and that. Albert, the old man who was showing us round, told us that you," she said, looking straight at Arthur Conan Doyle, "had given the magic lantern to the old theatre I was visiting with my school. He even read out a letter that you sent with it. I don't remember exactly what it said, but it was something about the future of us all depending on the magic lantern being used that night. We all thought that it was just a story the old man made up to make the magic lantern sound more interesting."

"What do you mean before you came through the magic lantern's beam?" asked Sir Arthur. This boy wasn't making any sense.

"That's how I got here. Through the magic lantern's beam. We were supposed to stay up looking for ghosts, but we all fell asleep. Then something woke me up and the magic lantern was on. It might have been the light coming from it that woke me up, and when I tried to get up, I felt dizzy and I fell. At least I think I fell, or the floor fell away from under me. I can't really describe it but I was falling for ages and then I ended up here, in this time. I don't know how or why," Sandy babbled on.

Sir Arthur didn't quite know what to make of this story. This must be some sort of hoax - an inventive one at that.

"I left the magic lantern in 1916 to a music hall in 2016? Interesting," he mused.

"Yeah. Albert, the man at the theatre in my time, said you had left the magic lantern and letter in your will," mumbled Sandy.

"Well, where is this magic lantern now? I assume it is still in 2016, was it?"

"No, it's not," piped up Bobby. "It's upstairs in the music hall."

"And is the music hall upstairs the very theatre you were in, in the future?" asked the author.

"Yes," replied Sandy.

It was the most bizarre tale he had ever heard. His good sense and logic told him that this was just a story made up by this group of ragged boys and utterly impossible, but his heart told him that anything was possible, that the world was full of unknown possibilities, and his instincts told him this strange-looking lad was telling the truth. Perhaps his journey to Glasgow would offer more mystery than even he could imagine - and he could imagine quite a lot.

"Forgive my incredulity, but this is absolutely the most extraordinary story I have ever heard," voicing his thoughts.

"Show him your future Bell with the moving pictures," Jimmy told Sandy, who looked at him mystified, before realising he meant her mobile. She shook her head. Showing her mobile to the boys was one thing but entrusting it to an adult was something entirely different. But then again, he was the reason she was there. She slowly and cautiously pulled her phone out of her pocket and switched it on.

Sir Arthur could not believe what he was seeing. He sank onto the arm of the chair that Jimmy had offered as the footage of the boys dancing the cancan flashed in full colour before his eyes. It looked and even sounded so life-like as the stamp of the boys' hobnails hit the stone floor. This strange little black rectangle was obviously not a technology of 1908. Even the material it was made of was strange; smooth like metal, warm like polished wood, but truly unlike either. Was it some kind of Bakelite? And what was making these images? How did they move? Where was the sound coming from?

"Phenomenal!" he exclaimed in wonder as Sandy locked the screen and it went dark again. "Truly amazing! Why, I could never even have envisaged such a thing. What is it? How does it work?"

Sandy shrugged. "It's a mobile phone, but I don't know how it works. I've never really thought about it. We all have them in the future," she explained as she tucked the phone back in her pocket.

"Can I see this magical magic lantern now?" Sir Arthur asked after taking a few moments to gather his thoughts and try to accept the miracle he had just seen.

* * *

The music hall was empty and the floor was sticky with the mulched mess of dropped food, spilt beer, and more unpleasant debris left behind by the 2:30 p.m. crowd. Two cleaners foraged noisily through the balcony above, bottles clanging against one another as they stowed them in sacks.

Sir Arthur Conan Doyle inspected the magic lantern from every angle in the gas-lit gloom. It was very old - the oldest he had seen. It had obviously been modified a few times over the years, and most recently it seemed to have been adapted for electricity. He switched on the electric bulb.

Sandy and the boys watched him for a moment, then all four of them turned and looked at the stage, waiting for an image to appear on the back wall.

"I haven't put a slide in yet, boys. There aren't any here," Sir Arthur said, searching around him.

"It doesn't need a slide," said Jimmy. "At least, it didn't the other night."

"What do you mean?" Sir Arthur uttered. "What other magical properties does this ancient - looking machine have?"

"Well, I tried to go back through the beam to my own time and, well, a message appeared, and there was no slide," explained Sandy.

"It said something about counting backwards and finding a diamond," interrupted Bobby.

"And A.B.," added Jimmy.

"A.B.?" asked Sir Arthur.

"Aye. I think it said 'Count back with A.B. and find the diamond.' " Jimmy added, as Sandy nodded in agreement.

"Well, it doesn't appear to be saying anything at the moment," said Sir Arthur as he began to fiddle with the lens, turning the brass cylinder that focused the picture this way and that. "Are you sure it wasn't a slide that someone had put on for a joke?"

"There was no slide," Jimmy responded. "And we all saw it. It was a ghost or sumthin'."

"Well, I suppose it could have been some sort of automatic writing," Sir Arthur mused as he stroked his moustache and stared at the projector.

"What's that?" asked Bobby.

"Ghost writing," answered George. "I've seen mediums do it during ghost shows. They go into a trance and write messages from dead people. The words magically appear in chalk on a slate. It's a trick."

"Yes, I suppose sometimes it is. I have seen automatic writing used in bogus ghost shows, but I have also seen what appears to be genuine channelling of spirits. In all instances, though, a living person held the pen or chalk. I have never seen a message from the other side projected," Sir Arthur pondered.

"Do you think it could have been Tam?" Sandy asked the boys.

"Who's Tam?" Sir Arthur quizzed.

"He's ma big brother. He was working the magic lantern on Monday night. He went missing, then his body was found in the zoo yesterday morning," Bobby answered sadly. "He was stabbed."

"Oh, my boy, I am so sorry to hear that," Sir Arthur commiserated, placing a hand on the small boy's shoulder.

"He was murdered," Bobby sniffed.

"And we think it has something to do with the murder of a rich old lady in the west end," Jimmy added.

"Miss Gilchrist?" Sir Arthur queried, remembering the column in The Scotsman.

"Aye," the boys replied in unison.

"How is your brother Tam connected to Miss Gilchrist?" Sir Arthur asked gently.

"He was stepping out with Nellie Lambic, Miss Gilchrist's maid, sir. She's the one who found the old lady deid." Bobby snuffled, tears now streaming down his face, leaving clean trails on his grubby cheeks.

"And he might have seen the murderer," George added.

"Ah, I see. Have you informed the police about this connection? That the murderer may have claimed two victims on that fateful night?"

"Aye, we tried. We even went up to the west end and met a detective at Miss Gilchrist's house. We told him about

Tam, but he didn't think they were the same murderer," continued Jimmy.

"The detective also told us that there were at least two people involved in the murder, but we didn't find out anything to do with the initials A.B.," Sandy added.

Sir Arthur pondered for a moment. First, the anonymous note written in a hand identical to his own which led him to this music hall and to a time travelling boy, then a ghost in a magic lantern, and now a murder too? It was all so unbelievable, and this ancient device seemed to be at the centre of the whole story.

"I wonder how long this magic lantern has been here?" he asked.

"Not long," Jimmy answered.

"Harry told me that Mr Pickard bought it from an auction in London," Sandy replied.

"Aye, and old Harry and Tam just fixed it up for the 'lectric a couple of days ago," Bobby proudly stated.

"An auction in London? Interesting…" Sir Arthur mused. "I wonder..."

The boys waited for the man to continue. He didn't. He simply stood staring at the magic lantern and stroking his moustache.

George broke the silence. "Wonder what?"

"For centuries there have been tales of an ancient magic lantern - perhaps the first - that belonged to a succession of great magicians and wizards, each of whom imbued it with their own spells. It was said to have the power to transcend the border between the worlds of the living and the dead.

Some people called it a Phantoscope, others the Lantern of Terror," Sir Arthur said, his gaze still fixed on the projector.

Sandy and the boys looked at the magic lantern with awe.

"You said you wondered if Tam might have projected the message you all saw. Tell me more about Tam," requested Sir Arthur.

"There's no much more to say. He was ma big brother and he worked here, in the Panopticon, and lived in the room at the back of the monkey house where you found us. He wanted to show moving pictures and marry Nellie," Bobby sniffled again.

"And when, exactly, was the last time you saw him?" Sir Arthur asked.

Bobby and Jimmy told him the events of Monday night right up to the point when Sandy had appeared on the stage - when she had fallen from the beam of the magic lantern.

"Fascinating." Sir Arthur pronounced when the boys had finished.

"And Sandy found his pocket watch this morning," added Bobby.

"I found it when I was cleaning out the monkey house. I don't know how it got there. We thought that maybe Tam or the phantom pickpocket had dropped it," added Sandy.

"A phantom pickpocket, eh?" asked Sir Arthur.

"Aye, we've been trying to catch him for ages," Jimmy piped up.

"We call him the Phantom Pickpocket of the Panopticon," declared George.

"And you found the watch in the monkey house?"

"Not exactly in the monkey house. Solomon the chimp put it in my pocket," she replied.

"The chimp gave you the watch?" Sir Arthur asked, incredulous.

The door to the stalls suddenly banged open and Mr Saprini, the stage manager, walked in.

"What are you lot doing in here? The music hall's closed, next show is at half seven!" He yelled across to them.

"We're just going, my good man," Sir Arthur called back cheerfully. "These scamps just wanted to show me your magic lantern. I shall be sure to return later and see it working. I apologise if we are trespassing."

Sir Arthur ushered the boys out of the music hall, smiling and waving at Mr Saprini as he did so.

"I would like to meet this chimp, Solomon," requested Arthur Conan Doyle once they had left the auditorium. The little gang led the way back down the stairs to the basement zoo.

Chapter Fourteen

The Monkey House Hoard

Sandy and the boys escorted their celebrity visitor back down to Noah's Ark. The crowds had gone and only a few people milled about, most of them gawping at the Russian bear and the Dog-Faced Baboon. Free from the press of people, Sir Arthur was able to walk around the outside of the chimpanzee cage and inspect it. Solomon and Betsy watched his every move. Betsy approached their new visitor and reached for him through the bars of the cage. Sir Arthur paused in his inspection to shake her hand.

"How do you do?"

Betsy then climbed a couple of feet up the bars until she was face to face with her new visitor. She pushed her chimpanzee face as far through the bars as she could and kissed Arthur's cheek. "Why, thank you, Betsy, but I must warn you that I am a married man," he joked.

Solomon furtively approached, his big, brown eyes fixed on Betsy's new admirer.

"Tell me, this phantom pickpocket, where does he strike?" Sir Arthur asked, turning his back on the chimps to face the little gang.

"All over the building. Sometimes it's people in the music hall who have stuff stolen and sometimes it's folk up in the carnival, but most of the time it happens down here," Jimmy answered.

"Well, I think I know the identity of your phantom pickpocket," observed Sir Arthur, as he turned and tickled Betsy under her chin with his right hand and grabbed Solomon's right hand with his left, causing Solomon to drop a key, which clanged as it hit the concrete floor.

"Caught red-handed," Sir Arthur quipped. He bent down, retrieved the key, and put it back in his trouser pocket.

"You mean, it was Solomon all along?" Jimmy asked.

"How can Solomon have robbed people in the music hall?" asked Bobby.

"He probably didn't. He picked their pockets down here before they went up to the music hall. They just didn't discover anything missing until later and then assumed it was one of the crowd in the music hall," Sir Arthur explained.

"Where's all the stuff he robbed then?" asked Jimmy, looking around the sparse cage, unable to see where the stolen goods could be hidden.

"I think I know. There's a hole back there." Sandy pointed to a pile of straw at the back wall of the monkey house. "That's where he pulled the watch out of. Clever, isn't he, picking pockets." She was in awe of the thieving chimp. "It's such a human thing to do."

"Where was Tam's body found?" Sir Arthur then asked gently.

Jimmy, George, and Bobby pointed across to the other side of the room where large, red curtains concealed the construction of the new bear and baboon cages.

"Over there," announced Bobby.

"Well, then, it appears Tam was either murdered down here or brought here afterwards - but, at some point, his watch must have fallen out of his pocket near the monkey house. I'm curious to know what else that chimp might have. How do we get into his cage?" Sir Arthur asked.

Sandy went to fetch the key and unlocked the door of the cage. The boys stood outside while the author searched the back wall and found the hole where Solomon kept his booty.

He pulled out a small pile of goodies; empty sweet wrappers, coins, coin purses, hat pins, buttons, conkers, penny whistles, assorted marbles, various keys, and something wrapped in a bloodstained handkerchief. He quickly stowed it in his pocket.

The detective-author's investigations had attracted the attention of the visiting public, who had started to flood in for a quick ogle before the 7:30 p.m. show. They crowded round, craning their necks to see what he was up to.

"Stand clear!" he called at them as he left the monkey house, with Solomon's hoard gathered in his hands and spilling from his coat pockets.

He pushed through the crowd, the boys following close behind, and made his way to the little back room, where he dumped the booty on the workbench. The boys had closed the door behind them and now began enthusiastically rummaging through the collection, seeking out the coins and other more interesting goodies.

"Go through that stuff carefully, boys. Remember, you're looking for clues, not treasure." Sir Arthur pronounced as he pulled the bloodstained handkerchief from his trouser pocket and unfolded it. Everyone's eyes lit up with surprise when a diamond brooch was revealed. A large, pear-shaped diamond surrounded by smaller stones glinted at them.

"That looks like the brooch they described in the newspapers," Sandy declared. "It was the only thing missing from the old lady's house."

"But I thought it was supposed to be a fake. Wow, it really does look real," said Jimmy.

"I very much doubt it is real. If there is a diamond this big in the world it would be in the possession of a rich Sultan, not an old woman living in a Glasgow tenement. But I suppose the smaller stones might be real," Sir Arthur commented. "And it proves one thing, that Miss Gilchrist's murderer was also down here on Monday night."

He handed the brooch to Sandy, who held it in her open palm. The stones glittered and twinkled like real diamonds in the dancing lamplight.

"Which means the two murders were quite probably by the same hand. A woman's hand," he muttered half to himself as he continued inspecting the bloodstained handkerchief. It was lace-edged and delicately feminine, embroidered in one corner with two floral letters. "A woman with the initials A.B."

"A.B.? That's what was on that message from the magic lantern!" exclaimed Jimmy.

"Count back with A.B. and find the diamond. Isn't that what it said?" questioned Sandy.

"Yes. It seems our little find corresponds to the message you saw," Sir Arthur stated.

They had almost forgotten about the message.

"Aye. An' A.B. is a woman!?" asked Jimmy, incredulous at the thought of a lady murderer - and in the west end, too.

"It would appear so," said Sir Arthur, holding up the elaborate, monogrammed silk and lace square. "Whether she is the murderer, I cannot say, but I can venture a guess that the blood that stains this belongs to Miss Gilchrist. Though I am puzzled as to why anyone would be interested in a fake diamond."

Sandy and the boys stared at the bloodstain with as much wonder as they had stared at the brooch.

"So, who do you think she is?" asked Jimmy.

"Whoever she is, this handkerchief tells us quite a bit more than just her initials. This A.B. is a wealthy lady with expensive tastes, used to the finer things in life - even just to wipe her delicate nose on."

"She is not the usual kind of murderer, if indeed she is the murderer, and I suspect she was well known to the victim - perhaps a relative. If not for the pickpocket chimp, we would never have found her out. That is a very clever chimp," he concluded.

"That detective did say that there were two people involved in the murder," Sandy piped up.

"Aye," agreed Jimmy. "But why would she come here after murdering old Miss Gilchrist?"

"Perhaps Tam did indeed see the murderer, or murderers, leaving the scene of the crime and they followed him back to the Panopticon to ensure his silence. Perhaps it is his ghost in the magic lantern," Sir Arthur pondered.

Bobby stopped his gleeful rummaging as he was reminded of his brother's murder. He looked up as if Sir Arthur had suddenly slapped him in the face, his chin and bottom lip trembling as tears welled in his eyes. George put an arm around his shoulder to comfort him.

Sir Arthur's heart went out to the small boy. "I'm sorry, Bobby. We will get to the bottom of this, and I promise you Tam's murderer will receive justice."

"I have an idea," suggested Sandy, who felt terrible for Bobby, who was now sobbing so hard he was shaking. "Why don't I try to go back in time and stop Tam from being murdered? Maybe I'll be able to find out who A.B. is and what the rest of the message means. Like, who S is?"

The boys and Sir Arthur stared at her.

"The message said, 'Count back with A.B, full stop. Find the diamond, full stop. S, full stop.' wasn't that what it said? 'Count back with A.B?' Count what back? I'm just wondering if it means go back in time to find A.B," Sandy explained.

Bobby stopped crying as hope filled his eyes.

"You could be on to something, Sandy," Sir Arthur remarked.

Chapter Fifteen

Sandy's Return Through the Magic Lantern

The cleaners had finished their work and the floor, though still sticky, was minus the mulch. The stage manager was nowhere to be seen, so the detective-author and the small gang entered the music hall and again crept across to the magic lantern. They knew they had to be quick, as the audience would soon start filtering in to get the best spot for the next show.

"Sandy, quickly! Go stand on the stage and get ready," commanded Sir Arthur as he walked towards the magic lantern, which sat in darkness on the small platform at the back of the music hall. He switched it on. Sandy did as she was bid and stood waiting in the lantern's beam. Nothing happened.

"It's still not working," Sandy pronounced, after a few seconds had passed.

"Perhaps we need to try a different approach," said Sir Arthur. "Working on the assumption that a ghost or some sort of mystical force was working the magic lantern, perhaps you need to use a little psychic energy."

"You mean, like mind reading?" asked Sandy.

"Yes, simply put. I suggest that you concentrate hard on the time you want to travel to. Concentrate very hard."

"How do I do that?"

"Imagine where you want to go. Project the thought with your imagination. Visualise the music hall at the time Tam was last seen," Sir Arthur suggested.

"But I wasn't here when Tam was last seen," Sandy said. "I don't know where he was."

"He was standing right where you are now, sir, right at the magic lantern," Bobby supplied. "He was working it when you arrived."

"Aye," agreed Jimmy. The other boys nodded.

She closed her eyes and tried to concentrate on the night she had arrived. She tried to imagine Tam standing at the magic lantern, even though she didn't know what he looked like. Nothing seemed to be happening.

"It's really hard. I don't know what he looks like so I can't imagine it properly," Sandy explained, her eyes still closed.

"Well, perhaps you could try a rhyme? Maybe that will focus your mind onto that particular time," Sir Arthur mused.

She tried to think of a rhyme, but she wasn't very good at rhymes.

"I can't think of a rhyme," she said.

"Try this." The author paused for a moment, then said, "Take me away to Tam's last day. How's that? Not my best work, but it might do."

Sandy closed her eyes and repeated it over and over in her head. Take me away to Tam's last day, take me away to Tam's last day, take me away to Tam's last day…still, nothing seemed to be happening. Then her head began to swim and, suddenly, Sandy's whole body began to tingle with static electricity. She felt a giddy sensation, as if the world was spinning around her. But, instead of the jolting drop she had experienced before, she felt herself being pulled upwards, as if invisible strings were lifting her like a marionette, higher and higher through an intense, bright, white light, and all at once she heard the sound of snoring.

She hadn't travelled back in time; she was forward in time. She had returned to the 21st century.

Her friends and teachers were all still snoring away, just the same as when she had left. Why had she ended up here? The magic lantern had turned off, and she felt a wave of disappointment mixed with the feeling of relief that she was back in her own time. Was that it, then? Was that the end of her adventure? She squeezed her eyes shut and tried the rhyme again, muttering it under her breath, but the magic lantern remained dark. *That can't be it,* she told herself, *what was the point of sending me all the way back in time if I wasn't supposed to stop the crime happening, or save Tam, or at least help catch the murderer?*

Not wanting to disturb the sleepers, she tiptoed her way through the auditorium to the toilets. She hadn't washed for two days and she stank. Washing with soap and hot water, even if it was just in a sink in the lady's loos, seemed like a luxury. And as for using a real toilet and toilet roll…

When she had finished washing and patting herself dry with paper towels, she sniffed her clothes - they were beginning to smell pretty bad. She stripped them off completely, not even bothered by the cold of the music hall, she had become so used to the conditions of 1908. In just her underwear, she bundled up her clothes and carried them with her as she snooped around the various rooms off the auditorium looking for a fresh outfit.

The first door led her into Mr Pickard's old office, only in this time it was full of computers, printers, and modern office equipment. She opened a second door to the left, which led to a room full of sewing machines and, as she had hoped, clothes rails full of costumes. She dumped her 21st century clothes and rummaged through the rails, chittering in her underwear. There wasn't any modern clothing; it was all costumes. It would just have to do.

She pulled out heavy wool trousers, a heavy cotton shirt, a woollen waistcoat, and put them on. Then she found drawers of socks and pulled out the thickest she could find. After dressing in the warm winter clothes, she found a large rack of shoes of every size and kind. She selected a pair of heavy leather boots that were near enough her size when worn with the thick, woollen socks. She caught sight of herself in a full-length mirror that stood at the end of one of the rails. Now she looked like one of the gang she had left behind. She had left them behind. The thought jarred her; she didn't feel right being here in her own time. She wanted to go back. She wanted to help solve the mystery. She wanted to rescue Tam.

Sandy looked at her phone. It read 4:30 a.m. and was running out of charge. "Well, what are you going to do, then?" she said to her reflection. "Sit around doing nothing for the next three hours until that lot wakes up? And then how are you going to explain your clothes?"

Her reflection stared back at her.

"No, I'm going back, and I am going to save Tam and solve the murder," she told herself sternly. She knew now that she could get back to her own time. So, after grabbing a thick woollen coat from one of the rails, she marched back out into the old music hall and tiptoed past her classmates as quietly as the squeaky floorboards would allow, over to her back pack. Retrieving her power bank to charge her phone, she switched the magic lantern back on, and stood in its beam.

With her eyes closed, she concentrated hard on the music hall she had left in 1908. She visualised what it looked like and how it smelled. She imagined the crowds that had been there when she had first arrived. She tried to think of Sir Arthur Conan Doyle's rhyme…what was it he said again? "Take me away to Tam's last day?" Was that it? What if she couldn't get back? She imagined the faces of the boys and Sir Arthur Conan Doyle, and suddenly, without any rhymes at all, she felt the familiar dizzy sensation. A moment later her stomach pitched as the 21st century fell from beneath her and she plummeted back through time.

When she landed with a wallop in 1908, it was as if the thirty minutes or so she had spent in her own time hadn't happened at all. Everything was exactly as it had been the moment she had left it.

"Are you ok?" George shouted. "That was quite a fall."

"Yeah, I'm fine," she called back. Sandy sat on the stage rubbing her right elbow, which seemed to have borne the brunt of the landing.

"Jings, how'd you do that?" asked Jimmy.

"Do what?" Sandy replied, a little confused.

"Change your clothes like that. I was watching you the whole time and nothing happened, except you suddenly fell over and now you're dressed, well, like us," Jimmy replied.

"I've been back to my time and I got changed when I was there. I found these clothes in a room full of old costumes," Sandy explained.

"Did you manage to go back and save Tam?" Bobby asked hopefully.

Sandy looked sadly at the boy. Her expression was answer enough. Bobby resumed his sobs.

"I'm so sorry. I tried. Honestly, I did. I concentrated as hard as I could, but the magic lantern wouldn't send me back to save him," Sandy apologised. "It would only send me back to my own time."

"Then there may be nothing that can be done to save him. We must instead concentrate on catching his murderer," announced Sir Arthur.

***

It was barely 6:45 p.m., but the first small groups of men, boys, and women were beginning to trickle in through the doors.

Sir Arthur switched off the magic lantern. "I feel we have learnt enough for today. I have a lot to digest and so, boys, if you will allow me, I must bid you goodnight and find myself some lodgings. I will meet you tomorrow morning in your room behind the monkey house."

The boys and Sandy nodded, and Sir Arthur Conan Doyle left.

Chapter Sixteen

The Prince of Wales's Feathers

Arthur Conan Doyle found himself a comfortable and spacious suite at the St. Enoch Station Hotel, not far from the Panopticon, where he sat turning the brooch over and over in his fingers, pondering its worth. He had also brought back with him a couple of newspapers containing reports about the murder. Why was this piece alone taken from the old lady's house when so much valuable jewellery was left lying around? What had they been looking for in the workbox, and did they find it?

The brooch's pin pricked his index finger, which he instinctively put to his mouth. As he did so, the brooch caught in the light, which highlighted a tiny mark just underneath the pin's hinge.

He pulled a small magnifying glass out from his jacket pocket and gave the mark a closer inspection under the bright light of an electric table lamp. His eyes practically popped out of their sockets when he saw the tiny mark.

"Good God!" he exclaimed to the empty room. The mark was in the shape of a crown with three protruding plumes. "The Prince of Wales's Feathers!"

It was the heraldic mark of the Prince of Wales. Had this brooch once belonged to him? Was it a real diamond after all? And how did it come to be in the possession of an elderly spinster in Glasgow? What was her connection to the once prince, now King Edward VII?

Tomorrow morning, he would get the boys to introduce him to the detective they had met at Miss Gilchrist's. Perhaps he could shed more light on this darkening mystery.

Chapter Seventeen

The Brooch is Stolen

It was Christmas Eve and the Panopticon was busy. The building was crammed, from attic carnival to basement zoo, and the air was filled with laughter and chatter. Sandy had been up early feeding the animals and had just finished eating her own breakfast when the boys came ambling in.

"He's not here yet, then?" George queried.

"Who?" asked Sandy.

"Sir Arthur."

"No, not yet. I'm sure he won't be too long, though," answered Sandy.

"I like the new clothes," commented Jamie, motioning to Sandy's attire. "It's funny, but it's like I've seen you like that before."

"Oooh, deja vu," said Sandy.

"Day shar what?" asked Jamie.

"Never mind," Sandy replied. "You totally missed out last night. Sir Arthur Conan Doyle found the diamond brooch in the back of the monkey house and it was wrapped up in a handkerchief with, you'll never believe this..."

"The initials A.B. sewn on it. Bobby and George told us," supplied Jamie. "And Sir Arthur thinks it's a woman."

"I didn't think a woman wid dae that, you know. Bash an auld woman's brains in," remarked Andrew.

"I dunno, I bet she would for a sparkling jewel. I know my sister probably would," joked Jimmy.

George, who had been standing reading the morning paper, suddenly shouted, "Listen to this, 'The police are busier than ever in their investigations, and the fact that they are taking particular precautions against information leaking out indicates that matters are now reaching an important stage. From what can be gathered, there is not the slightest doubt that the police KNOW THEIR MAN,' " recited George.

"See, it's a man," Andrew interrupted.

"Shush, Andrew, let me finish. 'We understand the police surrounded a house in the city yesterday, but no arrest was made,' " George looked up from the newspaper. "Do you think they have tracked down the man in the pale-coloured overcoat?" he asked.

"If they have, why haven't they arrested him?" questioned Jamie. "If you ask me, they're just telling people that so they'll think the police are doing their job. No mention of Tam, then?"

George scanned the rest of the paper before shaking his head. "No, I wonder if Sir Arthur has seen the newspapers yet?"

It was nearly an hour later before Sir Arthur finally showed up. He came staggering into the basement zoo with a gash on his head which had dripped blood down the front of his coat and scarf. The gawping crowds parted for the injured man as he stumbled towards the monkey house. Harry, who was sitting on his stool reading his newspaper, looked up and saw the author. He jumped from his seat and ushered the injured man onto it, then ran into the back room to fetch hot water from the kettle.

"Sir Arthur is injured!" he shouted as he ran into the back room, disturbing the gang, who had still been debating the likelihood of a woman being the murderer. Sandy and the boys jumped up and dashed out of the door to assist their wounded friend.

"What happened, sir?" asked George.

"I'm not sure," he replied. "I was attacked from behind. I must have hit my head when I fell."

"Did they get anything, sir? Should I send one of the boys to fetch the police?" asked Harry. He returned with a bowl of water and set about cleaning the wound.

"No, no, it's all right; it's nothing to bother the police with. I'll be fine. I just need to sit down for a minute," assured Sir Arthur.

Harry tried to shoo the boys away, but they congregated around the man, watching as Harry played nurse. "It doesn't look too bad, not when you wipe the blood away. It's just a wee cut, really. You might want to get a doctor to have a look at it, though."

"I will do just that," Sir Arthur assured his nurse.

"I'll fetch a bandage meanwhile," Harry said, picking up the bowl of water.

Sir Arthur protested. "There's really no need, Harry. I am fine. All I need is a moment to gather myself."

Harry wandered off to throw out the pan of warm water, looking a little dejected that the famous author had refused his treatment.

"The brooch?" asked Jamie when Harry had left.

"Is gone," replied Sir Arthur.

"Who was it?" Sam asked.

"I didn't see him, but I suspect he wasn't simply a mugger. He must have been following me." Sir Arthur reflected on the events of that morning.

"Then it must have been him," George gasped.

"Who?" Sir Arthur asked.

"The man in the pale-coloured overcoat that Nellie saw in Miss Gilchrist's hallway," answered George.

"He was here before," Andrew reminded them.

"Aye, that's right," piped up Sam. "He came round the other night when we got back from Miss Gilchrist's house. He came nosying around Tam's room. We hid in the corner."

"He must have been looking for the brooch!" announced Jimmy with sudden realisation.

"And he had a foreign accent," offered Andrew.

"Did you hear his voice?" Charlie asked Sir Arthur.

"No," said Sir Arthur. "but you are quite possibly right. Last night I discovered something very interesting about Miss Gilchrist's brooch, which might not be a fake after all."

The gang looked at him with surprise.

"The brooch is at the very heart of this mystery. I couldn't understand why a piece of costume jewellery was so important; then last night I discovered something. I found a small hallmark of three feathers and a crown. It is the Prince of Wales Feathers." The author explained.

"You mean, as in the King?" asked an amazed George.

"Yes," Sir Arthur affirmed.

"Do ya think it belongs tae the King?" asked Jimmy in surprise.

"It certainly seems to be a strong possibility," answered Sir Arthur.

"An' it's a real diamond?" Bobby asked, his eyes wide at the prospect that they had perhaps seen the largest diamond in the world.

"Very possibly. If it belongs to our King, then it can be assumed that the gem is indeed real," Sir Arthur proclaimed.

"But why would Miss Gilchrist have a diamond brooch that belongs to the King?" queried George.

"Exactly! And how did she come to possess it?" questioned Sir Arthur.

Harry returned. "These lads bothering you, sir?"

"No, not at all. Thank you for the seat and for attending to my wound. I feel much better, apart from a little headache, which I am sure will clear in the fresh air," Sir Arthur replied. "I'll take these boys with me in case I take a dizzy turn."

He ushered the boys out of the Panopticon and hailed a motor-cab, which he managed to squash the whole excited gang into. They were all delirious with joy at the prospect of their first ever journey in a motor car. All except Sandy, who didn't seem very interested at all.

"Are there motor cars where you're from?" George asked Sandy as Sir Arthur pulled the small boy and his sticks onto his lap.

"Yeah. Thousands of them," she replied as she squashed herself in next to the others. It was cramped, and Bobby, Charlie and Jamie had to sit on the floor, but that didn't seem to detract from the excitement of this first car ride.

"Queens Crescent, West Princes Street, if you please, driver," Sir Arthur instructed once everyone was in.

"Are we going to Miss Gilchrist's?" asked Charlie.

"Yes, to interview Mr. Adams, the downstairs neighbour," Sir Arthur answered. "I want to see if we can find out some more about Miss Gilchrist, A.B., and this man in the pale-coloured overcoat. And then we are going to pay a visit to the detective you spoke to the other evening. Do you remember his name?"

Sandy fished around in her pockets for the card the detective had given her, then remembered she had left it in her puffer coat back in 2016. "His name is Lieutenant Detective Trench and he's from the west end office," Sam supplied.

"Very good. Then we shall visit Lieutenant Detective Trench and see what we can find out from him," Sir Arthur announced as the motor cab rumbled through the city centre.

Chapter Eighteen

The Testimony of Arthur Adams

Twenty minutes later, Sir Arthur Conan Doyle was standing with his new friends outside the front of a west end tenement building and looking up at the windows of Miss Gilchrist's apartment. In the gloom of the December noon, it looked dark, empty, and lifeless. Sir Arthur stepped to the front door and rang the bell marked Arthur Adams, Flautist.

Arthur Adams answered. He was a nervous, grey, little man who peered at them warily through thick, bottle-bottom glasses.

"What do you want?" he queried sharply.

Before Sir Arthur could answer, a shrill lady's voice called out, "Who is it, Arthur?" A moment later, a plump lady dressed all in purple frills from her three chins to her two, purple silk-slippered feet, appeared at Arthur's side. She instantly recognised the celebrity on the doorstep, and her round, rosy face split with a wide smile. "Well, don't leave our guests standing out in the cold, Arthur, invite them in," she dictated, beaming graciously at the author before scowling at the dirty children that followed the famous man in.

"Thank you, Madam," replied Sir Arthur, as he entered. "Forgive me for troubling you..."

"Not at all, not at all! It is an honour to have Sir Arthur Conan Doyle, the famous novelist, visit our humble abode," she shouted, perhaps hoping the whole street could hear her whilst she lowered herself into a deep, though somewhat wobbly, curtsey.

"Please, just call me Arthur," he answered, a little embarrassed at the woman's grandiose greeting.

"Certainly, Sir Arthur," she simpered, deepening her curtsey.

"Mr. Adams, I presume?" Sir Arthur held out his hand to the man, who had opened the door and now closed it behind the visiting group as they traipsed in.

The man took the hand and weakly shook it. "I am, Sir Arthur," he replied and then turned to the purple lady to help her up from a curtsey so deep she appeared to be stuck. He then led the guests up a long hallway lined with gilt mirrors and framed portraits of portly pug dogs and prim predecessors - or so Sir Arthur assumed, as the family resemblance to both the spectacled man and the plump, purple woman were quite remarkable. "What a charming home you have," Sir Arthur commented as he was ushered into a room crammed with overstuffed sofas, cluttered curio cabinets, and tables piled high with sheet music and books. It was almost suffocatingly hot and heavy with the scent of lavender.

Another lady, stick thin and sharp-featured, sat in front of the fireplace sewing. She put down her work as the author and scruffy-looking urchins entered the room.

"Why, you're Sir Arthur Conan Doyle! What an unexpected surprise!" she exclaimed, her eyes wide with surprise. "Introduce us, Arthur, where are your manners?" she snapped at the timid man.

"Yes, yes, of course, how rude of me. Sir Arthur Conan Doyle, may I present my sisters Miss Adams," the plump lady in the purple frills bobbed another brisk curtsey, "and Mrs. Liddell." Mrs. Liddell, who was dressed in widow black, smiled demurely and gave a little nod.

"Oh, and please take a seat, sir," Arthur added in response to a pointed nod from his sisters, before gesturing in the direction of a cushion-laden, violet, velvet couch.

The boys and Sandy began to make their way towards the proffered seat.

"You boys can stand over there. I don't want any dirt on my rugs and furnishings," Miss Adams snapped at them. They retreated to the door and stood in a line like scolded children.

"No need to ask you why you're here," said Mrs. Liddell, as she put her embroidery hoop on her lap. "Murder."

"Yes, your neighbour upstairs. A tragic case," Sir Arthur murmured.

"Oh, it was terrible, Sir Arthur," added Miss Adams. "Just like one of your Sherlock Holmes stories. To think we were down here making merry whilst that poor, old lady was being battered to death. Oh, I feel faint just thinking of it," she said as she slumped into one of the overstuffed chairs, fanning herself with a handkerchief.

"Did you know her well?" Sir Arthur asked, his voice laced with sympathy for the trauma these two genteel ladies must have experienced. Although, he suspected both ladies were enjoying the excitement it had added to their own lives, a new-found celebrity status, a result of living beneath the victim of one of the most gruesome and shocking murders in Glasgow's history.

"Well? No, sir, she was not the type to take visitors or engage much in conversation. Kept herself to herself. We knew her maid much better, poor girl," Mrs. Liddell replied.

"Did you notice any strangers watching the apartment, or unusual visitors?" Sir Arthur enquired.

"No, not really. Though the poor old thing was convinced she was being watched and that her dog had been poisoned," said Miss Adams. "Nellie - that's her maid - told me that it quite upset the old lady when her dog died, and she became sure someone was going to murder her next. She had Nellie check under her bed every single night after that, looking for would-be murderers, I suppose. We thought she was just being foolish, but now it seems she was quite right." Miss Adams sniffed and pulled out a lace-edged handkerchief from her sleeve which she delicately used to dab her eyes, then blew her nose loudly.

"Her niece had taken to visiting her recently. What a nice lady. French, you know, and very elegant. Such a delight to talk to, and so kind coming to see her aunt, who, quite frankly, didn't seem to appreciate the kindness much..."

"Her niece is French?" Sir Arthur confirmed.

"Oh, yes," supplied Mrs. Liddell. "Miss Gilchrist and her sisters were all educated in Paris, you know, and the youngest sister stayed and married a Frenchman. She only returned to Glasgow with her husband a few years ago when she became ill. I believe she wanted to be near her sisters in her final days. Her daughter stayed in Paris."

"So why has Miss Gilchrist's niece come to Glasgow now?" Sir Arthur asked.

"Her father, Mr Birrell, died in October and, as she is the only child, Miss Birrell returned to settle her father's affairs. I believe she had every intention to return to Paris in the New Year," Miss Liddell replied. "Though, I suppose now she will have to stay longer to settle her aunt's affairs, the poor dear."

"How did she get on with her aunt?" Sir Arthur inquired.

"Oh, I think Miss Birrell was very patient and kind to the old lady. To be honest, we have always found Miss Gilchrist to be…" Miss Adams began.

"Careful now, you mustn't speak ill of the dead," Mrs. Liddell cautioned her sister. "She was a bit short-tempered, didn't have much patience for people, especially not her family. But she was a good, Christian woman and lived a blameless life of modesty and humility. She was always involved in some charitable work or other."

Miss Adams nodded her agreement.

"Have any other members of the family been around?" Sir Arthur continued his questions.

Both ladies shook their heads. "No, only her niece. The family have never got on with her, you know. Miss Gilchrist inherited every penny of her father's estate and her sisters have never forgiven her for it," informed Miss Adams.

"Do you know if her niece perhaps visited Miss Gilchrist on the day of the murder?" Sir Arthur queried.

"Yes, she did. She came in her new horseless carriage. Do you remember, Mrs. Liddell?" asked Miss Adams.

"Yes, indeed I do, Miss Adams. Quite shocking, I thought," said Mrs. Liddell, her lips pursed with disapproval.

"She is so very modern and continental," Miss Adams explained with a slight note of admiration. Her sister glared at her.

"Surely it isn't seemly for a lady, even a continental lady, to drive one of those dangerous contraptions," Mrs. Liddell argued. "I remember Miss Gilchrist was quite awful to her, shouting at her to get out and leave her alone. We could hear every word quite clearly. Not a very warm reception, given the season. That was around eleven in the morning, was it not, sister?"

Miss Adams nodded again in agreement.

"And you didn't see her again later in the day?" quizzed Sir Arthur.

"No. Whatever are you implying, Sir Arthur? Surely you can't suspect the girl of the crime? Goodness, no, what woman would be capable of such a horrific act of violence? Miss Gilchrist's niece is assuredly of a gentle and kind disposition for all her foreign accent and continental ways," declared Mrs. Liddell.

"Mr. Adams," Sir Arthur said, turning his attention to the man who hovered at the back of Mrs. Liddell's chair like a faithful servant awaiting his next instruction. "I believe you saw the suspect in the hallway?"

"Yes, sir, I did, and I told the police all I know," he curtly replied. "I believe they will catch him very soon."

"Arthur, that was rude," Mrs Liddell snapped at her brother.

"I am sorry, our brother is a little bit sensitive about the case. He won't even discuss it with us, and, lord knows, it is the most interesting topic of conversation we have had in many a long year," Miss Adams cheerily said, then, as if realising her jolly tone was inappropriate, she lowered her voice and smile to a more sombre level and added, "as awful and tragic as it may be."

"It was all printed in the newspapers," uttered the henpecked and goaded Arthur.

"Indeed, and I have read some of the various reports," Sir Arthur agreed. "At about the time of the incident, you heard a bang from Miss Gilchrist's apartment. You thought that perhaps it was the maid chopping kindling for the fire, but your good lady sisters," Sir Arthur smiled and bowed to each in turn, "fearing that the lady had fallen, sent you up to her apartment to check that everything was all right. You knocked upon the door and received no answer. You returned to your own apartment and your sisters sent you back up to knock again and not to return until you had made quite sure that your elderly neighbour was quite well. You returned to Miss Gilchrist's door, and it was then that Miss Gilchrist's maid, Nellie Lambie returned. You explained what you had heard, and Nellie suggested that it was probably her mistress raising the washing on the pulley. She unlocked the door of the apartment and let both of you into the hallway. Is that correct?"

"Yes," answered Mr Adams.

"What happened next?"

Arthur Adams looked at his two sisters who glared back at him. Their expressions warning him to tell or else.

"I stood at the door on the threshold, half in and half out, and, just when the girl had got past the clock to go into the kitchen, a thin, scarecrow of a man appeared. I thought he was very odd, but she said nothing, and he came up to me. I thought the man was going to speak to me, till he got past me, and then I suspected something really was wrong. By that time, the girl ran into the kitchen and put the gas up and said it was all right, meaning her pulleys. I said, 'Where is your mistress?' and she went into the dining room. She said, 'Oh! Come here!' I just went and saw this horrible spectacle..."

"Then the man bolted out of the door and rushed down the stairs like greased lightning, slamming the front door behind him," Miss Adams added enthusiastically.

"You didn't recognise him? You hadn't seen him anywhere before?" asked Sir Arthur.

"No, he was a stranger," replied Adams, wringing his hands nervously.

"Well, thank you for your help," expressed Sir Arthur Conan Doyle as he pushed himself up from the cushion-swamped couch. One of the cushions suddenly developed legs and a head as Sir Arthur disturbed a sleeping pug who stretched, sniffed him briefly, snorted, and curled back up.

"Are you leaving so soon? You haven't even had a cup of tea. Arthur, make our honoured guest some tea," ordered Miss Adams.

"No, please, Madam, I do not wish to impose. My friends and I still have much to do today. But I do have one last question. Who lives in the apartment above Miss Gilchrist's?"

"No one, sir," answered Miss Adams. "It's been empty several months since."

"Thank you again," Sir Arthur replied, nodding a short bow to each lady before earnestly shaking Arthur by the hand. Sandy and the boys followed him out of the flat and onto the street.

Only George turned to the Adams's and said, "Thank you for your help," before leaving. The others felt like they had been treated worse than flea-ridden mutts, and weren't inclined to be so polite.

***

"Why did you ask about the apartment above Miss Gilchrist's?" George asked Sir Arthur as they walked to the tram stop.

"Merely because I hadn't realised that there was an apartment above Miss Gilchrist's, and an empty apartment might afford a murderer or thief a place to hide, either before or after the crime was committed," Sir Arthur explained as the tram arrived.

"Next stop, Detective Trench," Sir Arthur announced as they jumped on the new electric tram. As it trundled further west, the boys ridiculed Arthur Adams and his sisters.

"That Arthur is a right wet blanket," remarked Jamie.

"Yeah, a total muppet," agreed Sandy. Sir Arthur and the boys looked at her with quizzical expressions. "It means idiot."

"Aye, and his sisters are right ugly," concurred Bobby.

"Yeah, like the ugly stepsisters in Cinderella," laughed Sandy.

Sir Arthur reprimanded them for being rude, but had to agree that Arthur, who had been one of the only witnesses to see the suspect in the pale-coloured overcoat, had been less than helpful. He had seemed reticent about telling them anything. In fact, he had seemed almost frightened of talking to them.

Chapter Nineteen

The Meeting of Two Great Detectives

When they arrived at the west end police office, a vast crowd of people were squashed into the entrance, all clamouring to tell the police what they knew about the Gilchrist murder. Posters on the walls announced that there was a fifty-pound reward for any information which might lead to the capture of the murderer. This was almost a year's wages, and every man, woman, and child was desperate to get their hands on it.

Sir Arthur Conan Doyle and the ragamuffin gang forged a path through to the front desk, where a sergeant and several constables were trying to get the crowd under control.

"We're here to see Detective Trench," Sir Arthur announced loudly so that he could be heard above the noise.

The desk sergeant, a small, sweaty man with a red face and a large, white, handlebar moustache stared at the well-dressed visitor for a long moment before his eyes lit up with recognition. "This way," replied the sergeant, smiling at the celebrity author. "Detective Trench will want to see you, of that I am sure," he added as he led them down a short corridor lined with panelled wooden doors. He stopped at one and knocked briefly before poking his head in and proudly announcing, "Sir Arthur Conan Doyle here to see you, sir."

When they entered, they found Detective Trench sitting at his desk reading through a report. He didn't seem the remotest bit surprised when he looked up to see the boys from the other evening and the famous author standing at his office door. He almost seemed to be expecting them - like bad news.

Sir Arthur stepped into the room, extending his hand in greeting. "Detective Trench? I'm Arthur Co..."

"Yes, I know who you are, Sir Arthur Conan Doyle," the detective interrupted, standing from his chair and politely accepting the handshake. "You have a lot of fans here in the Glasgow force. How can I help you? As you can see, I am a little bit busy at the moment," Trench stated, seating himself back down at his desk and peering at them over the piles of papers stacked as high as his chin.

"Ah, the murder of Miss Gilchrist. Yes, I am sure that this is a case that will keep the Glasgow police busy for a while yet. In fact, it's this very case that I would like to ask you a few questions about," Sir Arthur stated.

"With respect, sir, I am not at liberty to answer questions about the case, only to ask them," the detective replied, nervously glancing towards the door.

"I understand. But, you see, my young friends here..." he indicated to Jamie and Bobby. "Their brother Tam has also been murdered and we believe it may be because he witnessed something connected to the Gilchrist case. I believe the boys told you this when they met you a couple of evenings ago?"

"Yes, they did, but we simply do not have the manpower to investigate every crime and the pressure is rather on us to solve the Gilchrist murder."

"Well, it is possible that Tam was murdered because he saw something - surely that's worth investigating?" Sir Arthur prodded.

"As tragic as the boy's murder is, there is no real reason to connect the two murders. As I explained to your young friends here the other evening, the two murders happened at opposing ends of the town and were carried out in two different ways. It is just a coincidence that they happened on the same night," the detective replied.

"Other than the blood and gore in Miss Gilchrist's apartment, was there any sign of a struggle in the vicinity of the murder - in the back lane, for example?" Sir Arthur asked, further pushing his line of inquiry.

"Nothing suspicious was found outside the apartment, or in the lane behind it," Trench replied. "Though you are welcome to check for yourself. Now, if you don't mind, I have work to get on with," Trench said a sharp note of finality in his voice. He glanced towards the door again, as if gesturing to them to leave.

"What about the man mentioned in the newspaper?" asked Sandy. "The one Nellie saw in the hallway?"

Trench stared at her blankly.

" 'The Police Know Their Man, ' " George quoted from the newspaper he had read aloud earlier to the gang.

"We are currently following several lines of inquiry and, yes, we believe these will send us in the direction of the suspect. I would recommend following the newspaper reports for any further developments. They obviously know more than we do," Detective Trench said rather sarcastically.

"So, there is only one suspect in this case then?" Sir Arthur questioned again

"Well, it's no secret that we believe more than one man could have been involved. The man seen in the hallway was perhaps a look out. But once we have him, I am sure we'll manage to persuade him to tell us the identity of the real murderer," Trench replied.

"So, are you looking for another *man*?" asked Sir Arthur.

Trench thought it was strange the way that the author had phrased this question, emphasising the word 'man' in a curious way.

"Well, it certainly wouldn't be a woman," the detective replied incredulously.

"I don't see why not," Sir Arthur retorted.

A woman? Trench certainly had never considered that the murderer was a woman, nor to his knowledge, had any of his colleagues. He glanced nervously at his door again. Did they know Arthur Conan Doyle was here?

"That kind of brutal attack was surely by a man. Murderesses generally prefer less aggressive methods, such as poison," Trench replied. "Not violent bludgeoning." He stood up and walked to the door, which he opened. "Now, if you don't mind, I am rather busy…"

"Lizzie Borden," stated Sir Arthur.

"What?" asked Trench.

"Lizzie Borden took an axe. She gave her mother forty whacks. After she saw what she had done, she gave her father forty-one," Sir Arthur sang.

"Yes, I am familiar with the murder. But, I think you will agree, hers was a rather exceptional case," replied Detective Trench as he waited, holding open his office door.

"I am just illustrating that, though it is rare, it is not impossible for a woman to commit such a violent crime. And where did this murderer go? Surely, they would have been covered in blood. Someone must have seen him - or her," said Sir Arthur, ignoring the open door.

"We are still waiting for witnesses to come forward, but we suspect he escaped out of the dining room window and into the back lane," Trench replied, continuing to hold open the door.

"Thank you for your time, Lieutenant Detective Trench. I will be staying in town for a few days at the St Enoch's Station Hotel. If you should discover anything connected to the murder of young Tam, please do get in touch," he requested, and ushered the little gang out of the detective's office.

* * *

"I told you he wasn't very helpful," Andrew remarked as they wandered back to the tram stop.

"I am not sure if Detective Trench is the right man to ask. He was certainly eager to get us out of his office," said Sir Arthur.

"What do you mean?" asked George.

"I'm not certain yet, but something isn't adding up. Your friend Detective Trench seems to be hiding something. He seemed nervous, on edge. Did you notice the way he kept glancing at his office door? And the way he dismissed the possibility that your brother Tam's murder is connected. Any policeman worth his salt would be just as interested in your brother's murder, especially given the possibility of their connection. Clues around Tam's murder could well lead to the perpetrator of Miss Gilchrist's. And then there's Arthur Adams. Why was he so reluctant to speak to us? No, something is definitely not right with this investigation."

"You didn't tell him about the brooch or A.B.," said Charlie.

"Or about the Prince of Wales's Feathers," added George.

"No. I think we will keep that information to ourselves for a little while longer, notably since we no longer possess the brooch. It would be both foolish and dangerous to go around implicating the King without proper evidence. I believe it is wiser not to let the police know what we have uncovered thus far."

* * *

After Trench had closed the door behind Sir Arthur and his little gang, he resumed his seat behind the pile of folders he had accumulated on the Gilchrist murder. This was turning out to be the most frustrating case of his career, and his superiors weren't helping. Evidence was being hidden, statements were being ignored, and he seemed to be the only officer who had noticed. Every time he mentioned it to his fellow detectives, they told him he was reading too much into what was simply a burglary gone tragically wrong. But he knew in his gut, it just didn't add up.

He barely sat back down when the door opened again. This time Superintendent Douglas walked in with Chief Inspector Ord. His two superiors closed the door behind them as they entered and stood glaring down at him. He felt himself shrink in the intensity of their gaze.

"What did they want?" asked Ord.

"Nothing. One of the boy's brothers was murdered, he was the boyfriend of Gilchrist's maid. They think his murder is connected to Miss Gilchrist's and wanted to know if we will be investigating," Trench answered.

"And what's Conan Doyle got to do with them?" asked Ord.

"I don't know, sir. I didn't ask," he replied, and thought to himself that he should have. *Why was the famous author running around with a gang of east end urchins?*

"I trust you told him to stay away from the case?" demanded Douglas. The threat in the superintendent's face was crystal clear. "This investigation is very delicate - very sensitive - not just to us, but to the public as well. We don't need an amateur celebrity sleuth stirring things up in the press. I cannot impress upon you strongly enough the importance of keeping that man away."

"Yes, sir," Trench nodded, though he knew it was more likely that the real reason they wanted Conan Doyle kept away was because he might manage to uncover the truth.

Although the man was an author, he was no amateur sleuth. It was well known that he had a talent for finding the facts. It wasn't so long ago that the press was full of praise for Sir Arthur Conan Doyle's detective talents when he saved an innocent man from false conviction in the Edalji case and left the police looking like incompetent idiots. As for suggesting that a woman was somehow involved in the murder...Detective Trench thought the idea was ridiculous. Anyway, he couldn't ask Ord, or Douglas, they wouldn't tell him anything, even though he had been the first detective on the scene.

What were they hiding? Not just from Arthur Conan Doyle - that was understandable - but from their own detectives. Could they somehow be involved in the murder?

What could this old lady have done that warranted her death and the concealment of the facts of the case? And what did the author detective know? It was obvious to him that Arthur Conan Doyle and his little gang hadn't told him everything they knew, either.

"Anyway, we came to tell you a new witness has come forward. His name's Alan Mclean. He claims he was offered a pawn ticket for Miss Gilchrist's missing brooch. He's waiting for you in the interview room," stated Douglas.

"I suggest you listen very carefully to what he has to say," added Ord. "And we strongly encourage you to follow that line of inquiry."

Chapter Twenty

Trench Pays a Visit

Sir Arthur and the gang retired to the comfortable luxury of Sir Arthur's suite at the St. Enoch Station hotel. The boys had never seen such opulence and they were wide-eyed with awe when they entered the grand apartments. Even Sandy was impressed. There was a drawing room with sumptuous couches, a dining table that could seat twelve diners, a separate bedroom with a bed big enough to accommodate two large families, and an indoor bathroom which contained not just a huge white bath with hot and cold running water, but also a toilet and a sink. To the boys it seemed like a palace.

"Jings!" Jamie exclaimed when he saw the porcelain toilet bowl. "You could drink out of that, it's so clean. What's the paper for?" he asked, referring to the little stack of white paper next to it.

Sandy had, by now, experienced enough of the facilities available on the Trongate to understand that a clean toilet and toilet paper were luxuries unfamiliar to the poorer folk of the city. When she told Jamie and the boys what the paper was for, they looked at her with utter disbelief.

"How the other half live," muttered Sam wistfully. Just like the other boys, he and his family lived in a 'single end', which was a one room flat in which the family ate, slept, and relaxed. There was one toilet shared by over forty people which was outside in the back court. In the winter, it was so cold that the water in the bowl froze.

When the tour of the suite was done and the boys had finished marvelling at the wonders of wealth, Sir Arthur ordered afternoon tea for himself, and hot chocolate and a tray of eclairs and French fancies for the boys, which they eagerly tucked into.

A knock at the door disturbed their sweet feast. Sir Arthur looked at the eight children, who had frozen like statues at the sound - mouths open wide, full of half-chewed cake. He stood up, walked to the door, and called out, "Who's there?"

"It's Lieutenant Detective John Thomson Trench, sir," a voice called back.

Sir Arthur opened the door.

"Detective, please come in. How can I help you? Hot chocolate?" He asked, holding up the pot that he had carried to the door in case he needed it as a weapon.

The detective entered the room, a little taken aback to see the boys sitting there, though not entirely surprised.

"Uh, no. No hot chocolate for me, thank you," replied the detective.

"Please, take a seat." Sir Arthur indicated to a vacant chair at the cake-laden table and Trench sat down. Sandy and the boys chewed silently, staring at him.

"Look, I'll come straight to the point," said Trench. "I know you suspect something is wrong with the murder investigation of Marion Gilchrist." Trench looked directly at Sir Arthur. "I know that you don't just write about crimes, but that you have solved them in real life too."

"Well, yes, I have been involved in one or two cases…"

"It's one in particular that I'm thinking of. The Edalji case," Trench elaborated.

"Are you implying that there is some similarity between that and the Gilchrist murder?" Sir Arthur enquired.

"What's the Edalji case?" interrupted Charlie.

"A couple of years ago, I was involved with freeing an innocent man, George Edalji, who was wrongly convicted for mutilating animals and sending threatening letters. He was regarded with suspicion, because he was partly of foreign extraction - half Parsee Indian, on his father's side. The evidence against him had obviously been fabricated by the police investigating the case and, when the mutilations and letters continued after his conviction, I simply pointed out that Edalji must be innocent, as he couldn't possibly continue his vile crimes from a prison cell. His only crime was being half Indian," Sir Arthur explained. "Are you suggesting that the same is going on here? Is there an innocent man being framed simply for being a foreigner?" he asked, turning to Trench.

Trench considered his answer for a moment, then replied, "After your visit this afternoon, I interviewed a man called Alan Mclean. He claimed that, on the night of Miss Gilchrist's murder, a German man called Oscar Slater offered him a pawn ticket for a diamond brooch at the bargain price of fifty pounds. According to Mr Mclean, Slater was selling a pear-shaped brooch, studded with diamonds and worth thousands of pounds. He said he was selling it cheap because he needed the money fast."

The boys and Sandy looked at each other.

"The missing brooch from Miss Gilchrist's apartment?" asked Sir Arthur.

"Yes, so it would seem," replied Detective Trench. "What McLean told me certainly fit the description and Oscar Slater is well known to the west end police office. He's been arrested several times for gambling and dealing in stolen diamonds. My superiors seem determined that I should follow this line of inquiry and find him guilty - but I'm sure he has nothing to do with the murder."

"The man certainly sounds like a plausible suspect. What makes you so sure he's innocent?" Sir Arthur asked.

Trench shook his head, "I was the first detective at the murder scene. I spoke to the maid, Nellie Lambie, and took down her statement. She told me about the man she saw in the hallway. She described him as a living scarecrow in an ill-fitting, pale-coloured overcoat. She said he was sallow, hollow-eyed, and looked like death. I've met Slater, and he is far from being a scarecrow. He is well fed to the point of portly. So, when Mclean left, I paid a visit to the pawnbroker on Sauchiehall Street and discovered that Oscar Slater had indeed been in, but he had pawned a diamond ring, not a diamond brooch. I went back and told Ord what I had discovered, but he ordered me to omit the truth from my report and state that the pawn ticket is for the missing brooch. Later today, I am to go to Slater's house and arrest him for the murder."

"But why would your colleagues want to arrest the wrong man? Are they that desperate to close this case?" asked Sir Arthur.

"That's just one of the questions I've been asking myself. Douglas and Ord are not Glasgow detectives. They were brought across from Edinburgh to help with the case. I don't understand why, Glasgow detectives are the top in the world. I've solved dozens of cases and have never had to have specials from Edinburgh hold my hand. There's something going on and it's at the highest level. Not only do they want me to lie about the pawn ticket, they want me to lie about everything else, including the murder weapon and the maid's statement."

"The maid's statement?" Sir Arthur prompted.

"Yes. Nellie Lambie didn't just tell me about the man she had seen in the hallway, she also told me that, when she found Miss Gilchrist, she had still been alive and, with her last gasp whispered, 'It was A.B.' "

Eight little jaws dropped at once. Sir Arthur knew what they wanted to say but he hushed them with a glance and a slight shake of his head. Trench noticed.

"I know you know something. I've told you what I can, now it's your turn. What do you know?" The detective demanded.

The boys and Sandy squirmed in their seats. Sir Arthur glanced at them, sat back in his chair, steepled his fingers and thought for several seconds before jumping up and pacing back and forth across the hotel room floor. He clasped his hands behind his back as he considered what

Trench had told them and tried to piece it together with what they knew.

Everyone in the room watched him in pensive silence.

"We found a large, pear-shaped, diamond brooch wrapped in a bloodstained handkerchief at the back of the monkey house in the Panopticon Zoo. It was a woman's handkerchief monogrammed with the initials A.B.," Sir Arthur explained.

"Good grief! Do you have it here?" Trench asked in disbelief.

Sir Arthur shook his head. "Unfortunately, it seems that we were being followed. I was attacked this morning and the brooch was stolen, hence my war wound," replied Sir Arthur, indicating the gash and lump at his hairline which had already bloomed into a deep bruise. "But I can tell you that the brooch is inscribed with the Prince of Wales's Feathers."

Trench's eyebrows lifted and his moustache twitched. "Are you saying that this murder is somehow connected to the King himself?" he asked, incredulous.

"It seems it is a possibility," Sir Arthur concurred.

"And the handkerchief?" Trench queried.

"Gone too, I'm afraid. The brooch was still wrapped in it," Sir Arthur expounded.

"Do you have any idea who this A.B. is?" Trench asked.

"Apart from being a woman, I have no idea," Sir Arthur replied.

"A woman," Trench shook his head in disbelief. "How is a woman connected to this brutal murder? And how did the brooch happen to end up in the monkey house of the Panopticon Zoo?"

"My brother, Tam, he worked there," stated Jamie.

"Ah, yes, the other murder victim of the same evening. I remember your friends here telling me about him." Trench turned to Sandy and the other boys. "You said he had been in the west end at the time of the murder and had, in fact, been with Nellie Lambie when she had gone to fetch the evening paper. You believe he may have witnessed the murderer fleeing the scene?"

"Aye, an' we think he followed Tam back to the Panopticon," offered Sam.

"Or she," added Sir Arthur.

Trench thought for a moment. "So, you think that because the brooch was wrapped in a lady's handkerchief the murderer could be a woman?"

"I believe it is possible and must be considered. Surely it cannot be a coincidence that the brooch was wrapped in a handkerchief with the initials A.B., the same initials as Miss Gilchrist's dying words to her maid. And the more I think about it, the more I suspect that whatever papers or documents they were looking for in the workbox will somehow explain how Miss Gilchrist came to possess such a valuable jewel with a royal connection. Perhaps that is why your colleagues from Edinburgh are asking you to lie about the evidence," suggested Sir Arthur. "Perhaps they are covering up some kind of royal conspiracy."

"Hmm, seems a bit far-fetched to me - but then again, in this modern world, anything is possible. I will get to the truth," Trench promised. Then addressing Arthur Conan

Doyle, directly, he stated, "I should warn you that they know you have become interested in the case. They told me to make sure you stay away. I've taken a chance coming here, but I need your help. I can't trust them."

"Are you suggesting that we work together?" asked Sir Arthur.

"Yes, I suppose I am. Ord and Douglas are watching me, I'm sure of it, and if they find out that I'm here to ask for your help, instead of warning you off, there might literally be hell to pay. Whatever we do, we must not let them find out," Trench warned.

"And we won't," Sir Arthur declared and looked over at the boys. He winked at them. "Where do you buy your newspaper, Detective Trench?" Sir Arthur asked.

"Same as most people, from a newsboy," Trench replied with a quizzical look.

"Which corner do you buy your paper from?" Sir Arthur asked.

"Great Western Road, at the Botanic Gardens," replied Trench. "What does my newspaper buying habits have to do with anything?"

"Just remember to buy your newspaper there every morning and evening," said Sir Arthur. "We will use the newsboys to communicate."

Chapter Twenty-One

Nellie Lambie

After Trench left, the boys and Sandy finished off their cakes and hot chocolate, chatting enthusiastically about Detective Trench's visit. A police cover-up, Miss Gilchrist's last words - it was all like something from a penny dreadful mystery and they were going to solve it.

As the evening wore on, they began to feel drowsy in the comfortable, luxurious, heated rooms.

"I'd better go," said Sam, yawning and stretching. "Mum will be expecting me home for the Christmas Eve feast."

The yawn spread through the gang as they all agreed, rather reluctantly, that it was time to leave.

"I think I'll join you for the walk back to the Trongate. I feel a brisk walk will do me the power of good and clear away the cobwebs," remarked Sir Arthur as he went to fetch his coat and hat.

Together, they joined the late afternoon crowds and headed to the Panopticon. The street was full of chatter and laughter.

"Mum's doing a goose tomorrow. She says you're all welcome to come if you want. She says there's plenty.

Dinner's at six," invited Sam as they approached the tenement where his family lived.

"I never turn down a feast!" called Jimmy.

"Me neither," said Charlie. "I love your mam's cooking."

Bobby and Jamie looked at their feet. They were in no mood for festivities. Their brother's murder lay heavy in their minds and hearts. The others suddenly felt their grief and their merry chatter was replaced by silent guilt.

"We will get to the bottom of this, I promise," assured Sir Arthur.

"Aye," agreed Sam, addressing his two grieving friends. "I know we will." He waved goodbye as he disappeared through the door to his tenement close.

The rest of the gang continued along the Trongate to the Panopticon.

The queue for the next show was pushing its way through the front doors when they arrived. Andrew and George said goodbye and headed home while the others made their way up the lane to the side entrance and the spiral stair, on which the crush of people pushing and jostling continued. They were carried along in the crowd. Finally, they found themselves safely shut in the back room behind the monkey house, the noise of the crowd muffled beyond its confines. Sir Arthur stoked the last embers of the little stove, adding some lumps of coal. Within moments, fresh flames licked the metal grate.

"So, what do we do next?" he asked as he settled himself into a chair. Before anyone could answer, there was a knock on the door and a woman's voice called softly, "Jamie, Bobby, you in there?"

"It's Nellie!" Bobby announced, leaping up to open the door. A young woman stepped inside.

Sir Arthur stood up and bowed as Nellie entered. Nellie looked at the well-dressed stranger nervously.

"It's alright, Nell. He's a friend," Jamie explained.

"Hullo," she cautiously hailed.

"You must be Nellie Lambie, Miss Gilchrist's maid. I am so sorry about what you must have been through. It must have been truly horrifying," Sir Arthur said gently, taking the young woman's gloved hand in both of his.

"Thank you, sir," she responded, before politely withdrawing her hand.

"Nellie, this is Sir Arthur Conan Doyle," Jamie announced proudly when he realised that Nellie hadn't recognised their new celebrity friend. "He's come to help find the murderers."

"Sherlock Holmes?" asked Nellie, wide-eyed and a little taken aback.

"Aye," replied Charlie. The others nodded vigorously in agreement.

Nellie curtsied. "Oh, sir, I am sorry I didn't recognise you. I went to see one of your plays at the King's Theatre only last week with Tam. It was wonderful."

"Thank you, Miss Lambie," Sir Arthur said, as he cleared Sandy and Charlie off of the seat they had just settled themselves into and offered it to the suddenly star-struck maid.

"We're awfy glad to see you, Nell. We, well, we…" Jamie began, and Nellie pulled the boy towards her and hugged him as he burst into tears.

"It's alright, Jamie, it's alright," she soothed.

Bobby dashed to her side and she embraced the small boy too, holding them both as they bawled.

"Your maw's worried about you both. She said you ran off this morning and you've no been home for yer tea. She asked me to come find you. I knew you'd be here, but I didn't expect to find Sir Arthur Conan Doyle here too." Nellie looked up from the two boys and met Sir Arthur's gaze. She smiled sadly. "If you don't mind me asking, sir, how is it that you are here?"

"Now, that is a long story," he said, and began to tell the tale, with considerable help from the boys, about how he and Sandy, a stranger from the future, ended up trying to solve the murders of Miss Gilchrist and Tam and the mystery of the diamond brooch.

Nellie Lambie listened to every word. When the story was finished, she was utterly speechless.

The back room was silent, save for the noise of the crowd outside as Sandy, Sir Arthur and the boys watched her with expectation, allowing her time to absorb the extraordinary tale.

Bobby, who was now sitting on the maid's knee, broke the silence. "We're gonna find out who did it, Nell. Sir Arthur promised we would."

"I am sure you will," she replied, looking into the small boy's earnest, little face. She affectionately brushed his unkempt hair out of his eyes. "If you lot can't, then no one can."

"Do you mind if I ask you a few questions?" Sir Arthur requested.

"About Miss Gilchrist's murder?" she asked, cautiously.

"Yes, that's if it's not too painful for you. I will understand if you would rather not," Sir Arthur offered.

Nellie considered the matter for a moment. "I will do my best, sir, but I don't know if I will be very helpful."

"Thank you, Nellie. I am sure you will be very helpful. I am curious to know about Miss Gilchrist's little dog. Is it true that it was poisoned?"

Nellie frowned and looked down at her hands. "Poor little thing. I didn't think he was poisoned at first. I thought he had choked on a caramel. Loves caramels, he does. They always stick his teeth together, though."

"Caramels?" Sir Arthur enquired, intrigued.

"Aye. Miss Gilchrist had left a box of chocolates on her side table in the parlour and when I went in to fix the fire I found them scattered on the floor, with Pepper in the middle of the mess chewing on a caramel. I picked the lot up and told Pepper off for eating the mistress's chocolates, then went to the kitchen to put them in the bin. When I got back to the parlour, little Pepper was choking and then he just keeled over and died. Poor wee thing," murmured Nellie.

"Where did Miss Gilchrist get the chocolates?" asked Sir Arthur.

"I don't know, sir. They weren't her usual brand. I usually pick up her chocolates from Buchanan Street every Saturday, but I didn't pick up that box," Nellie explained.

"Were they perhaps a gift?" suggested Sir Arthur.

"I suppose they must have been," Nellie replied, "but I don't remember them being delivered and I can't imagine who they were from. I must have been out at the time."

"Had Miss Gilchrist received any strange visitors around that time?" continued Sir Arthur.

"No. Just her niece and a couple of ladies from her church. She didn't really get many visitors. She liked her privacy."

"Did she have many friends?"

"She knew a lot of people. She did a lot of work for charity and for the church and she was very well known in her circle," Nellie tactfully answered.

"What about enemies?"

"Oh, I don't think so, sir. Not that I can think of, anyway. Most people just thought she was a bit cold and unfriendly, but I don't think anyone disliked her enough to kill her. Her family doesn't like her, though I can't imagine any of them killing her in such a horrible way. Oh, it was awful." Nellie sniffed and looked back down at Bobby on her knee to hide the tears welling in her eyes. Then she looked up at the boys. "Do you really think the same person that killed Tam killed Miss Gilchrist?" she queried.

Sandy and the boys all nodded.

"We think that Tam saw the murderer after he left you, and they followed him back here," Sandy offered.

"Where was he found?" she asked suddenly. "No one will tell me what happened."

"He was found behind the curtain where they're building the new cages," Jamie replied. "He was stabbed."

Nellie went pale, pulled out a handkerchief, and began to weep into it.

Sir Arthur snatched the handkerchief from the girl's hand and held it closer to one of the oil lamps. Nellie gasped at the sudden snatch.

“A.B.!" he exclaimed.

"It's my new mistress's, sir. I have recently been employed in the service of Miss Gilchrist's niece, Miss Birrell. She took pity on me, sir, when I suddenly found myself without both a home and a position and said that, since she needed a maid, I could work for her. Her father died a few weeks ago and she has come from Paris to close his house. She gave me the handkerchief though, sir. I didn't steal it. Since Miss Gilchrist…since she was…you know…I just seem to keep bursting into tears," wailed Nellie as she erupted into a fresh flood.

Sir Arthur handed the handkerchief back. She thanked him through a hiccup.

"I'm sorry, Nellie, I didn't mean to snatch it from your hand. It's just that this handkerchief is identical to the one we found in the monkey house. The initials…”

But Nellie finished the sentence for him. "A.B." She looked up at the detective with fear and realisation in her eyes. "When I found Miss Gilchrist, she was still alive and with her last breath she said 'It was A.B.' "

She looked down at the white, lace-trimmed square in her hand and suddenly dropped it as if it had grown teeth and bitten her. It floated to the concrete floor, as all eyes stared at it.

"No, you can't think...no, no, it's not possible. Miss Birrell is a lady. She couldn't have!" Nellie looked at the famous author-detective, her glistening eyes wide with shock. "It was horrible - the work of some kind of monster, not an elegant lady like Miss Birrell. She wouldn't be capable of something so, so..." she paused, trying to find the words, "...just so horrible." She paused again, thinking for a moment, and seemed to fortify herself. She was suddenly composed again.

"It couldn't have been her," she said with conviction, "I saw the murderer coming out of Miss Gilchrist's bedroom and he definitely wasn't Miss Birrell. He was like death himself. A skeleton in an overcoat and hat."

"I think that was her accomplice. The real murderer would have been covered in blood, and you yourself described him to the newspapers as a tramp, but you didn't describe him as covered in gore. Now, Nellie, think. Are you sure you didn't see Miss Birrell at Miss Gilchrist's on Monday night?" Sir Arthur pressed.

"No, sir. I mean, yes, sir. I'm sure," she replied. "Are you sure it isn't a coincidence? There must be lots of A.B.'s in the world. I mean Anne is a common name and there's hundreds of surnames beginning with B. Brown, Burnett, Burrell, Baxter..."

"I don't believe in coincidence," stated Sir Arthur. "And there can only be one A.B. with this exact monogrammed handkerchief connected to Miss Gilchrist," he added, picking up the delicate square from the floor.

"Oh, how horrible! What am I going to do? I can't go back now. I can't! And I only started there the other day," Nellie cried.

"Of course you can go back," Sir Arthur said soothingly. "You'll be absolutely fine. Simply act normal. Miss Birrell probably doesn't know you suspect a thing," Sir Arthur reassured her, as he patted the girl on the shoulder in an effort to be comforting.

Nellie looked up at him. "I'm not going back there," she asserted.

"Nellie, I know it must be frightening for you, but it would be invaluable to our investigation, to finding the truth about what happened to Miss Gilchrist and Tam. You could help bring their murderer to justice," Sir Arthur reasoned.

Nellie's eyes filled with fear again. "I can't, I just can't! She'll know I know," she nodded. "I'm no good at lying, sir. My face always gives me away."

"All you have to do is get on with your daily work, just as you would normally," Sir Arthur reassured the girl.

"But I don't understand. Why would Miss Birrell want to kill her aunt to steal a brooch?" she asked. "Everyone knows that brooch is fake."

"Well, it transpires that the brooch might not be fake after all. You can help us find out more," Sir Arthur gently explained.

"I don't know, sir," began Nellie. "I don't feel comfortable about going back there, let alone spying on her. If I go back now, it'll be to collect my things and hand in my notice."

"No, Nellie. If you hand in your notice, she'll know something is wrong. I suspect she only employed you to find out what, if anything, you know. You must go back to work as normal. You will be absolutely fine, I promise. You want to help us get justice for Tam, don't you?" Sir Arthur persuaded the maid, looking her straight in the eyes.

"Yes, sir," she replied.

Sir Arthur pulled a silver whistle out of his coat pocket and handed it to her. "We'll be there to keep an eye on things. You won't see us, but we will be watching. If you feel threatened or frightened at any time, you blow this whistle and we will be there in an instant." The boys nodded earnestly in agreement.

Nellie took the whistle.

"Well, I suppose I had better get back then," she sniffed as she stood up.

"I'll come with you, if you like?" Jamie asked.

"No, Jamie, you and Bobby had best go back home. Your maw needs you," Nellie replied, smiling at the boy who seemed so desperate to protect her.

"I'll come with you," suggested Charlie.

"That's a very good idea," affirmed Sir Arthur. "You can escort Nellie back to the west end and take the first watch. Look out for anything suspicious and wait until all the lights are out for the night. But remember to stay hidden. What time does your mistress rise in the morning?"

"Never before ten, sir."

"Well, then, my personal gang of irregulars," Sir Arthur, addressed Sandy and the boys. "I suggest we all meet at eight o'clock tomorrow morning in my hotel room."

With that, the gang dispersed.

* * *

When Sir Arthur arrived back at the St Enoch Station Hotel, there was a message waiting for him at the reception desk. Sir Arthur opened the small, folded piece of paper, which had been sealed with a splodge of red wax, and read, "Edalji has fled. I will come and see you as soon as I can."

It was from Lieutenant Detective John Thompson Trench.

Chapter Twenty-Two

25th December

Discovery of a Blood-Stained Cloak

The next morning, the boys and Sandy met up at Sir Arthur's hotel suite and were treated to a breakfast like they had never seen before. They piled their plates with kedgeree, kippers, poached eggs, and cured ham. Sandy longed for Coco Pops but she tried to nibble around the edge of her plate. As they munched their way through the small banquet, Sir Arthur told them about the note from Trench.

"Do you think the German man Detective Trench told us about has legged it then?" asked Sandy.

"If you mean left Glasgow, then yes, I believe so. I expect Detective Trench will provide us with more details soon enough, but in the meantime, we have other fish to fry," he replied as he popped a forkful of kipper into his mouth and chewed it thoughtfully. "How did you get on last night?" he asked, turning to Andrew.

"I got frozen to the core," moaned Andrew.

"Did you see anything?" Sir Arthur pressed.

"Naw. Just rain. Nellie drawing the curtains was the only action I saw," he replied as he stabbed a thick slice of ham, shoved it in his mouth, and chewed blissfully.

"Well, who's going to be next to have the thrill of standing outside in the cold then, eh?" Sir Arthur pondered aloud.

Sandy and every boy, including Andrew, thrust a hand eagerly in the air. Sir Arthur regarded them all with a thoughtful eye. "You'll all get your chance," he said, and began organising them into shifts.

***

Although he had already done his duty the night before, Andrew volunteered for the first shift of the morning since he usually sold his newspapers from that end of Sauchiehall Street. He lugged his heavy bag of newspapers up to Hill Street and positioned himself right on the corner of Rose Street where he would have a good view of the Birrell house and could still sell his papers. It would be a lot more comfortable than squatting behind the large clump of holly bushes which had concealed him the previous evening. He stood there, battered by the wind and rain for two hours, until finally his waiting was rewarded by the departure of Miss Birrell, who got into her motor car and drove off.

He didn't get a good look at the lady driver. Her face was obscured by a large hat, tied down with a scarf against the cold weather, but she was tall and elegant. That much Andrew could see.

After the motor car had disappeared around the corner, Nellie suddenly appeared at his side.

"Morning paper, miss?" he asked.

"Yes, thanks," Nellie replied and handed him a coin.

As Andrew handed her the paper he asked, "Have you found out anything?"

"No, nothing at all. I barely see her, except when I need to take coal or tea into whatever room she's in. She spends most of her time in the study," Nellie replied.

"Doing what?" he queried.

"I don't know. She doesn't exactly tell me her business," responded Nellie.

"Any visitors?" Andrew checked to see if anyone was watching them.

"Not since I've been here. Unless you include the delivery boys and postman. I certainly haven't seen that man again, the one from Miss Gilchrist's…I'm sure Sir Arthur is wrong about her, you know. She is very nice and I simply can't imagine her killing her aunt like that." She shivered at the memory of the battered old lady. "Or consorting with the likes of him," she observed, referring to the man in the pale-coloured overcoat. "I'd best go back. Miss said she wouldn't be long." Nellie turned and walked back across the street.

A few minutes later, Andrew saw Jimmy, who was to take the next watch, turn the corner at the bottom of the street. Andrew casually strolled towards him. The boys glanced at each other as they passed.

"She's out in her automobile," Andrew whispered out of the corner of his mouth. He then headed onto Sauchiehall Street, where he made his way to his usual pitch to sell the last of his morning papers. Meanwhile, Jimmy took over the vigil.

Jimmy was pulling a hand cart. His dad had told him he might as well collect some rags while he was up in the west end. All those posh houses meant rich pickings and his rag collecting was a better cover than hiding in a bush. It had taken him just over an hour to push the cart uphill all the way from the east end, and he was glad that the journey back was downhill the whole way.

Once he was at the top of the street with the empty cart, he knocked on the first door and waited, all the time glancing towards Miss Birrell's house. A maid answered the first door, from which he managed to get a set of old sheets and an old pair of worn-out ladies' boots. The next house provided him with an assortment of rags, the next some old broken pans and chipped crockery, the next an old rug and a broken stool.

All the time he was filling the cart, he was also watching Miss Birrell's house and he saw her return just as he was two doors away. She pulled up in her motor car and pulled out a large trunk which had been wedged into the back seat. *Interesting,* thought Jimmy. He was dropping the latest hoard into his cart when she started the struggle up the steps, contending with her long skirts as she battled with the bulky box. He ran over and offered his services in helping her carry it to the front door, ascertaining that the box was empty and managing to get a good look at the woman at the same time.

He thought she looked about the same age as his Aunty Agnes, who had just celebrated her fortieth birthday. She certainly appeared to be a lady of means. She was dressed in the latest fashion and obviously enjoyed the best things that money could buy.

Miss Birrell happily accepted help from this rag-and-bone boy and, as they got to the top step, Nellie opened the front door.

"Ah, Nellie," Miss Birrell declared wearily. "Wonderful timing, dear. Be a love and take this, will you?"

Nellie took the trunk off her mistress and helped Jimmy drag it over the threshold. Once inside, the lady shut the door, and removed her driving gloves and hat which she placed on an ornate marble-topped console table. She looked Jimmy up and down and smiled at him.

"Wait here. I have some old rags you can take," she said and stepped over to the wide stairs that swept up to the floors above. "Nellie, bring that case up, will you?"

Nellie followed her mistress, dragging the large trunk up behind her, step by step. Jimmy instinctively offered to help, but Nellie refused and told him haughtily, "Stay there, boy. I can manage. It is not heavy." Then a few steps up, she leaned over the bannister and shouted down, "And don't touch anything!" Then winked and silently mouthed, "Look around, I'll keep her busy."

Jimmy found himself standing on his own in the hallway of the large townhouse. It was vast and very grand with a marble mosaic floor, and an ornate ceiling with plaster details so thick it looked like icing on a wedding cake. A large crystal chandelier glittered above his head and enormous, gold-framed mirrors showed him his pale, ragged reflection. He took his cap off and held it in his hands, wringing it nervously. He felt very uncomfortable shut in with a woman who was quite possibly a murderer. He gingerly stepped over to the large marble console table where Miss Birrell had left her gloves and hat. Like the handkerchief, the gloves bore her embroidered initials. He slowly, carefully, pulled open the drawer and, after glancing up to the top of the stairs, rummaged through its contents, looking for anything that might be a clue. There was nothing - so he slowly and carefully closed it again, then stepped back to where they had left him and resumed wringing his cap.

The lady reappeared a few moments later, with Nellie dragging a large cloth sack down the stairs.

"Here, boy," she called. "This is for you."

Jimmy ran up the stairs and met the lady and her maid halfway up.

"Thank you, ma'am," he replied, and took the surprisingly heavy bundle. He dragged it down the rest of the stairs. At the bottom, Miss Birrell caught up with him.

"Something extra for your help," she said, opening a small coin purse that hung from her chatelaine and handing him a shilling.

"Jings, thanks miss!" Jimmy said, pleasantly surprised as he pocketed the coin. She opened the front door and he made his way back out onto the street. He even turned and waved and she waved back, smiling, before she closed the door. Nellie was right - she seemed quite a nice lady. It was hard to imagine her going around bashing old ladies' brains in.

Jimmy continued his way down the street, stopping to look back at 9 Hill Street from every door. By the time he got to the corner, his cart was as full as he could manage. His dad would be very pleased with the haul, so he began the long walk back to the east end, passing Charlie on the way, who was selling newspapers at the top of Buchanan Street. As Jimmy passed, he nodded at Charlie, signalling it was his turn to leave his pitch for sentry duty.

* * *

When Jimmy got back to his dad's yard, he and his little sister, Maggie, set about the task of sorting the odd collection of west end junk. Jimmy sifted through the broken pans and chipped pots whilst Maggie sorted through the rags, pulling out the stuff that still had good wear left in it and separating the worn-out rags that would be reused to make paper and rugs.

"Look at this," she said, pulling out a big, heavy, black wool cloak with a shiny, red satin lining. "There's nothing wrong with this. It's like new." The little girl stood and held the heavy cloak up, which was so long that, even with her arms extended above her head, it still swept the floor. "It's just got some kind of mark on the front, dead in the middle, like something got splashed on it. Clean that out and it would be good as new. People in the west end got too much money, if you ask me."

Jimmy looked at his little sister and the cloak she was holding up. "A mark? Like a splash? Let's see." Jimmy dashed over to his sister, grabbed the cloak from her and inspected it. He saw exactly what she had meant. On the black wool, the stain was a brownish mark in the light of the oil lamp. But it didn't look like mud. Could it be blood? "What other stuff was with this?"

Maggie pulled the hessian sack from the pile of clothes. "It was the first thing I pulled out. I haven't pulled out anything else yet."

Jimmy recognised it instantly as the bag that Miss Birrell had handed him. He grabbed it off Maggie and stuffed the cloak back in.

"What are you doing with that?" she asked.

"Never you mind - and don't go telling Da," he snapped at her, then ran out of the door to the Panopticon.

The Panopticon was only a five-minute walk from the yard, but the bag felt like a dead weight, made heavier by the wind and rain that battered him. By the time Jimmy got there, it was nearly 6:00 p.m. and Sandy was sitting in the zoo guarding Solomon to make sure he didn't pick any more pockets.

"What's that?" she asked, pointing at the cloth sack.

"I'll tell you later. I'm just dropping them off until we get back," Jimmy said, placing the sack on the ground.

"Get back? Oh, of course, we're going to Sam's for Christmas dinner," Sandy suddenly remembered. She had never had goose before, but it couldn't be worse than her gran's turkey.

* * *

It was 8:00 p.m. when the whole gang came cheerily down the stairs with full bellies. Sandy had never been in a single-end before, but she had heard about them. Sam and his family had their own room, which they didn't share with anyone else. It was a lot bigger than she had expected. In fact, it was bigger than the living room and kitchen in her tower-block flat. The ceiling was quite high, and it had one large window where a table had been piled high with food for dinner. On the opposite side of the room was a curtained recess. The curtain was open enough for Sandy to see a large bed behind, covered with a patchwork quilt. There was a large stove within the fireplace on one wall with a mantelpiece adorned with China dogs, a mantel clock and a sepia-toned photograph of the Spisman family. Sam was only a small boy when the picture was taken and was sitting on his mother's knee while his father stood behind them and his older brother and sister, Jakub and Maria, stood on either side. A large, patterned rug covered the floor, and four chairs and a couple of stools comprised the rest of the furniture. It was cosy and homely.

Sandy was used to a 21st century Glasgow Christmas where the streets are adorned with Christmas lights, tenement windows sparkled with Christmas trees, and people generally celebrated the holiday with presents and too much food. In the Glasgow of 1908, there was hardly anything festive. In fact, it was like an ordinary day for most people. Sam's family, however, were Polish Catholic. His mum and dad, Mr. and Mrs. Spisman, had moved to Glasgow in 1901, and they cheerfully celebrated Christmas. A real Christmas tree stood in the corner to the left of the window and filled the room with the smell of pine. It didn't have any tinsel or plastic decorations, but it did have a few glass baubles which twinkled in the light of the little candles that had been pegged to the branches. The other branches were adorned with apples, walnuts and little gingerbread stars and hearts. The gingerbread treats were delicious. Mrs Spisman told her that they were called pierniks and that her mother had always made them on Christmas Eve, which is when they traditionally have their Christmas feast.

"But today is the day for celebrating with friends and sharing what little we have," she said, as she handed a plate full of pierniks to Sandy.

Sir Arthur had brought with him two bottles of wine and a fruit cake, which was added to the table. For a couple of hours, he and the little gang feasted, sang, chatted and made merry with the Spisman family.

Now, as they filed into the room behind the monkey house, the chatter turned from Christmas celebrations back to the business of the day, the murder of Marion Gilchrist - and, most importantly, Tam. Bobby and Jamie were already waiting for them.

Jimmy dragged the bag of rags out from under the workbench.

"What's in the sack?" Bobby instantly demanded.

"Bloodstained clothes," announced Jimmy as he pulled out the cloak and held it up, pointing out the stain down the front. He then pulled out the other items; a pair of men's boots, which were also stained, and a pair of men's striped trousers which had splashes up the lower part of the legs.

"Blood," Sir Arthur instantly announced. "Where did you get this collection of bloody clothes?"

"From Miss Birrell," Jimmy replied.

The others gasped in amazement.

"How did you manage to get Miss Birrell to hand you the very clothes the murderer was wearing?" asked Sir Arthur.

"She gave them to me after I helped her carry a trunk into her house. They're men's clothes," Jimmy remarked.

"That doesn't mean that Miss Birrell couldn't have worn them. Look at the size of the boots," Sir Arthur said as he picked up the pair of black leather boots. "They are more like a boy's boots than a man's. They would certainly be more likely to fit a woman," Sir Arthur explained. "You helped Miss Birrell carry a trunk into her house?" he suddenly added.

"Aye, a big trunk. She was struggling wi' it," Jimmy replied.

"Was the trunk heavy?" Sir Arthur asked.

"Not really, sir. It was empty and bulky. Do you think she's going to stuff a body in it?" asked Jimmy, voicing what he'd been thinking as soon as he had seen the lady trying to heft the large travelling trunk up the steps.

"I think it unlikely, but it is curious why she needs such a large trunk. She must be planning to travel," Sir Arthur said, and then added, "Has anyone got anything else to report?"

"I saw Nellie. She didn't really have anything to say, other than Miss Birrell seems to spend most of her time in the study," Andrew said.

"You spoke to Nellie? Where? On the street?" asked Sir Arthur, a little abruptly.

"Yes, sir. I sold her a newspaper. Miss Birrell couldn't have seen us, she had already gone off in her motorcar," Andrew replied.

"Did Nellie say anything about what Miss Birrell was doing in the study?" Sir Arthur asked.

"She didn't know."

"Interesting," the author mused, and considered what the boys had told him. "So we have bloodstained clothes from Miss Birrell which appear to be her size. Is it Miss Gilchrist's or Tam's blood? Is she indeed guilty of these brutal crimes? And what kept her busy in the study? We need to speak directly to Nellie and see if she has found anything else out."

"It's Sunday tomorrow. It's likely Miss Birrell will be at church in the morning. We could go up then and see Nellie," suggested Jamie.

"We could, but we can't all go together and knock on the front door. I'm sure we are still being watched," Sir Arthur said, unconsciously touching the gash on his forehead. "Sandy, how do you fancy a shift tomorrow morning?"

"Aye," answered Sandy. "What are you thinking?"

"After Jimmy's success collecting door to door, I think you should go disguised as some sort of hawker. Maybe you could try a disguise as a peg seller. If the house is being watched, they would never suspect a girl," Sir Arthur suggested. "Jimmy, could you find us some suitable clothes for a girl, a gypsy peg seller, in Sandy's size?"

The boys looked horrified. Dress Sandy up as a girl? The indignity and humiliation of it!

"You can't dress him up as a lassie!" exclaimed Andrew.

"Why not? Sandy is, after all, a lassie," Sir Arthur replied, matter-of-factly.

There was a sharp intake of breath from all the assembled boys. Never, for one moment, had it occurred to them that Sandy was anything but a boy. She had short hair, wore breeches, and wasn't at all like a girl. They looked at Sandy, waiting for her to laugh and say it was only a joke, that of course she was a boy, but Sandy just looked guiltily at them.

"Well, you never asked," she said. "When you assumed I was a boy, I just thought it was easier to pretend to be a boy."

"So, you are a lassie?" asked a disbelieving Jimmy.

"But you don't wear girl's clothes. My mam would faint if she saw you," Jamie said and started laughing. "My sisters would die if they had to wear breeches and cut their hair short." Then he looked serious again, "Did you have your hair cut off as a punishment?"

"No," Sandy laughed. "It's fashionable for girls to have short hair, and everyone wears trousers in the future - if they want to, that is."

"Isn't it difficult to tell who's a man and who's a woman?" asked George.

"Well, no, of course it isn't. Women still look like women and boys still look like boys…well, a lot of the time anyway. And girls do still wear dresses and skirts and some girls have long hair and some men have long hair. We just have the choice to wear whatever we want," Sandy concluded.

The boys all shook their heads in disbelief.

"Jings. What a weird world you live in," stated Charlie.

Sir Arthur had known for a while that Sandy was a girl. He had thought she was a strange kind of boy when he met her. He had never met such a clean urchin. In fact, the child seemed to have a fear of the dirt that her cohorts delighted in. And the way the child had delicately carved and picked at his dinner with a knife and fork, while the other boys hacked and shovelled with their knives, leaving their forks clean and unused on the tablecloth, suggested not all was as it seemed. Then there was the boy's shyness when it came to relieving himself, which, amongst the balcony boys, was practically regarded as a sport. Therefore, Arthur Conan Doyle concluded that this unnatural boy must be a girl.

"So, what do I do? Just go door to door selling pegs?" Sandy asked, not quite sure what a peg seller did.

"Aye," said Jamie simply. "Most maids will buy off a Gypsy. They're always worried they'll get cursed if they don't."

Chapter Twenty-Three

26th December
The Letter

The next morning, Sandy, in her gypsy peg seller disguise, caught a tram up Sauchiehall Street and walked the rest of the way to Hill Street.

A couple of years ago, she had gone door to door with her mum and Gary, a charity worker who had been mum's boyfriend at the time. They were trying to get people to donate money to help save a rare species of turtle from extinction. Most of the time, people just slammed the door in their faces and they were left on the doorstep feeling stupid, but some people took them seriously and dropped some change into their collection box. Not many people signed up for the newsletter though, including Sandy's mum, who dumped him the next day. Surely selling pegs in Edwardian Glasgow would be easier than raising money to save endangered turtles.

It was a freezing cold, but dry, day. A watery sun shone weakly through the perpetual smog that enveloped Glasgow. The outfit Jimmy had supplied for her was as warm as her boy's rags, with a heavy, brown, woollen skirt that swept the pavement, beneath which she still wore her trousers; a thick, mustard-coloured, cotton blouse, brown woollen jacket, a plaid shawl, topped off with a battered, old hat with some faded silk flowers around the crown, hiding her short, boyish hair. She wore the boots she had borrowed from the future music hall's wardrobe store with thick woollen socks, but her feet still felt like blocks of ice on the frosty, cobbled streets. Over her arm, she carried a wicker basket that Jimmy had half-filled with wooden dolly pegs.

Sandy wanted to appear like a genuine gypsy peg seller in case Miss Birrell saw her, so she walked up to the first door on Hill Street and pulled the bell. When no one answered, she made her way to the next door. This time, a maid cautiously peered out and instantly slammed the door closed when she saw the ragged girl. At the next house, there was no answer, nor at the next. It seemed that the houses of Hill Street were deserted. Everyone, it appeared, had gone to church.

She got to Miss Birrell's house and rang the bell. No one answered, so she rang again. As she was about to ring for a third time, Nellie answered the door and Sandy smiled her biggest, most engaging smile, "Buy some pegs, miss?"

"Not today, thanks," replied the maid, who began to close the door.

"Please, Miss," Sandy called through the narrowing gap, pleading as engagingly as she could, "I haven't sold a single bundle all morning and they're only a ha'penny. My father will beat me if I go home without selling any."

Nellie opened the door a little wider and peered out at the waif on the doorstep. "All right," she said, taking pity on the poor, frozen child. "I guess we could use some, even though it ain't drying-outdoor weather this time of year. Here," she offered Sandy a ha'penny. "What you're doing out selling pegs on the Lord's Day, I'll never know. You won't make much money round here on a Sunday."

As Sandy moved forward to take the ha'penny in exchange for the peg bundle, she whispered, "It's me, Sandy. You probably thought I was a boy. You met me the other day in Tam's room," and handed the ha'penny back with a bundle of pegs.

Nellie's eyes widened. "Yes, I remember you. Why ever were you dressed as a boy?"

"Long story," replied Sandy. "Has anything happened? Have you seen anyone or anything suspicious?"

"Well, yes - there is one thing. I told Andrew yesterday that Miss spends a lot of time in her study," Nellie said.

"Yes, he told us."

"Well, I'm not sure if this is important or not, but last night, when I was fetching her tea tray, I noticed a letter sitting on her desk. It had a red wax seal on it of three feathers in a crown. Miss Gilchrist had a letter with the same seal on the back. I think it's the same letter," Nellie said, glancing anxiously over her shoulder

Three feathers and a crown - wasn't that what Sir Arthur had found on the brooch? "Thanks, Nellie. I think that's quite important." Then the two girls said goodbye.

Sandy kept up her door-to-door ruse until she came to the end of the street so as not to raise suspicion, selling two more bundles in the process. At the corner, she turned right and began to run as fast as her boots would let her. She trotted down Sauchiehall Street and met Charlie at the top of Buchanan Street. After telling him what Nellie had discovered, they jogged together down the hill to the St. Enoch Station Hotel, where they hoped they would find Sir Arthur Conan Doyle.

Chapter Twenty-Four

Doyle Works the Twilight Shift

Sir Arthur Conan Doyle had spent the last couple of hours strolling along the Clydeside. The river was swathed in grey smog from the cloud-belching steamboats that crammed the quaysides. The haunting sound of fog horns drifted through the thick air. It gave his meander a dream-like quality.

He stood, gazing into the cold, dark river, and pondered the extraordinary events of the last few days which had left him feeling as foggy as the river itself. He was not used to feeling like this. He prided himself in being a great detective writer because he was a great detective, able to clearly see clues and deduce motives where no one else could. But from the moment the mysterious letter had arrived, his crystal-clear powers of deduction and reason had become cloudy and dull.

A murder was not unusual, and even the connection to a member of the royal family was not beyond belief. But, a haunted magic lantern, a time-travelling child from the future, and a mysterious letter in his own hand, were difficult to digest, even for a man as open-minded to all possibilities as Sir Arthur Conan Doyle. What more bizarre twists would this Christmas mystery present?

He had hoped that a riverside walk would help him put it all into perspective and perhaps even result in an epiphany. But, sadly, all he achieved was cold, damp feet and a deeper feeling of desolation. He turned and headed back to his hotel.

As he walked across St Enoch Square, he saw Sandy and Charlie running toward the hotel doors. He "hallooed" them, so they stopped and waited for him to catch up. He could see by their excited expressions that something had happened and, as soon as they were in his room with the door securely shut behind them, Sandy blurted out what Nellie had said about the letter with the crown and feathers wax seal.

"The Prince of Wales's Feathers. This is very interesting news indeed," commented Sir Arthur when Sandy had finished. "The letter could well be what was taken from the work box. What we need to know is what is in that letter. Is it connected to the brooch? Does it explain how Miss Gilchrist came to possess it?"

He walked over to the fireplace, squatted down in front of the fire and, grabbing a poker, prodded at the glowing coals, goading them into life, provoking a burst of sparks and fresh flames. He gazed into the red heart of the coals and thought for a while.

"I think it's my turn to watch the house," he said at length and disappeared into the bedroom. He pulled a hanger of old clothes out of the wardrobe and threw it on the bed. He had decided last night that he would take a leaf out of his own Sherlock Holmes books and had given

Jimmy enough money to provide him, as well as Sandy, with disguises.

"What are you doing?" Charlie asked, surprised as Sir Arthur reappeared from the bedroom carrying what appeared to be a bundle of rags.

"I am going to disguise myself as a lamplighter and take the Hill Street twilight shift," Sir Arthur explained. "Now, you two get about your business and I will see you here, with the other boys, at about six o'clock tonight. Make sure you're all here. I'll provide some dinner."

So saying, he shooed the two children out of his hotel room and put on the old clothes, throwing his heavy winter coat over the top to hide his disguise until he left the hotel and was safely in the subway station. Then, when he was sure no one was looking, he shoved his overcoat in a cloth bag, slung it over his shoulder, and caught the subway train heading west.

It was still murky daylight when he got to the bottom of Hill Street at about 3:30 p.m. so he waited, peering up the hill to where Miss Birrell sat in her grand townhouse. It was at least fifteen minutes later before the lamplighter - a small, gaunt, grey man - arrived, huffing and puffing his way up the street. Sir Arthur gave the poor leerie quite a fright when he stepped out from the deepening shadows.

"I am so sorry. I didn't mean to startle you. I wonder if I might borrow your pole and ladders for a couple of hours?" he asked the bemused lamplighter. "I am willing to pay, of course."

“How much?" asked the man, eyeing the ragged stranger with a sceptical look.

"A pound for your trouble. And I will return your equipment to you when I have finished," Sir Arthur offered, opening his purse and showing that he had more than enough money to keep his bargain.

"I'll take a guinea," the lamplighter replied. "I still got the whole of Sauchiehall Street to light, as far as Buchanan."

"Well, how about I finish your shift for you and pay you a pound and return the pole to your home," Sir Arthur bartered, thinking a guinea was just a little too much.

"Well, I don't suppose I would mind that too much. Bring my pole and ladders back to Lauder's Bar. I'll be in there, with my pound," the wily old man stated, sticking out his woolly, gloved hand, palm up, for the payment which the author duly provided.

Sir Arthur took the pole and ladders and slowly began to make his way up the left side of Hill Street. He had thought this task would be a simple one. He hadn't considered the vile December weather or the practised skill of the lamplighters, who could illuminate whole sections of the city in just a few minutes with their magic poles. But the pole was not so easy to wield. The bottom was weighted by a reservoir of kerosene oil which fuelled a wick, providing a small, continuous flame to light the tall street lamps. Adjacent to the flame was a hook to open the glass cover that protected the gas jet inside.

At the first lamp, Doyle fought for several minutes in the wind and rain to hold his balance on the short ladder and fish for the little ring on the glass door. He finally managed to hook it and pull it open. Then he spent a couple of minutes trying to unhook the pole before twisting it clumsily round so the flame would ignite the gas jet, which it did in a small, explosive poof. Then he used the hooked side to push the glass door shut again.

He felt rather pleased with himself as he basked in the brilliance of his first lit lamp. His second lamp took him at least as long as the first, but by the time he had managed to get to the top of Hill Street, he had developed a technique. Now it only took him a few seconds to illuminate each one. Enjoying his task, he started to sing the old lamplighter's song from his Edinburgh youth:

My tea is nearly ready, and the sun has left the sky;
It's time to take the window to see Leerie going by;
For every night at teatime and before you take your seat,
With lantern and with ladder he comes posting up the street.
Now Tom would be a driver and Maria go to sea,
And my papa's a banker and as rich as he can be;
But I, when I am stronger and can choose what I'm to do,
O Leerie, I'll go round at night and light the lamps with you!
For we are very lucky, with a lamp before the door,
And Leerie stops to light it as he lights so many more;
And O! before you hurry by with ladder and with light,
O Leerie, see a little child and nod to him tonight!

He was so engrossed in his song and his task that he had almost forgotten the real purpose of his west end visit. He nearly missed a man in a pale-coloured overcoat and cloth cap walking down the front steps of Miss Birrell's house. Sir Arthur covertly watched the man as he continued to light the lamps - hook, flip open, unhook, twist the pole, light the gas, push the door closed, down the ladders and move onto the next, repeat. He watched the man walk down the hill before disappearing around the corner. Doyle closed the door of the lamp he had just finished lighting, jumped down the ladder, and trotted to the corner. He peeped round. He could see the man in the pale-coloured overcoat buying a newspaper. The man handed the newsboy a coin and walked off.

A moment later the boy called after him, "Oi, Mister, what kind of coin dae you call this?" The man did not respond and disappeared into the smoggy gloom.

Interesting, thought Sir Arthur as he walked to the corner where the newsboy stared at the coin under the unlit lamp.

"Let me help you with that," he said as he jumped up the ladder and lit the gas, bathing the boy in a pool of amber light. "What's wrong with the coin, laddie?"

"I huvnae ever seen a coin like that. I don't know what it is, sir. Is it worth anything?" the newsboy asked.

"May I see it?" asked Sir Arthur. The boy eyed him suspiciously before handing over the coin. Sir Arthur turned it round in his hands. It was not just wrong - it was French! Its front was embossed with the head of King Louis XVI and the date read 1791. An antique French coin, from the time of the French Revolution. Why would the man in the pale-coloured overcoat have an antique French coin?

How was this possible? He realised the boy was staring at him. "Aye, laddie, it's worthless. Some kind of foreign coin. Here lad, have a real one in exchange and an extra one for your trouble," said Sir Arthur, handing the boy two shiny copper pennies. The boy was delighted.

* * *

It was nearly 6:00 p.m. by the time he got back to his hotel room. It had taken him just over two hours to complete the task of lighting the lamps and delivering the pole back to its owner, who was merrily drinking away his pound.

During his walk back, he puzzled the coin over and over in his head, and each time the conclusion was the same. The coin was over a hundred years old and from another country all together. What did it mean? Who was the man in the pale-coloured overcoat? Was he a time-traveller, like Sandy? Had he also travelled through the magic lantern and, if so, why? Why would someone who can travel through time choose to travel to 1908 and steal a diamond brooch and a letter? Surely the gold of King Solomon's mines or the riches of ancient Egypt would have more appeal to a time-travelling thief. The letter Nellie had seen must be the key to this mystery, and on the walk back to St. Enoch Square, he began to hatch a plan of how to get it.

Back in the warmth of his rooms, he sat at the desk and wrote a letter to Nellie Lambie instructing her to block the fireplace in the study. He told her not to allow Miss Birrell to call for a chimney sweep and instead offer to fetch the man Miss Gilchrist always used. She must then go to the Panopticon and find him. When Sir Arthur finished the note, he sealed it in an envelope, ready to be delivered, then penned a brief note to Trench asking the detective to meet him the next night at his hotel room.

He had just completed this when Sandy and the boys arrived. He let Sandy tell them about the letter with the Prince of Wales's seal, then he told them about his escapade as a lamplighter and how he had seen the man in the pale-coloured overcoat.

"I didn't notice him at first. I have to say that the task of a lamplighter isn't as easy as it appears, especially not on cold, windy nights like tonight. I had quite a time of it at first, I can tell you, and I was so engrossed with my task that I did nearly miss him, but I saw him on the bottom step of Miss Birrell's and followed him as far as Sauchiehall Street."

"Well, that's not very far. You mean you only followed him to the bottom of the hill?" said Charlie, disappointed by the story so far.

"And, at the bottom of the hill, I discovered a very interesting piece of evidence indeed," Sir Arthur continued and pulled the coin out of his pocket.

"It's a coin," stated Charlie, clearly unimpressed.

"The very coin the man in the pale-coloured overcoat used to buy a newspaper with. Is it an ordinary penny?" asked Sir Arthur.

Charlie took the coin from Sir Arthur and inspected it. "Who's that? That's not King Edward!"

"No, that is Louis the sixteenth, and it's French. Note the date on the other side," Sir Arthur prompted.

Charlie turned the coin over in his hand, Sandy and the boys crowding round him to get a look. "1791!" he exclaimed. "Cor, is it valuable?"

"I doubt it," Sir Arthur replied.

"So, the man in the pale-coloured overcoat is from France in 1791?" asked Sandy, a little confused.

"Or visited it. I have a sneaking suspicion that he's a time-traveller too," Sir Arthur offered.

"Do you think he came through the magic lantern as well then?"

"We can only assume that he did," Sir Arthur observed. "After all, how many other ways are there to travel through time?"

There was a knock at the door.

"I believe dinner is served," Sir Arthur announced as a trolley full of silver-domed dishes was wheeled into the room. As Sandy and the boys scoffed their way through the three-course meal, he outlined the plan he was hatching.

"To get into Miss Birrell's study, I will disguise myself as a chimney sweep and take one of you with me. Sandy, I think you could pass as my apprentice; you're certainly small enough. Then we can quickly search for the letter," proposed Sir Arthur.

"But what if she doesn't need her chimney swept?" asked Bobby.

"I have already written a note to Nellie instructing her to block the chimney in the study. We just need to get it to her," explained Sir Arthur.

"I'll go," said George. "I'm up at Mr. MacBrayne's tonight anyway, and it's not far from Miss Birrell's."

"Then I will leave it in your hands to deliver the note. Remember to be careful and stealthy," cautioned Sir Arthur.

"Yes, sir. I will make sure I am not discovered," George assured enthusiastically. He was thoroughly enjoying this new life as a detective.

"Well, that's settled then, George will deliver the note and, Jimmy, can you gather some clothes and brushes that would suit a pair of chimney sweeps and bring them to me here tomorrow morning?"

"Aye," Jimmy replied through a mouth full of beef.

"And there is one final task I would ask of you," requested Sir Arthur as he pulled out a second letter and waved it in the air. "This letter is for our detective friend, Trench, and needs to be given to the newsboy that will be working at the Botanic Gardens tomorrow morning when he passes on his way to work."

"I know who that will be. I'll go," piped up Jamie as he stabbed a roast potato with his knife.

Doyle was sure these boys had never eaten so well, and it was evident in the rosy glow that now painted their usually pale cheeks. He felt heartened that he could provide these poor children with something that he had always enjoyed and taken for granted - a decent meal.

When the last lick of plum pudding was cleaned from every bowl, George left to deliver the note. The boys and Sandy followed him out.

***

At 8:30 p.m., George arrived at 9 Hill Street. A cosy light glowed through the drawn curtains and, being careful not to slip on the icy steps, George cautiously made his way up the front steps to the door, trying hard not to make too much noise with his sticks. He pulled the bell lever and waited for Nellie to answer, but the face that greeted him was not the pretty, smiling face of the young maid. It was the gaunt and skull-like visage of the man in the pale-coloured overcoat.

* * *

Miss Birrell had somehow found out that Nellie had spoken to Sir Arthur and the boys, and she had been waiting for Nellie's return from the shops. The young maid was greeted in the kitchen with a look of cold, hard evil dancing in her mistresses' usually sparkling green eyes.

"I know what you've been up to, Nellie, dear," Miss Birrell had said in her soft, lilting French accent. "And I know what you, that nosey writer and gang of urchins think, but understand this," she cooed in a soft but threatening voice as she had soothingly stroked the maid's hair. "If you lead the police to my door, you'll be the one that hangs for the old lady's murder." Nellie had looked at her mistress with terrified eyes. Miss Birrell nodded and said, "I'll make sure of it. I'll tell them that you murdered your boyfriend too and they will believe me because I am a respectable lady of means and you are nothing but a wretched servant."

When George had arrived later that evening with the note from Sir Arthur Conan Doyle, Miss Birrell and her friend, the man in the pale-coloured overcoat, had taken the boy and tied him up in the windowless attic room.

Nellie had been warned by Miss Birrell that she would kill him if Nellie said a word of it to anyone or disobeyed, reminding Nellie she would be hanged not only for the murders of Miss Gilchrist and Tam, but for the murder of George as well. The poor maid had no choice but to do as Miss Birrell instructed, which was to go to the Panopticon and play along with Sir Arthur Conan Doyle's plan as if everything was alright. She was ready to cry, ready to scream, but she knew he was watching in the shadows.

Chapter Twenty-Five

27th December
George Didn't Come Home

The morning of the 27th of December was bright and clear. Even the perpetual smog had thinned to let the watery, winter sunshine through. Frost had painted every rooftop and railing white, and the icy cold nipped at Sandy's nose, toes, and fingers as she washed the morning's breakfast dishes at the water pump. She had just finished this task when Andrew appeared, looking as white as a sheet.

"George didn't come home last night, Sandy," he spluttered.

"What do you mean, he didn't come home last night?" repeated Sandy, a chill running down her spine.

"Just that. He didn't come home. He's gone, maybe dead! Maybe that man in the pale-coloured overcoat, or Miss Birrell, murdered him when he delivered that message last night. George has never not come home. Mam is mad with worry. He's her favourite - and after what happened to Tam..." Tears welled in his eyes, and he stared pleadingly at Sandy. "She's sent me out to find him. We've got to find him!" Andrew practically wailed.

"Let me take these things back downstairs," said Sandy, lifting the tray of clean dishes, "and we'll go and get Sir Arthur and start a search for George."

"Jamie, Sam, and Charlie are already out looking for him and telling all the other newsboys."

"Well, that's good." Sandy tried to sound reassuring as they walked down the steps together.

"Well, I was…" but Andrew didn't get to finish the sentence.

The sound of running footsteps behind them made them stop and look round. Nellie rounded the corner of the spiral stairs looking worried and harassed.

"Is Mr Doyle here?" she asked.

"No, not yet," Sandy answered. "We're just about to go and look for him after I've dumped this lot," she said, indicating the tray of dishes.

"Huv you seen my wee brother George?" Andrew quizzed.

"Aye," Nellie answered. "He came to Hill Street last night and delivered a letter. That's what I'm here about."

"What time did you see him, Nellie? Was he alright?" Andrew asked anxiously. "He never came home last night and mams at her wit's end wi' worry. Something's happened to him, Nellie, I know it!"

"He was fine when I saw him," Nellie lied, trying to sound as reassuring as possible.

The three entered the zoo together and as they stepped into Tam's little room behind the monkey house, Nellie felt a pang of loss and loneliness wash over her, sharpening her fear for herself and George.

Harry was sitting next to the small stove, sipping tea from an old enamel mug.

"You all right, Nellie?" he asked as the trio entered the small room. "You look a bit pale."

Nellie tried to give Harry a big, everything's wonderful, smile, but she couldn't quite manage it.

"I'm just missing Tam, that's all," she wearily replied. "Being in here, well, you know…"

"Aye, of course. I am so sorry about Tam and Miss Gilchrist. You've really been through it, eh? Here, have some of this," Harry said, as he took the teapot from the stove and poured steaming hot brown liquid into a stained and chipped cup. "Och, and the police are useless an 'aw…"

Nellie took the cup and held it as the tears flowed unchecked down her cheeks. Harry didn't know what to say to console the maid. "Are you here to collect Tam's things?" he, rather tactlessly, asked in an attempt to fill the awkward silence.

Nellie glanced at Andrew, then shook her head. "No," she responded weakly. "I just, well, I just wanted to see Bobby and Jamie really," she lied and took a sip of her tea.

"Huv you seen George?" Andrew blurted.

Harry looked up from his cup. "George? No. Why?" A look of concern spread across his face.

"He's missing," Andrew declared, sniffing back the threatening tears.

"No, not wee George. When? What happened?" He felt his heart sinking to his stomach.

"We don't know. All we know is he didn't come home last night from Mr MacBrayne's," Andrew replied.

Harry put down his mug on the small, wooden table. "Well, that's it, first Tam and the old woman are murdered and now George is missing. Something is going on and there's something you lot aren't telling me." He stared at the new boy, Sandy. Sandy looked across at Andrew and then both looked guiltily down at their hands.

"Well, what is it?" the young zookeeper with the fuzzy moustache demanded.

"We don't know, honest, Harry. We're as much in the dark as you are, but we are trying to find out," Andrew replied honestly. "We're going to go and find Sir Arthur next. He'll know what to do."

Harry grunted. It was clear they weren't going to tell him what was going on. Now that he was a man, the boys had stopped trusting him with their secrets. He was no longer a part of their gang, but they seemed to be quite happy to let Sir Arthur Conan Doyle in on the mystery. And what was this strange new boy's story? Where had he come from and how had he suddenly become such an important part of the gang?

"Aye, well, Sandy won't be going anywhere until he's finished his chores. The monkey house and aviary are no gonny clean theirsel's," Harry declared as he stood up. He walked to the door and turned back to the small group, who were also now standing. "Let me know if you hear anything about George," he said, addressing Andrew. Then, turning to Nellie, he added softly, "I really am awfy sorry for your loss, Nell. If I can be of any help at all, please don't hesitate to ask me. I am always here." Then he turned and left, closing the door behind him.

Sandy counted to five after the door closed, making sure that Harry was gone before asking Nellie, "Have you blocked the chimney?"

"Yes, that's what I've come to tell you. It's done. Miss Birrell has asked me to get a chimney sweep in directly, so tell Mr Doyle to come as soon as he can." Nellie's hands shook as she placed her teacup on the small wooden table and stood up.

She desperately wanted to say something - tell them that Miss Birrell had George locked up, that she knew their plan and was setting a trap. She opened her mouth to speak, but nothing came out. She couldn't tell them or, rather, didn't dare tell them. Somehow Miss Birrell would know, so instead she said, "I have to go. Miss Birrell will be expecting me back," and she left.

Sandy looked at Andrew. "Do you think Nellie was acting a bit strange?" asked Sandy.

Andrew shrugged. "Aye, a wee bit, but she's had a bit of a strange time of it."

"I s'pose," Sandy replied, then, trying to sound more positive added, "well at least we know that Nellie saw him last night and got the note."

Andrew brightened up a bit. Sandy was right. Nellie had said George had been fine when she'd seen him the previous night. Maybe George hadn't met his doom at the hands of Miss Birrell after all.

"Aye," he agreed. "Maybe he was working later than usual for Mr. MacBrayne, so the ol' man told him to sleep in the shop rather than walk all the way home. Especially with his legs being the way they are."

Sandy was surprised. "Does George often sleep in the shop?" she asked.

"Well, he's never slept there before, but then, George has only worked for Mr. MacBrayne for a few weeks. The other boys do if they work late. Some of them live there all the time, they just kip in the back shop. I'm sure he'll be hame soon if he's no back already. Then he'll come to the Panopticon, well, as soon as mam has finished making a fuss of him, that is." Andrew's tone revealed he was trying to convince himself, more than Sandy, that his little brother was okay.

"I bet you're right," encouraged Sandy. "Well, I'll just muck out and then we can go and find the others, if you like. You never know, maybe George will get here before I'm finished."

"Do you need a hand?"

"Thanks, that'd be great. You can save some of it for the music hall shows if you like." She laughed at the thought of throwing monkey poo at the comedians.

"Save it? Sell it, more like. Tam got a ha'penny a bag."

Chapter Twenty-Six

Trench Stands His Ground

In the west end police office, Lieutenant Detective Trench was sat at his desk reading the note which he had found concealed in his morning newspaper. It was from Sir Arthur Conan Doyle.

Regarding news of the Edalji case, it is imperative that I see you. I have kept information from you for no other reason than I thought it too unbelievable. Now it has become apparent that, however strange the truth is, I must share it with you. I ask that you keep an open mind. Come to my hotel this evening and I will tell you the unbelievable truth.

ACD

What did Sir Arthur mean by *unbelievable truth?* Nothing, right now, seemed unbelievable to Detective Trench.

Since his visit to Sir Arthur's hotel room on Christmas Eve, he and Chief Inspector Ord had led a team of officers to arrest Oscar Slater. When they got to his house, though, Slater had gone. According to the maid who answered the door, he had left with his lady friend to spend the New Year in New York.

Ord had the officers search the house from top to bottom, seeking out any tiny bit of evidence that could be used to implicate Slater. A small, rusty hammer was discovered amongst some old tools. Ord was now claiming that the rust was blood and that it was the murder weapon. Then he declared that Oscar Slater was without doubt the murderer, and his sudden departure for New York was an attempt to flee justice. Trench was told to track down the man's travel arrangements and he discovered that the ocean liner ticket had been booked several weeks ago, long before Miss Gilchrist's brutal demise. To Ord, however, this was simply more proof that the murder was premeditated. He then forced Detective Trench to hide or lie about any evidence to the contrary. He was told to forget his original report in which he recorded the dying woman's last words and to lie about the witness accounts. He was told to lose the fingerprints taken at the crime scene along with the photographs of the real murder weapon.

Anything that might point to the truth was to be destroyed. But Detective Trench couldn't. He would never forget what he had seen that night, the blood splatters on the wall and hearth rug, the dining room chair leg covered in blood, gore, and hair from the old lady's fractured skull, which had been without doubt the real murder weapon.

The pile of collected evidence and paperwork sat on his desk, taunting him. If he refused to rewrite his report, adding the rusty hammer, the pawn ticket, and the testimony of Alan Mclean, he knew it would cost him dearly. His job, or even his life, could be at risk.

And now this note from Sir Arthur…what had the detective writer discovered that could possibly be more unbelievable than two senior detectives covering up the truth behind the most brutal and vile murder of recent years?

As he pondered this, the door to his office was suddenly pushed open and Ord strode into the room. Trench surreptitiously pushed the note back into the newspaper, which he now folded and casually flung on his desk as if he had just finished reading it.

"Anything interesting in the papers?" asked Ord.

"No, not particularly," Trench casually replied.

The door opened again and Superintendent Douglas entered. He eyed the newspaper briefly before settling his cold, blue eyes on Trench.

"Everything all right, John?" he quizzed.

"As well as can be expected," replied Trench.

"Are you sure? Only you haven't handed in your report yet," remarked Douglas.

"It's nearly finished. I'll get it to you tomorrow."

"I look forward to it."

"Have you heard from Sir Arthur Conan Doyle and his gang of newsboys and urchins recently?" Ord asked.

"No," Trench lied.

Ord smirked as if he knew full well that Trench was hiding something.

Trench suddenly felt angry. Why should he feel anxious and intimidated by Ord and Douglas? He wasn't the one who was covering up a murder and falsifying evidence. He was just following orders, but not anymore. He wanted an explanation.

"Why are you falsifying the evidence?" he asked, suddenly and quite bluntly.

"Falsifying evidence, John? What exactly are you referring to?" Ord retorted impatiently.

"The fingerprints, the maid's statement, the pawn ticket, the murder weapon. Why?"

Ord moved over to Trench's desk and stared down at the papers. He lifted one of the brown paper folders and waved it at Trench. "Believe me, we are not trying to prevent justice being done. Trust me when I tell you there is far more going on here than murder," he stated and then placed the folder back down on top of the teetering pile.

"Then tell me the truth," Trench continued. "I am in this job for the same reasons as you; to solve crime, preserve justice, and protect people."

"A worthy speech, but if you really wanted to protect people, you would listen to us. Heed us when we say to stay clear."

"It is my job to find out the truth, no matter who's trying to conceal it," retorted Trench. He was not going to be bullied.

Ord reached across the desk, picked up Trench's newspaper, opened it out and shook it. The note from Sir Arthur Conan Doyle fluttered down onto the pile of folders.

"And sometimes it's our job to protect the truth," Ord suddenly snapped, "from nosey amateur detectives. Even famous ones. Which is why you are suspended."

"Suspended?" Trench wasn't really surprised.

"You have knowingly and purposefully discussed highly sensitive police matters with a civilian. You are suspended, forthwith, pending an investigation which will result in your dismissal from the force."

Ord continued. "Detective Pyper will take over the Gilchrist case. Tomorrow, witnesses will be sent to New York to identify Oscar Slater as the man in the pale-coloured overcoat seen in Miss Gilchrist's hallway. He will then be returned to Glasgow and tried for her murder. He will be found guilty, and the murder case of Miss Marion Gilchrist will be closed, justice will be seen to be served and people can get on with their lives." Ord asserted all in a single breath; then walked around the desk to where Trench was sitting, placed a hand on his shoulder, and leaned down until his mouth was just an inch from his ear. Trench could smell the tobacco on Ord's breath. "And you will do nothing to interfere."

The suspended detective did not reply. He just stared back into the man's face, refusing to break eye contact until Ord turned around and walked to the door.

Douglas followed, stopping briefly to say, "Well, look on the bright side, at least you no longer have to worry about submitting your report." He smiled weakly before following his Edinburgh colleague out the door.

Trench was a good and honourable man and a great detective - reliable, dedicated, and diligent. But Douglas knew that he was also too honest and would never give up his pursuit of the truth, and the truth was just too devastating to be revealed. He and Ord were under the orders of a much higher authority to make sure that Oscar Slater paid the ultimate price, and that the truth stayed deeply buried. The future of the world depended on it. He felt a pang of regret that such a good policeman's career had to end this way, but they had been left with no other choice.

Chapter Twenty-Seven

Rescue From a Fire

Arthur Conan Doyle awoke to Jimmy banging on his door.

"What time is it?" he blearily asked as he opened the door and let the boy in.

"It's nearly half-seven. Where do you want these?" he asked, showing the author a bag of soot-blackened rags.

"Pop them over there, would you, please?" The sleepy man pointed in the general direction of the other side of the room.

Before he had a chance to close the door again, his breakfast arrived along with the morning newspaper. Sir Arthur grabbed the newspaper and settled himself in an armchair to read while the waiter bustled around him.

Jimmy put down the bag and watched the waiter set up the breakfast on the large dining table. He eyed it, his mouth watering at the smell of eggs and bacon.

"Will that be all, sir?" asked the waiter as he eyed the grubby boy with suspicion.

"Yes, yes, thank you. That will be all," Sir Arthur replied without taking his eyes from the newspaper.

Jimmy hovered near the table. Sir Arthur sensed the boy's hungry eyes on his breakfast - a sense that was confirmed by the loud rumbling from the lad's stomach.

"Help yourself," Sir Arthur replied in response to the gastric request.

As Jimmy munched his way through a plateful of eggs, bacon, sausages, fried tomatoes, sautéed potatoes, and buttered toast with strawberry jam. Sir Arthur scoured his newspaper for any new information regarding the murder of Marion Gilchrist as he sipped a cup of coffee.

The articles about the murder were shorter than previous days. There was nothing new of any consequence reported, which surprised him. Trench's last note stated "Edalji has fled," implying that the man the police were about to arrest had gone. So why weren't the newspapers full of the suspect's passage from Glasgow? He would ask Trench about it later, but now he had better get to the Panopticon and change into his latest disguise.

He grabbed the bag of clothes that Jimmy had provided and slung them over his left shoulder. Jimmy, full to bursting, grabbed the chimney sweep's brushes and poles which he slung over his right shoulder, and the two unlikely friends left the hotel together, merrily walking the quarter of a mile to the Panopticon.

When they arrived, the little zookeeper's room was empty. However, the sound of laughter led them to the Aviary where they found Sandy and Andrew struggling to clean out the cage. The colourful collection of cockatiels, parrots, budgies, and myna birds were crammed together, perched on both children's arms and heads. A group of boys were doubled up laughing heartily at the scene.

Sir Arthur entered the bird house, chortling at the boy's predicament, and shooed the birds off their human perches, freeing the boys so they could get on with their task. When the last of the dirty sawdust had been swept into a bucket, Sandy and Andrew came out of the cage, covered in feathers and spattered with bird poo.

"Are you finished?" he asked, suppressing a chuckle at the sight of them.

"Yeah," Sandy replied.

"Then you might as well get changed into these." Sir Arthur pulled out a set of the sooty chimney sweep's clothes from the bag and handed them to her. "Nellie will no doubt be here soon."

"She's already been."

"She was here first thing," Andrew added.

Sir Arthur raised his eyebrows in surprise. "My, that was quick."

They went to Tam's room and put on the disguises whilst Andrew told Sir Arthur about George.

The news knocked the cheeriness out of the author as he felt a dark cloud of disaster descending. "He didn't come home? What was I thinking, asking him to deliver the note? Miss Birrell and her accomplice are clearly dangerous and now I have led little George to his doom," he observed solemnly.

"It's all right. We asked Nellie and she said he was fine when she saw him last night. He delivered the letter and left," explained Sandy.

"An' he might have just stayed at Mr MacBrayne's last night. He never has before, but it must be what happened. I'm sure he'll turn up soon," added Andrew confidently, trying to convince himself more than Sir Arthur that this was the case.

"Ah, I see," said Sir Arthur, not entirely convinced. *If Andrew hadn't been worried, why had he mentioned it?* "Did Nellie say she had blocked the chimney?" he enquired, turning to Sandy.

"Yep, we're to go up as soon as we can."

“Excellent!" He added the finishing touches to his costume by placing a tatty old flat cap on his head, pulling on a pair of frayed black fingerless woollen gloves and rubbing some soot from the stovepipe on his face. "We'll go straight there." But Sir Arthur now felt very cautious about his plan. Something was definitely not right.

At 10:30 a.m., Sir Arthur Conan Doyle and Sandy emerged from the basement zoo. Andrew and Jimmy had decided to stay and wait at the Panopticon, hopeful that George would appear there soon.

They had just begun the walk to the subway station when they met Jamie, who was rushing along the Trongate to find them.

"None of them…have seen him…since last night," Jamie gasped between breaths. "Mr MacBrayne…was the last to see him…and said George left at half eight..."

Sir Arthur turned to Sandy. "When you saw Nellie this morning, how did she seem?"

"She seemed okay. A bit sad because of Tam, I suppose."

"What did she say, exactly?" Sir Arthur pressed.

"She just said that George had delivered the letter and we were to go up as soon as we can and that she had to go, as Miss Birrell would be expecting her back," explained Sandy.

"Did she seem nervous?" asked Sir Arthur.

"A bit, I suppose, but I can't blame her after what she's been through."

The author pondered this for a long moment. "I suppose she has been through a lot. But I am not convinced by what she told you this morning."

"Do you think Nellie lied and they've got George locked away somewhere?" Sandy asked. "Or worse?"

"I don't think that Nellie wanted to tell you a lie. Perhaps she didn't have a choice." Sir Arthur paused, then said, "Jamie, go and fetch Andrew and Jimmy from the Panopticon and take them, and whoever else you can find, to 9 Hill Street as soon as you can. Hide where you can see the house and wait for my signal."

"What signal?"

"Any signal. You'll know when you see it or hear it. Sandy, you take the tram to Maryhill and fetch Lieutenant Detective Trench. You must be extremely cautious. I'm going to carry on with the plan on my own," pronounced the author as he began to rummage in his pockets for tram fares.

Sandy was stunned. "But if they do know about our plan, then they'll be ready for you."

"Yes, the element of surprise is lost, but I shall have you, the other boys and Detective Trench waiting to come to my aid if it all goes wrong," Sir Arthur answered, still digging through his pockets for change.

"No!" Sandy shouted, louder than she had intended "If you change your plan, she'll know something's up. We mustn't change our plan, or she'll know Nellie told us and she might do something awful to her and George.

"Look, we just have to be prepared for the worst, but we have to try and find that letter and get George back," she declared with such conviction and determination that Sir Arthur couldn't argue with her.

Sir Arthur paused to think. "Well, if you're coming with me, you must do exactly as I say and when I say it. If I tell you to run, you run as fast as you can, you don't look back, you just run. Is that clear?"

"Yes, sir," she agreed.

"Jamie, you send Andrew and Jimmy to fetch the others, then you go and find Detective Trench. Take this for the tram fares." Sir Arthur gave Jamie a handful of coins he had pulled from his pocket.

"Yes, sir," Jamie said as he pocketed the money and ran off towards the Panopticon.

Sir Arthur and Sandy made their way to Miss Birrell's, and forty minutes later they were standing outside 9 Hill Street, looking up at the four-storey townhouse.

They looked at each other, both knowing a knock on the door was probably a mere formality, sure that the occupants within were already expecting them. Sandy rang the doorbell. Nellie promptly answered and let them in.

They followed the maid silently up the stairs to the first floor, then along the hallway to a room at the end. She opened the door. "It's in here, sir." Nellie announced loudly as they entered the study. Sir Arthur pulled the door closed behind them. The study was a dark room, lined with bookcases of dusty old volumes and cabinets filled with curious objects. It was cold without a fire in the hearth, and dim with only two gas-lamps on either side of the door to light it. Sir Arthur lit the oil lamp on the paper-strewn desk. He looked out of the barred window and realised the flaw in his plan. The room was on the first floor at the back of the house so he wouldn't be able to signal to the boys unless they were hiding in the lane.

"Where is your mistress?" he asked the maid, who stood nervously near the door, watching his every move.

"Downstairs in the front parlour, sir," Nellie replied.

Sir Arthur walked over to the fireplace. He handed Sandy the brushes and took a blanket from his bag which he spread across the floor, then reached up inside the chimney and pulled out the rag blocking it. A cloud of soot followed - a small, billowing, black flurry that speckled the grey blanket. He then took off his woolly gloves and ventured to the desk to look for the letter. It wasn't amongst the letters and papers that covered the leather desktop.

He tried the drawers - but they were locked. He wasn't surprised. "I don't suppose you have a key?" he asked, turning to Nellie.

She shook her head. "She keeps all the keys on her own chatelaine."

"Good thing I have these then," Sir Arthur remarked as he pulled a cloth bag full of small, metal picks from his pocket. He selected one and started trying to pick the locks, and as he fiddled with the delicate, hooked tool, there was a clicking sound at the door as a key was turned in the lock. He marched to the door, cursing under his breath and muttering, "Damned idiot - of course she's going to lock you in! Call yourself a detective writer..." Then, pale, grey smoke began to seep beneath the door. It seemed that her plan was to burn the house down with him, Sandy, and the maid trapped inside.

Nellie squealed when she saw the smoke.

"Where's George?" he demanded.

"In the attic," she cried. "I'm so sorry, sir, I couldn't tell you. They threatened to kill George if I said anything, and they said they would make sure I was hanged for it."

"That's alright, Nellie. It's not your fault. I'm the one who got us all into this. I'm a stupid, old fool obsessed with adventure."

He walked to the window. It was barred and nailed shut. He walked back over to the fireplace and stuck his head up the chimney. It had a large fireplace and a wide chimney breast. It was the only way out of the room. He turned back to the girls. "Sandy, you will need to climb up the chimney and get help. It will be very difficult and quite dangerous, but you are just small enough to manage it and you are certainly strong enough. When you get onto the roof, shout for the boys, they should be nearby, and Jamie might have arrived with Trench. Tell them to run for the fire brigade." Sir Arthur took the rag off from around his neck and gave it to Sandy. "Put this round your nose and mouth."

"Okay." Sandy hesitated before tying the grubby rag around her face. It smelt of his cologne. She had never thought of herself as remotely strong. She couldn't even climb the rope in gym class at school, let alone scale a chimney. There was little choice, though, and no time to think about it. Nellie gave Sandy a boost and Sandy began the dangerous and difficult clamber up the chimney.

"Quick as you can!" Sir Arthur shouted up behind her, before turning his attention back to the desk and his lock picking.

"What are you doing?" Nellie called, coughing as the smoke began to fill the room. "We should be trying to open this door and get out."

"The fire is on the other side, we won't get out that way. Sandy will get the fire brigade and warn the others. Hopefully the doors will hold the fire back for a few more minutes. We'll be fine, but I still need to try and find what we came for, or this was all for nothing," he stated as the lock on the first drawer relented and he rifled through its contents.

"Smash the window open," he ordered. Nellie, grabbing the fire poker, smashed the panes of glass and stood with her head against the bars, gulping the outside air. The fire was now licking at the bottom of the door inside the room.

Sir Arthur kept rummaging through the drawers full of receipts, letters, bills, photographs, knick-knacks, and calling cards; but no letter with a royal seal. He dumped the contents and began searching for a secret drawer. He felt inside the empty recesses. Still nothing. Then he began to frantically search all the contents he had strewn on the floor, checking again in case he had missed it. But he could not find the letter with the royal seal. She must have taken it with her. He did, however, find a letter from a lady in Edinburgh confirming the rental of a house on Herriot Row, available from the 27th of December. That was today's date.

***

Meanwhile, Sandy's clamber up the chimney had been the stuff of nightmares. At first, she had thought she was going to choke to death on the bitter clouds of soot that rained down on her, even with the rag covering her nose and mouth. When she had recovered from the black avalanche, she began the climb.

At first, she found it hard to get a grip with her hands and feet; there was nothing to hold on to. She tried digging into the brick with her fingernails, but that just hurt. Then she worked out a technique of jamming her legs, feet and palms of her hands against the walls of the chimney and pushing herself up. She managed to inch herself up the bricks, but the progress was slow. Smoke began seeping around her. She ignored it and focused instead on looking up to the small hole of daylight high above. But the higher she went, the narrower and more claustrophobic the chimney got. The very last section of the climb was so tight she could barely move, and she felt the panic rising in her chest. She was desperate to get out. Her arms were stretched above her, the palms of her hands pushing against the brick, her fingernails digging in, her thighs and feet pressing against the sides as she shoved herself up. She wriggled, shoved, and clawed her way towards the light, tears rolling down her face as she gasped for every breath. She was suffocating on the smoke and soot. But she did not give up. She focused on that little bit of daylight above her and kept on moving, pushing, scrabbling, twisting, writhing, squirming - until, by some miracle, she made it out.

Squeezing herself up, shoving loose bits of chimney stack out her way, she emerged, blackened and squinting, into the daylight. She pulled the rag away from her mouth and nose and took in deep mouthfuls of cold, fresh winter air. Every muscle in her body ached from the physical effort of the chimney climb. Her fingernails were torn, her hands grazed; she felt dizzy and weak, but there was no respite. She still had to get down from the roof.

***

Andrew, Jimmy, Sam, and Charlie had been hiding in the bushes outside 9 Hill Street when Charlie spotted a small figure emerging from a chimney. At that exact same moment, the front door opened and Miss Birrell, dressed in men's clothes, and the man in the pale-coloured overcoat, came out hefting a large trunk.

From their leafy lair, Jimmy, Sam and Charlie watched Sandy tentatively shuffle on her bottom down the steep pitch of the roof. Andrew observed the couple as they loaded the trunk into the motor car and drove off. As soon as the car had disappeared around the corner, the four boys sprang from their hiding place to watch Sandy, who had now reached the guttering.

***

Slowly, ever so carefully, and whimpering slightly at the height and fear of falling, Sandy pulled herself out of the chimney and lowered herself onto the apex of the roof. She squatted down and turned herself to face the roof slates, then extended her legs and let herself slide down the slates to the guttering. She put her feet in the guttering and inched her way along it to the drainpipe, the only way down that she could see.

"You alright?" Sam shouted up.

"Never been better," Sandy called back, trying to sound sarcastic, but fear made her voice sound high-pitched and shaky. She felt the cast-iron guttering creak and shift beneath her weight. "We got locked in the drawing room, they set fire to the house, I nearly suffocated climbing up a chimney, and now I'm probably going to break my neck trying to get off this stupid roof. All in all, I would say things are definitely not peachy. Now, can you please go and fetch the fire brigade. Sir Arthur, Nellie and George are still trapped inside!" Sandy yelled down.

Sam instantly sprang into action and ran down the street to fetch help, while Andrew, Jimmy and Charlie watched Sandy with bated breath.

Sandy was terrified. One slip and she would fall four storeys to certain death. The guttering had held as she inched along it but now she had to step onto the drainpipe.

She leant forward and rested her body on the sloping roof as she felt for the top of the drainpipe with her left foot. She shifted her body along the roof a fraction. A slate dislodged under her right hand and went crashing to the ground. Her stomach pitched and she froze for a moment. She looked up at the grey sky, muttered a small prayer, then forced herself to move.

"Get a grip," she whispered to herself and took a few deep breaths before reaching down with her left foot again, blindly feeling for the top bracket that tied the drainpipe to the wall. She found it and cautiously moved her right foot onto the other side. Then, using the brackets as very deep ladder rungs, she began a tentative and painful climb down. Stretching her leg down as far as she could to reach the next bracket, and the next.

The cast iron pipe was so cold it burnt her fingers, which were already grazed and sore from the climb up the dark, narrow chimney. Her battered fingers clung on to the pipe as best they could as she cautiously stepped down each bracket-rung, but the sheer pain and exertion overwhelmed her at last and she just couldn't hang on any longer. She lost her grip and plummeted.

She fell eight feet into Charlie, Jimmy, and Andrew's linked arms, and the four of them tumbled to the ground.

"Are you alright?" asked Jimmy, as they helped each other up from the frozen ground.

"Yeah, I'm fine, thanks to you guys. I don't think anything's broken anyway. Did you see Miss Birrell?" Sandy replied.

"Aye, we saw her and the man in the overcoat leaving just as you came out the lum," answered Charlie. "An' they was carrying a huge trunk."

"Aye, the one I helped her with the other day - only, it wasn't empty. They looked like they were struggling with it a bit," said Jimmy.

"Do you think George is in it?" Andrew asked Sandy.

"Or maybe he is still locked in the attic of a burning house."

Andrew suddenly leapt into action. "Come on!" he shouted at the others as he dashed towards the front door. Together, they did their best to break the door down. They put their shoulders against it and tried to ram it open. They kicked it and battered it with their fists, but their efforts barely scratched the green paint. Sandy looked through the shiny brass letter box and peered into grey smoke that was building beyond. Sir Arthur and Nellie were nowhere to be seen. They must still be trapped in the first-floor room.

At that moment, the urgent sound of alarm bells ringing and horses' hooves clattering on the cobbled street filled the air. The fire brigade had arrived, with Sam standing proudly on the back of the gleaming fire-engine. Sandy thought the group of men that jumped off the two horse-drawn fire appliances looked incredibly heroic in their smart blue uniforms with shining brass buttons and brass helmets.

"Crikey, that was quick!" said Andrew.

"I bumped into them on Sauchiehall Street. They were already on their way here!" said Sam, grinning widely.

The firemen moved the children out of the way as one of them, the tallest and burliest, hefted an axe high and struck at the door. The wood splintered under the blow. He wielded it a second and third time and, on the fourth blow, the door caved in.

Smoke belched out as four firemen ran into the house, carrying hoses, whilst the others pumped water from the two fire engines. The four horses that had pulled the engines stood placidly waiting amidst the action and excitement. Sandy and the boys wanted to pet them, but a fireman pushed them back. A few minutes later, Sir Arthur and Nellie emerged, coughing and spluttering through the smoke, held up by firemen. Two of the firemen disappeared into the house to search for George or any other survivors.

Sir Arthur sat Nellie on the kerb and was trying to comfort the traumatised maid when Jamie arrived with Lieutenant Detective Trench.

"What's happened?" asked Trench.

"I was an idiot. I walked all of us into a trap and we were lucky to escape. I only hope that George is unharmed," Sir Arthur responded, his voice bleak

"George?" asked Trench.

"Ma wee brother. He disappeared last night," Andrew answered.

"I sent the lad to deliver a note to Nellie last night, but it seems the man in the pale-coloured overcoat and Miss Birrell intercepted it and George. They locked him in the attic," explained Sir Arthur. Nellie nodded in agreement. "The firemen are trying to find him."

As he said this, the two firemen emerged from the house with what looked like a bundle of clothes in their arms.

"Is this the missing boy?" one asked as he approached them.

"George!" Andrew exclaimed and ran to the firemen to retrieve his little brother. Holding him in his arms, Andrew pleaded with his brother. "Come on wee man, speak to me," he softly entreated, tears streaking his cheeks.

"Hullo," George answered weakly, opening his eyes and gazing at his big brother. He smiled. "You can put me down now, if you like."

Andrew placed his little brother down carefully on the pavement, supporting the frail boy as he struggled to find his balance without his sticks, which had been left behind in the burning building.

"Is there anyone else, sir?" asked one of the firemen.

"No," answered Sir Arthur as he surveyed his little gang. "Thankfully, everyone has survived the fire relatively unharmed. Thank you for your prompt arrival and rescue."

Then, turning to Detective Trench, he added, "We should alert your colleagues at the west end office. I think we can safely assume that Miss Birrell is indeed guilty of murdering Miss Gilchrist and attempting to murder myself, Nellie and Sandy. We can add kidnapping to the list as well," he added, looking at the small boy who was coughing hard and holding onto his brother's arm for support. His heart went out to the frail lad. "As for the man in the pale-coloured overcoat…"

"He went with Miss Birrell!" Jimmy burst out.

Charlie and Andrew nodded their heads in agreement, "Aye, they left in Miss Birrell's motor car. They had the big trunk with them and it seemed really heavy. We thought George was in it."

"Well, I am no longer a detective. I have been suspended," Trench announced sadly. "Superintendent Douglas and Chief Inspector Ord didn't like me talking to you and they know I went to your hotel the other night. They also know about the note you sent me in my newspaper this morning. I found this rascal," he said tousling Jamie's hair, "on Maryhill Road."

"Then they have been following you," Sir Arthur said.

"It seems so. And they aren't just hiding the truth about Miss Gilchrist's murderer. They have fabricated evidence to implicate Oscar Slater, who left Glasgow for New York a couple of days ago. They are sending witnesses to New York to positively identify him. They warned me not to interfere."

"Witnesses?" Sir Arthur asked, "What witnesses?"

"The downstairs neighbour, Adams, and Miss Gilchrist's maid, Nellie." Trench looked over at the girl, who was sat on the pavement recovering from her ordeal.

Nellie gazed back at Trench.

"They're sending me to New York?" she asked.

"Yes, they will be coming for you in the morning," confirmed Trench.

Nellie was aghast. *New York!?* she thought. But that was a long journey across the sea. She had never been outside of Glasgow. She had dreamed about leaving - her and Tam, together, on an adventure to the new world where new opportunities promised prosperity, and a better life. They had often stood on the quaysides and watched the big ocean liners steaming off up the Clyde, laden with waving passengers heading to America. But she had never really thought she would be one of them and, without Tam, the prospect was frightening, not exciting.

"And you are sure this Oscar Slater is innocent? I mean, sending officers and witnesses to New York is expensive business. Surely the police would not be investing such huge sums of money to falsely accuse an innocent man?" Sir Arthur queried.

"Ord and Douglas aren't interested in catching the real suspect," Trench explained. "They want someone convicted to satisfy the public, but not the real murderer. They told me that there is a lot more to this case than just a murder and that they 'have a duty to protect the truth' "

"Then it surely looks like somehow the King must be connected to this case. But how?" Sir Arthur pondered. "We need that letter with the royal seal."

"I'm not going to lie," Nellie announced. "I'm not going to accuse an innocent man."

"You probably won't have a choice. Douglas will be going with you and, believe me, whatever the secret is that they're protecting, your life will mean nothing in comparison." Trench warned her, solemnly. "You will be better just doing what he wants. At least until the case gets to court."

Nellie felt as if the weight of her terrible situation was crushing her. She was homeless, jobless, and about to be forced to send an innocent man to the gallows.

"Don't worry, Nellie. By the time you get back, we'll have captured the real criminals. Oscar Slater will be a free man and you, my dear, will have a new position with my sister in Edinburgh." Sir Arthur confidently promised as he stood up and turned his attention back to the detective.

"Your note said that you had an unbelievable truth to tell me," Trench said in a voice low enough that only Sir Arthur could hear him.

"Now is not the time or place," The author replied, conscious of the young woman beside him who would not have understood what he had to tell the detective. "We have to find Miss Birrell."

"But where has she gone?" asked Andrew.

Sir Arthur pulled out the confirmation letter from the landlady in Edinburgh. "I think I know exactly where they've gone, and I suggest we make that our next mission."

Chapter Twenty-Eight

28th December
A Slippery Chase

After her awful ordeal, Nellie was taken to spend the night with the Adams's. Sir Arthur himself had escorted the maid and asked that Arthur Adams and his sisters look after the distraught girl. He felt sure that she would be safe in their home. Perhaps the familiar people and surroundings would help calm Nellie, who had been through a lot over the past few days. Arthur and his sisters welcomed Nellie in, and did their very best to spoil her with comforting hugs, hot tea, and the finest Belgian chocolates money could buy.

At 9:00 a.m. the following day, the police arrived to escort Nellie and Arthur Adams to Glasgow Central, where they boarded a train headed to Liverpool. From there they would travel by ocean liner to New York. They were accompanied by several policemen and Superintendent Douglas. Arthur was as nervous and fearful as Nellie. Whilst the two witnesses sat huddled together, Nellie found his hand, which she grasped tightly for the whole train journey.

By 11:00 p.m., Sir Arthur Conan Doyle, Lieutenant Detective Trench, Sandy, and the boys from the Panopticon were getting on another train at Queen Street Station. The gang were dressed in their Sunday best and Sandy was in a new set of boy's clothes that Sir Arthur provided.

Sandy was astounded. She had been in Queen Street Station a couple of times with her mum, but in 1908 it looked very different. The huge glass canopy was the same but the modern concourse beneath was gone. The ticket machines, coffee shops, and fast-food restaurants were replaced by wood-panelled waiting rooms, a ticket office, and newspaper stands. But the most amazing and wonderful change of all were the trains.

At all four platforms, wooden carriages lined up behind enormous steam engines billowing smoke and steam out through their black iron chimneys. Sandy, Sir Arthur, and the boys walked up to the Edinburgh train, which stood puffing sooty clouds as it waited at platform two.

Sir Arthur opened the door to a first-class carriage and Sandy and the boys excitedly stepped on board. The compartment was otherwise empty and even Detective Trench seemed a little excited as he settled himself into his sumptuously upholstered first-class seat. Soon after they were comfortably seated, the engine whistle blew and the train slowly left the station, entering the momentary darkness of a smoky tunnel before emerging into a brilliant world beyond.

The train steamed through the open countryside between Glasgow and Edinburgh, which was sparkling white in a fresh, thick carpet of overnight snow. Sandy sat at the door side of the compartment, opposite Sir Arthur and Trench, whilst the boys squashed their faces against the glass of the window, watching with amazement as the pristine, white, open fields passed them, marred only by the occasional collieries with their huge wheel-shaped headstocks that stood like black giants against the glittering white landscape.

The boys had never seen so much space, as none of them had ever stepped a foot beyond the boundaries of their Glasgow lives. They had never known that so much open space existed, or so much sky. It was breathtaking.

Sir Arthur watched them, pleased that this adventure had opened their eyes to the world beyond, even if it had also exposed them to mortal peril.

"Do you have trains in the future?" asked Charlie, who loved trains, and was even more besotted with them now that he was actually travelling on one.

"Yeah, we do, but they're not like this."

Trench laughed. "What an odd thing to ask, 'do you have trains in the future?' As if you have travelled through time."

"I have," Sandy replied simply, looking at the policeman with a serious expression.

As the countryside sped past, Sir Arthur told Trench everything. He told him about the anonymous note he had received which had sent him to Glasgow in search of the boys, the magic lantern and the mysterious message, about Sandy and the man in the pale-coloured overcoat having both come from the future, perhaps both through the beam of the magic lantern. Sandy showed him her phone and shot a short video of Sir Arthur saying, "When you have eliminated all which is impossible, then, whatever remains, however improbable, must be the truth."

When she played it back to Trench he nearly fell off his seat. Then they showed him the antique French coin from 1791 that the man in the pale-coloured overcoat had used to buy a newspaper with. Sir Arthur Conan Doyle had not exaggerated in his note - this really was an unbelievable truth, yet, with his own eyes, he had seen a miraculous device from the future.

"And then there's the royal connection," observed Sir Arthur.

"Yes, the mark you found on the brooch," agreed Trench.

"Not just the brooch, my good man. Miss Birrell is in possession of a letter with the King's seal. I suspect that whatever is in that letter is at the heart of this case."

Trench was speechless. He looked down at the antique coin he still held in his hand and decided he wasn't sure about anything anymore.

* * *

It was after 1:00 p.m. when they arrived at Edinburgh Waverley Station and scaled the steep steps to Princes Street. As they emerged into Edinburgh, the boys gazed up at the looming, ancient castle swathed in fog. It was like they had entered into another world. It was so different from their familiar Glasgow cityscape.

The snow crunched underfoot as Sir Arthur Conan Doyle led them on the short walk to his family home at Picardy Place. It was the house he had grown up in, which now belonged to his sister. The boys lagged behind as they gazed in wonder at the sites of these foreign streets.

It wasn't long before they arrived at the warm and comfortable home where Sir Arthur's sister, Connie, and his wife, Jean, made a huge fuss of the little gang of urchin newsboys. He had kept the ladies up to date with events on nightly phone calls, so they knew all about the Panopticon gang. Connie and Jean provided warm blankets and a dinner of steaming hot meat stew, which the boys and Sandy washed down with cocoa and finished off with a large treacle pudding and custard. The danger they were in felt far away from the comfort of the large house and plentiful food. Before they had met Sandy and Sir Arthur Conan Doyle, all these boys had known were the basic, overcrowded hovels they lived in; meals of stale bread and potato, occasionally garnished with a lump of grey, tough meat, and the odd ha-penny bag of sweets, a luxury they could only occasionally afford. Now their bellies were so full it was difficult to move. Each child snoozed in blankets on the plush sofas in the cosy home at 8 Picardy Place.

At 5:00 p.m., Sir Arthur woke them all up. He produced the letter from his pocket and read it out to them. It had been written by a Mrs Coleville and confirmed the rent of a house on Herriot Row. It was not a long walk but, in the snowy conditions, Sir Arthur decided he would take his skis with him. Skiing was a passion he had discovered near the end of the last century, an exhilarating sport which he took every opportunity to enjoy. Trench, Sandy, and the boys followed the author into the large entrance hall and across to a cupboard which was crammed with all sorts of equipment; tennis rackets, golf clubs, roller skates, ice skates, and of course, skis.

"Going skiing without me, father?" enquired a tall boy, with neat dark hair, as he came sauntering slowly down the stairs with his hands in his pockets.

"Kingsley, my boy, you are welcome to join us on our perilous adventure. Meet the Panopticon gang. Boys, Sandy, Detective Trench, meet my son, Kingsley," hastily making introductions before turning his attention back to gathering his skis out of the cupboard.

Jean, who had appeared in the doorway of the drawing room, bustled into the hallway and tried to take the skis off her husband. "Kingsley, you are not going anywhere except straight back to bed with that terrible cold and you," she said pointedly to her husband, "are not taking these children anywhere on an evening like this. They should be tucked up, warm and safe in bed. What are you thinking of, traipsing these poor mites about in this weather, and so inadequately dressed," she berated.

"I have to say, old man, I do agree with your good lady," Detective Trench said.

"We have a man to save from the gallows and a mystery to solve, darling Jean. And, John, old chap, time is of the essence! The game is afoot!" Sir Arthur responded before pulling the skis from his wife's grasp.

"Well, at least let me find them something warmer to wear. I'm sure there are a few old jumpers and coats that would fit," Jean capitulated, her warm smile full of concern as she gazed down at George, who was obviously crippled by rickets. Sir Arthur read his wife's heart.

"Don't worry unduly about young George here," he said, tousling the small boy's hair. "He is far more capable than he looks."

George looked up at the author with a beaming smile. He was enjoying this adventure. He hadn't even minded being locked in the attic because he knew his friends would find him and he felt stronger every day.

She looked at the faces of boys that her husband seemed to have adopted. She thought sometimes her husband believed he was his own fictional detective, and now he had his own real band of urchins, just like Sherlock Holmes's Baker Street Irregulars. Each young face looked up at her with mischief and excitement gleaming in their eyes. George's eyes seemed to shine the brightest behind his glasses.

"Come on, Kingsley. Let's find them something warm to wear," she said, placing her arm about her son's waist and guiding him back up the stairs.

Sir Arthur propped his skis against the wall and dove back into the large hall cupboard. A moment later, he pulled out three wooden sledges, big enough to carry the small gang of boys and the detective. A few minutes later, Jean had bundled them up in woolly hats, scarves, mittens, and oversized jumpers. Feeling ready for anything, the gang ventured forth into the night.

The snow was now a thick, driving curtain of white, and the icy wind nipped at what little of their faces peered through their woolly armour. It was a bleak contrast to the delicious, luxurious warmth of the house at Picardy Place.

Sir Arthur Conan Doyle led the way as if he were leading an Arctic expedition. He pulled himself up the gently sloping hill using his ski poles whilst the boys and Sandy pulled two sledges behind them, trudging in the tracks Sir Arthur made. George sat merrily on one of the sledges and Trench reluctantly brought up the rear, dragging his sledge behind him in a pair of borrowed galoshes. He thought the whole idea was ridiculous - an adventure for boys; not a way to apprehend criminals.

Sir Arthur stopped and called back over his shoulder, "Just down here!" Then turning right and, pushing off with his ski-poles, launched himself down a steep street, swinging his body right and left as he effortlessly sped down the snowy hill.

Sandy and the boys jumped on their sledges and pushed off, quickly gathering speed. They whooped joyously as they zoomed behind him.

Trench hesitantly followed, his heels carving ruts in the deepening snow as the cautious detective tried to control the speed of his sledge.

Halfway down the hill, Sir Arthur swerved left and stopped. The boys and Sandy narrowly avoided crashing into him as they leaned hard to turn their sledges. Jimmy went tumbling off the back of the one he shared with Sam, Charlie, and Bobby, landing on his bottom and sliding into the middle of the road; while Trench, unable to turn his sledge fast enough, sped past the turning, spun one hundred and eighty degrees, and carried on down the hill backwards.

"Nineteen Herriot Row. It's just along here," Sir Arthur shouted into the wind as he pushed himself along with his poles for a few feet, stopping at the end of the row of tall townhouses where a snow-covered motorcar was parked.

"Is that Miss Birrell's motorcar?" asked Charlie.

"Aye," replied Jamie.

"Do you think she's here then?" asked Jimmy.

Sir Arthur looked up at the front of the house. None of the windows appeared to be lit and he could see by the glow of the streetlight that the drapes were open.

"I don't think the motorcar being here is an indication that Miss Birrell is. I doubt she would take the motorcar in this weather. It would never manage the snow and ice. Motorcars will never replace horsepower when it comes to the Scottish winter. It appears that the house is empty. However, we should proceed with caution. They may be at the back of the house," pronounced Sir Arthur.

Sandy resisted commenting about motorcars replacing horsepower. She felt they already knew too much about the future.

Steps led up to a grand front door, whilst a wrought iron gate opened onto a second set of steps that led down to the basement entrance, generally used by tradesmen and servants.

Sir Arthur unbuckled his skis and placed them against the railing, then carefully made his way down the icy steps to the basement. The gang left their sledges on the pavement and followed. When they were all gathered at the bottom, Sir Arthur and the boys searched the front and side of the house, peering through barred windows into the dark rooms beyond, looking for signs of life.

"It looks empty," observed Charlie.

"So it appears. Let's see if we can find a way in," suggested Sir Arthur.

"I suppose you mean find a way to break in," said Trench, who had caught up with them. He was stiff, cold, damp, and aching from his brief, terrifying sledge ride.

"Yes, I suppose I do," replied the author as he shook one of the iron bars that protected the basement sash windows from intruders. "The question is, how?"

The gang walked around, inspecting the basement windows, checking the bars to see if any were loose.

Then Sam suddenly shouted, "Over here! There's a coal hatch."

Sir Arthur walked over to the small wooden door at the base of the wall. It was locked with a simple bolt. The door was too small for a well-fed adult to squeeze through, but a boy would easily fit, and Bobby eagerly volunteered.

Sir Arthur held the hatch open as Bobby scrambled in, sliding a couple of feet down the chute to land on top of a mountain of coal.

Even with the hatch open, the coal cellar was dark as night. The mountain of coal appeared as shadowy valleys and peaks to the small boy as he cautiously picked his way down on his hands and knees. He finally made it to the cellar floor and stood up, but it was so dark he couldn't see a thing. He made his way across the cellar with his hands outstretched, feeling for the door. He found it with his head and let out a yelp.

"Bobby, are you ok?" Sir Arthur called through the coal hatch.

"Fine," Bobby called back up, feeling for the door handle. He turned it, then rattled it and pushed against it. "The cellar door's locked," he called. "I can't get out."

A moment later, something tinkled down the pile of coal. Bobby saw it glint in the light that seeped in from the hatch and grabbed for it. It was a long cravat pin.

"Use it to try and unlock the door. If it's anything like my coal cellar door, it will just have a simple catch holding it closed. Push the pin through the gap in the door about halfway down and move it up through the gap until you push the catch up." Sir Arthur instructed through the hatch.

Bobby did as the man ordered. He was right. He found the catch, pushed it up and the door swung open into a scullery.

Bobby found an old bread knife on the scullery windowsill which he grabbed and held in front of him like a weapon. Then, he headed through the scullery and into a large kitchen, out into a hallway and the servants' entrance. A large key hung on a hook beside the door. Bobby stood on tiptoe and just managed to reach it, took it down, unlocked the door and let the others in.

"So much for us getting in and out without a soul ever knowing," commented Sir Arthur as he entered the house and saw the black coal dust footprints all over the floor. "More important, are you ok?"

"Aye, sir, I'm fine," the boy replied.

"Right, you best wait outside. I don't want you getting any more muck around the place. You can keep watch on the street, but stay hidden. And if you see Miss Birrell or the man in the pale-coloured overcoat, give a whistle. George, you stay with him."

Both boys looked at Sir Arthur with disappointment in their eyes. They had wanted to join the search. They didn't want to miss out on the discovery of the letter and miss all the fun.

"But I don't know how to whistle," declared George hopelessly.

"Me neither," added Bobby.

Trench pulled a silver police whistle out of his coat pocket and handed it over to George, who accepted it as if it was some kind of valuable treasure. Bobby looked at it greedily.

"Here," he said, and handed Bobby his truncheon, which the small boy eagerly took. "Just in case. But only use it if you need to - and aim for their knees. Or a little higher up, in the man's case," he informed, winking.

The two boys left, Bobby leaving a trail of little black footprints in the snow behind him as the others ventured into the basement lobby.

"Before we do anything, we need to make sure that the house is indeed empty," asserted Trench.

"I agree," Sir Arthur concurred, pulling a revolver out of his coat pocket.

"Where the devil did that come from?" Detective Trench asked. The boys and Sandy looked at the gun with fascination.

"I got it from my study before we left. It's my W.G. I got it when I served in Africa as a medic a few years ago," he stated proudly, and walked up the hallway. Carrying the gun in front of him, Sir Arthur opened the door to the kitchen, then through to the butler's pantry and store cupboards. Each space was empty - not a crumb on the shelves or a dish in the sink. There was nothing to indicate that someone was living there. Trench grabbed an iron poker from beside the kitchen range to use as a weapon in place of his truncheon. He waved it in front of him just in case any murderers unexpectedly jumped out.

Next, the group silently crept up the stairs to the rooms above. Creeping down the hallway, past the large travelling trunk, Trench tentatively opened each door in turn and peeked in.

The large spacious rooms were bare. Only one - the parlour - contained furniture. A couch, a fireside chair, and a rug.

They crept up the next flight of stairs. Again, the apartments were empty, save for two bedrooms which contained two beds and empty wardrobes. The two floors above were completely vacant. When, at last, Trench was satisfied that no one was hiding in the building, they returned to the entrance hall on the ground floor where the trunk stood with a couple of other smaller pieces of luggage, each piece monogrammed with the initials A.B., Trench and Sir Arthur inspected each one in turn. There was nothing suspicious - just clothes, jewellery, hats, and shoes.

"It seems that this is not the end of the journey," Trench said as he lifted a luggage label that showed the on-going destination as the Hotel Manhattan, New York.

Sir Arthur inspected the label. "Interesting. Didn't you say that Oscar Slater is currently bound for New York?"

"I thought we had established that the two persons are not connected," Trench whispered.

"Hmmm, perhaps not, perhaps not," the author mused in response, though something still worried him about Oscar Slater. *Why were they implicating this man in particular when he was sure that Glasgow had many other villains that could easily fit the bill? If the police were looking for a scapegoat, why go to all of the expense of chasing a man to New York, and with witnesses?* "Keep looking for the letter and brooch. Check for secret drawers and panels."

They kept on looking; the boys as well. They pulled out everything and checked inside the linings, but there was no sign of the letter or the brooch.

"Probably got 'em with her," Jamie suggested.

"Yes, Jamie, you're probably right," agreed Sir Arthur.

Suddenly, they heard a whistle at the front of the house. Miss Birrell and the man in the pale-coloured overcoat were back.

"Quick, move!" Sir Arthur ordered and they ran to the front door. Trench opened it and peered out onto the street, the poker still gripped in his hand. It had stopped snowing and, in the distance, he could see the figures of a man and woman trudging their way towards the house.

Bobby and George were already seated on one of the sledges, and Trench and the others rushed out to join them. By the time Trench and the boys had got back onto their sledges and Sir Arthur had buckled his skis back on, Miss Birrell and her companion had spotted them and were rushing towards them as fast as they could, slipping and sliding on the snowy street, which slowed down their pursuit.

They were barely ten feet away when Sir Arthur shoved the boys off, shouting at them to "Turn left at the corner and head downhill!"

He and Trench followed. Sir Arthur pushed with his poles as hard as he could and headed to the corner. He turned and sped down the hill, overtaking the over-laden sledges to lead a fast path down the steep street.

Trench was lagging behind the others and was barely at the corner when he heard the sound of a motorcar being cranked. He jumped back off his sledge and ran it down the start of the hill as the motorcar shuddered to life. He jumped back on his sledge and began to catch up with the others, racing down the hill as fast as he could, the speed no longer bothering him in the light of an imminent pursuit by two murderers.

After cranking the car, the man in the pale-coloured overcoat jumped in beside Miss Birrell, who pushed on the accelerator, gradually moving forward, slowly picking up speed as she approached the corner. The car's wheels skidded on the snow as she tried to steer. She managed to get it back under control and followed them. As the car coursed down the hill it picked up more speed and began to close the gap.

Sir Arthur and the gang swooshed around another corner. Miss Birrell and the man chasing them, if somewhat haphazardly, fought to handle her skating vehicle. Sir Arthur pushed himself faster. This street was even steeper and all three sledges seemed to fly down it at thrilling speed, getting faster all the time. The detective and gang clung on for dear life.

"She's still behind us!" called George in a panic as he looked back over his shoulder and straight into the furious face of Miss Birrell. "And she looks really angry."

Sir Arthur skied as fast as he could, the sledges racing behind him. As he came to the bottom of the hill, a horse and cart ambled along from the street to the right. Sir Arthur elegantly swerved left and missed it with yards to spare. The sledges followed, Trench screaming a little, but Miss Birrell was not quite so lucky. With the car's wheels unable to grip the snow slick road, she couldn't steer or stop and she crashed into the front of the cart. The cart driver was thrown out from his seat, landing in a pile of snow in front of a set of school railings. The man in the pale-coloured overcoat jumped from the motorcar and vaulted over the railings, landing in the snow-covered playground.

Miss Birrell, however, was trapped between horses and cart. The panicked horses reared, then kicked out their back legs, smashing the windscreen and kicking Miss Birrell in the head. By the time the cart-driver, Sir Arthur, Trench, and the gang had calmed the animals down, Miss Birrell was unconscious and the man in the pale-coloured overcoat was gone.

As Sir Arthur checked her for signs of life, people from the nearby tenement buildings began to fill the streets, eager to see the cause of the commotion. The small crowd attracted the attention of a passing policeman, who blew his whistle when he saw the motorcar and its unconscious driver. By the time the lady came round, she was surrounded by police and spectators, with Arthur Conan Doyle and Detective Trench explaining to the Edinburgh constables that she was wanted by police in Glasgow in connection to the murder of Miss Marion Gilchrist and a young man called Tam Murray.

Miss Birrell wailed her protest as two constables helped her out of the wrecked automobile and placed a set of handcuffs on her.

"They won't try me for her murder," she hissed at Sir Arthur and Trench. "This is about far more than the murder of an old woman, and nobody cares about some poor east end boy. You have no idea what you are dealing with, believe me. It would be better for you all if you let me go."

Chapter Twenty-Nine

The King's Secret

It was nearly 9:00 p.m. when they arrived back at 8 Picardy Place. The rest of the Doyle family were playing bridge in the drawing room. Sir Arthur, Detective Trench, and the gang went to the kitchen where they could talk about their most recent adventure and thaw out in front of the stove. A pot of hot cocoa had been left on the hob, which Sandy and the boys gleefully shared between them.

Once they were all seated around the large kitchen table, Sir Arthur reached inside his coat and pulled out a small black velvet drawstring bag with little gold tassels. The gang looked at him and the bag with puzzled expressions.

"It's Miss Birrell's. I pulled it out from under the seat of her motorcar," he said, answering their quizzical looks.

They watched eagerly, desperate to know what secrets the bag contained as Sir Arthur carefully pulled open the draw strings and tipped out the contents. Coins, calling cards, a folded five-pound note, a key, and a small mirror clattered onto the wooden table - there was no sign of the brooch or letter. They searched through the coins, looking for anything unusual, but they were all completely normal. They inspected the two calling cards; one for Mr. William

Barrie, Solicitor, George Square; and one for Mr. Arthur Adams, her aunt's neighbour.

"What about this solicitor chap?" asked Trench, waving the card at Sir Arthur.

The boys looked up with a glimmer of hope. They were not entirely sure what a solicitor was, but it sounded sinister.

"Seems perfectly reasonable when you consider that Miss Birrell was in Glasgow to close her father's estate," answered Sir Arthur. "Perhaps he was engaged to deal with the legal business." There was a general disappointed muttering from the gang. "We shall keep the cards just in case we find some relevance to them later on," he continued, and popped them in his pocket.

"The key?" asked Sam, as he picked it up and inspected the structure of the mortice key.

Sir Arthur took the key from the boy and inspected it closely. "It seems like a perfectly ordinary door key to me. Perhaps it's the key for the house in Herriot Row? What do you think, John?" he queried as he passed the key over to the detective.

Detective Trench scrutinised every millimetre before agreeing with Sir Arthur that there was nothing remotely noteworthy or unusual about it.

Next, they inspected the mirror, a circular silver compact enamelled with delicate blue flowers and engraved with the initials A.B., there didn't seem to be anything unusual about that either. Sandy and the boys looked at the small collection of items with disappointment.

"What do we do with it all?" Charlie asked, staring at the coins and five-pound note.

"I suggest that we use the money to buy a slap-up tea when we get back to Glasgow and any change can be spent on sweets. What do you say?" Sir Arthur suggested, and the gang all gleefully agreed that this would be the best use of Miss Birrell's money.

"Morally, we should return the bag to Miss..." Detective Trench began, but the gang drew him such a disgusted look he decided to leave the sentence unfinished.

"Good. I am glad we all agree," Sir Arthur said, cheerfully picking up the bag again to pop the contents back in. As he picked it up, however, he could feel something else - not in the bag, but in the silk lining. "What's this?"

Trench and the gang watched with rekindled interest as he took a knife from the kitchen drawer and ripped open the stitching, put his hand inside, and pulled out the diamond brooch. He placed it on the kitchen table, where it gleamed in the lamplight. Jamie, Andrew, Sam, and Charlie leaned forward to get a closer look. They hadn't been in the zoo when Sir Arthur had discovered it in the monkey house.

"That is a big diamond," Sam noted, as he picked it up and inspected it with reverential awe. "It's bee-yooo-tee-ful."

"May I see it?" asked Trench.

Sam handed the brooch to the detective, who looked at it closely. The large, pear-shaped diamond was dazzling and so were the smaller stones that encircled it. Each of the smaller stones alone must have been at least a carat each, if they were real. He looked at the back and found the small mark beneath the pin. Sir Arthur pulled his magnifying glass out of his pocket and handed it to the detective, then he continued foraging through the lining of the bag, whilst detective Trench scrutinised the hallmark.

"Aha," Sir Arthur suddenly shouted as his fingers closed on what felt like an envelope at the bottom of the bag's lining. He pulled it out. Trench and the gang gathered round to get a closer look at the red wax seal on the back.

"It's impressed with the Prince of Wales's Feathers, just like on the brooch," observed Trench.

"Let's see if this will tell us why Miss Gilchrist was in possession of it, and perhaps why she was murdered," said Sir Arthur, as he opened the envelope and pulled out a letter. He unfolded it and read aloud,

26th February 1895
My dear Miss Gilchrist,

Disaster! Our safe place has gone up in flames and Magi has disappeared. I am still searching. I commend Stella to your keeping. I fear that our secret is in danger of being exposed. I am deeply sorry to place this burden on your shoulders, but in my position, I can do nothing else but entrust this matter to the only other person who knows the truth.
I beg of you to keep yourself and Stella safe. I do not need to remind you that all of our futures depend upon it.

Yours,
Albert Edward

"Who's Albert Edward?" asked Sandy, a little confused.
"The Prince of Wales," answered Sir Arthur.

The boys, Sandy, and Detective Trench stared at the letter with great reverence. This had been written by the King himself.

"However, it is unusual for a member of the Royal family to close a letter with such an informal signature. And note how he addresses the recipient with a formal salutation. He evidently had a great deal of respect for Miss Gilchrist," commented Sir Arthur.

"Or it's a fake," suggested Detective Trench, breaking the spell.

"No, I think it is indeed genuine. I have seen the King's handwriting before and this certainly appears to be a match," replied Sir Arthur, waving the letter in the air.

"Who are Stella and Magi?" asked George.

"That, my dear boy, is a mystery. Whoever they are they must be very important, as it seems that all of our futures depend upon them," Sir Arthur answered.

"Or did depend on them. This note was written over a decade ago," Detective Trench suggested.

"How could two girls be so important?" Jimmy asked, puzzled.

Sandy scowled at him. "And why wouldn't girls be so important?"

Jimmy blushed. He had forgotten that Sandy was a girl now that she was back in boys' clothes. "Well…och, well, you know what I mean. I-I-I dinnae mean that girls aren't important - it's just, well…"

"It's okay, Jimmy, I'm just messing with you," Sandy laughed.

"Can I have a look at that letter?" Trench requested. Sir Arthur handed it over. The others watched as the detective's eyes darted backwards and forwards, reading every line several times. He inspected both sides of the paper with the magnifying glass, looking for any other clues, like a hidden symbol or watermark. Then he re-read one line out loud. "I fear that our secret is in danger of being exposed." He looked up at the others. "And what exactly is the secret that only Miss Gilchrist knew?"

"Who Stella and Magi are?" suggested Jamie, tentatively.

"Yes, Jamie, but what exactly is the secret in relation to them?" Trench asked.

They read the letter to Miss Gilchrist again. What safe place had gone up in flames? What was the secret that only the two of them knew? The letter didn't explain anything; it only raised further questions.

For several minutes they sat in silence, sipping their cocoa, lost in their own theories about the deepening mystery.

At length Trench said, "Perhaps - and it's only a thought - but perhaps, well, when he was a younger man, the King did have a bit of a, uhumm…" he cleared his throat, struggling with how best to phrase his next sentence and not sound treasonous or improper. "Shall we say, he was rather popular with the ladies." He winked at Sir Arthur, who stared at Trench as if seeing him for the first time. His eyes suddenly widened as he understood what the detective was implying.

"You don't think Stella and Magi are lady friends?" Sir Arthur asked, a little confused. Then suddenly it dawned on him. As Trench opened his mouth to reply, Sir Arthur said, "My good man, do you think they are the result of a relationship with a lady? Daughters from an illicit union!?"

Trench nodded solemnly.

Sir Arthur looked as though he was about to faint. He took a deep gulp of his cocoa. "Well, that would explain a lot. If this is true, and Ord and Douglas know about it, then it would explain why they are trying to hide the truth. If news of the king's illegitimate daughters came out…well, that truly is a scandal that could end everything. Good God, the whole empire would be at risk!"

"Why?" asked Sandy.

The others around the table looked at Sandy in disbelief.

"An illegitimate child is born outside of wedlock," Sir Arthur explained.

"What's wedlock?" Sandy enquired.

There was a general gasp around the table. Even the boys seemed stunned.

"Marriage. An illegitimate child is born outside of marriage. I assume by your lack of understanding that illegitimacy doesn't exist in the future."

"My mum isn't married to my dad. Loads of my friends' parents aren't married," Sandy explained.

Sir Arthur Conan Doyle, Detective Trench, and the boys all looked at Sandy with utter astonishment and horror.

"It's really no big deal," Sandy stated, shrugging offhandedly. "Weddings are really expensive."

"Well, I can assure you it is most certainly a big deal in this time," Sir Arthur insisted forcefully. "It is simply not acceptable to have children outside of holy matrimony. And if anyone got wind of the King being involved in such debauched and immoral behaviour, then I can assure you it would compromise the very fabric of our society. It would start wars and rebellions across the Empire. Lord knows we are at the brink of war as it is."

Sandy still didn't understand why it was so important, but Sir Arthur obviously felt very strongly about it. And so did the others.

"But it doesn't explain how Miss Gilchrist is involved. How did she know the Prince of Wales and why would she be so deeply in his confidence? It just doesn't make sense," Detective Trench added, changing the subject. "Unless she was the mother?"

Another gasp circled the table.

Sir Arthur considered this for a moment "I do not think that this letter was written to a lover. I think perhaps that the missing lady, Magi, was the mother and that Miss Gilchrist was a friend, perhaps a servant. I would imagine the King would use her Christian name, or some form of term of endearment if she was a lover or a close friend. Though she was certainly close enough to him to be in his confidence. And it would seem that Miss Birrell found out and was perhaps intending to use the letter to blackmail the King?"

Andrew picked up the brooch and looked at it in the lamplight. "This brooch must be worth a fortune if it's real," he declared. Sandy and the others stared at it too, as if hypnotised by the glittering jewel.

"Yes, yes. If it's real it would be worth a king's ransom," Sir Arthur agreed.

"Then why would he give it to a servant?" Sam asked.

"Perhaps to buy her silence?" Sir Arthur suggested. "Though it doesn't seem like her silence needed to be bought. The tone of this letter is friendly, warm. Perhaps she was to keep it for Stella?"

"But Miss Birrell murdered her aunt for the brooch, so what happened to Stella? Where is she now?" asked Charlie.

"And where did Magi disappear to, do you think?" asked George.

"And why bother with blackmailing the King?" asked Andrew.

"Greed," Detective Trench replied. "And power. We can only guess the extent of her villainy, but money and power are strong motives for murder, blackmail, and theft."

"And she seemed such a nice lady an' aw," Jimmy added, the shilling she had given him still safely in his pocket.

"Greed can corrupt even the nicest of people. Take my word for it. I have seen all sorts of respectable people, even priests, turn to crime in the name of fortune," said Trench.

"And if we are right about the contents of this letter, then that knowledge is far more valuable to a blackmailer than any diamond, no matter how big. Miss Birrell was right. There is no way on earth that she will ever be tried for the murder of Tam or Miss Gilchrist lest the truth come out," explained Detective Trench.

"Yes, indeed. Miss Birrell was almost certainly trying to take advantage of the precarious situation with Kaiser Whilhelm. If the Kaiser found out, well, who knows what would happen?" Sir Arthur commented, a note of anxiety in his voice. "It could result in the worst war of all time…or it could mean that Kaiser Whilhelm will overthrow our King Edward and we will come under German rule."

"He couldn't really do that, could he?" Jamie asked, his brown eyes filled with concern.

"Well, theoretically, yes, he could. He is, after all, the oldest grandchild of our late Queen Victoria and therefore could be said to have a genuine claim to the throne of Britain in the event that our King was discovered to be morally indecent and therefore unfit to govern."

"You don't suppose Miss Birrell and the man in the pale-coloured overcoat work for the Kaiser, do you?" asked George. "I mean, Sandy did say he sounded German, didn't you?"

Sandy nodded. "Yeah, he sounded…." She nearly said that he sounded exactly like the Germans in old war movies, then thought better of it since neither World War had happened yet, so she simply said, "… German."

"It is not beyond the realm of possibility that they are working for the Kaiser, but I dearly hope not," Sir Arthur responded. He suddenly felt a sense of doom.

"So, what do we do now?" asked Andrew.

"Tomorrow, we will escort Miss Birrell back to Glasgow and make sure she is safely handed over to the Glasgow police," Sir Arthur replied. "I am sure that Chief Inspector Ord and Superintendent Douglas will continue to keep the truth under wraps."

"What about the letter and the brooch?" Trench asked. "What are we going to do about them?"

"Obviously we need to hand them over too. If they got into the wrong hands…" Sir Arthur gazed into the depths of his cocoa. "Well, it doesn't bear thinking about," he said, folding the letter back up. "Especially since Miss Birrell's associate is still at large."

"I'll telephone the west end office in the morning and speak to Ord. Maybe he can call Douglas back before they board the ship for New York. The evidence is safe now, so they don't need to use Oscar Slater as a scapegoat," added Trench, before he drained the last of his cup.

"New York!" Sir Arthur suddenly piped up.

"Yes, New York. That's where they are sending the witnesses to identify Oscar Sla…"

"No, John, New York! That's the destination written on the labels on Miss Birrell's cases!" Sir Arthur explained.

Trench yawned. "Slater is a diamond dealer. Maybe she was going to sell him the brooch?" he suggested drowsily. "Or maybe it's just a coincidence." He stretched.

Sir Arthur didn't believe in coincidences. There was something connecting Oscar Slater to this case other than him being used as a scapegoat. However, he knew it was not the time to consider this connection further. It was clear by the yawning around the table that it was time for bed. Tomorrow would be another day.

Chapter Thirty

29th December
The Train Bandits

The new dawn did not bring any new answers with it and, as the gang sat and ate their breakfast, they discussed the dilemma of the letter and the brooch.

"I still don't trust Ord and Douglas," Trench declared.

"John, my friend, their treatment of you was only to ensure you didn't discover the truth. We might as well give them what they were trying to protect. After all, what are we going to do with a diamond brooch?" Sir Arthur replied.

Detective Trench harrumphed. "I still say I don't trust them. There is still something not right … something we're missing. I mean, who is the man in the pale-coloured overcoat? You say he's a time traveller, like Sandy here. Why would someone from the future be bothered about the illegitimate children of a king from the past who is probably long dead? I say we hold on to the items for now."

Detective Trench certainly had a point. Why was the time traveller here? Why was he so interested in the brooch? What was his connection to Miss Birrell? Sir Arthur wondered.

Sir Arthur had spent a sleepless night pondering these very points. The letter provided a serious motive for murder and explained why Ord and Douglas were framing an innocent man. They were protecting their King and country from a hideous scandal. But how much did they know? Did they know that the man in the pale-coloured overcoat is a time traveller and that the magic lantern is a time machine?

"You don't suppose you're wrong about him being a time traveller?" Trench added, as if reading Sir Arthur's thoughts. "Perhaps he's an antiques dealer. Have you considered that? And that's why he pulled an 18th-century French coin from his pocket. It may be that he's just helping Miss Birrell find a buyer for that brooch," Trench suggested.

Sir Arthur had indeed considered this - but, somehow, the man being a time traveller made more sense to him.

"Well, we know that Sandy is a time traveller. Surely her journey from the future must relate to this case?" Sir Arthur replied. He was sure of it. It seemed the only reasonable answer to the girl having been sent back in time. And, when one has eliminated all which is impossible, whatever remains, however improbable, must be the truth. "There is a lot more to this mystery that we are yet to unearth."

* * *

When they arrived at Edinburgh Station later that morning, the police were already on the Glasgow platform with Miss Birrell, who was handcuffed and looking somewhat dishevelled after her night in the police cells. A large, horseshoe-shaped bruise she'd earned in the motorcar crash had spread across her forehead and blackened both of her eyes. She was a wreck of her former, elegant self. Trench and Sir Arthur left Sandy and the boys standing on the platform whilst they went to speak to the officers escorting Miss Birrell. Only Sir Arthur came back.

"Detective Trench is accompanying Miss Birrell back to Glasgow with the Edinburgh officers. We will sit in the adjacent compartment," he told them when he returned.

Half an hour later, the train was speeding through the countryside and the gang were comfortably seated in their compartment, discussing the man in the pale-coloured overcoat.

"Well, if he is a time traveller, he will head back to the Panopticon and the magic lantern at some point," Sir Arthur pointed out.

"An' he'll probably come for the brooch and letter an aw," added Andrew.

"If that is really what he's here for," reflected George.

"I wonder when in time he's from?" asked Sandy.

"Now that is a good question," said Sir Arthur. Suddenly the wheels of the train squealed on the tracks and they came to a jolting halt, throwing them all off their seats.

Sir Arthur got up and slid open the upper part of the compartment window. He stuck his head out and looked along to the front of the train, trying to see what had caused the sudden stop.

"By the Lord Harry!" he exclaimed. "It's a hold-up!"

The boys and Sandy jostled for a look, pressing their faces against the glass. Along the front of the train were two figures on horseback pointing guns at the driver and fireman.

"Is it the man in the pale-coloured overcoat?" asked Sam.

"Who else could it be?" replied Jamie.

Sir Arthur opened the door on the opposite side of their compartment.

"Wait here," he instructed as he dashed to the next compartment where Trench and the Edinburgh constables guarded their prisoner. He knocked on the door and Trench let him in.

"Move her!" Sir Arthur barked at the officers.

"What's going on?" asked Trench.

"It's a hold-up. Two bandits, possibly more, no doubt here to liberate Miss Birrell."

Trench dashed to the window. "You're right. I can see two of them." He ran to the compartment door.

"Where are you going, man?" Sir Arthur demanded.

"I'll try and create a diversion while you get her away," he shouted back over his shoulder as he made his way up the corridor to the carriage door, swiftly opening it and dropping silently down onto the snowy ground outside.

Trench crept his way along the side of the carriages as quietly as he could in the fresh, crisp snow. When he got to the engine, he crouched down and peered beneath the engine to the opposite side of the tracks. He could see the horses' feet and hear the bandits talking.

"Stay here and guard these two. I'll search the carriages and find the woman," he heard one of them say, though the voice was very muffled, as if the speaker's mouth was covered. He saw the legs of one of the horses move, turning and galloping away. The other horse remained where it was.

"Get down here," he heard the remaining bandit gruffly order. Trench watched the legs of the driver and fireman come into view as they climbed down from the cab. They stood next to each other with their backs to the engine.

"Keep your hands in the air and don't move, or I'll shoot."

Trench laid himself flat and crawled under the train. He could see the legs of the lead bandit's horse, two carriages up. Trench crawled across the tracks beneath the train with the aggregate biting into his knees and palms. He scoured the tracks, looking for something he could use as a weapon. There was nothing but the jagged stones. He supposed they would have to do.

"There!" he heard one of the bandits shout.

Trench, fearing he had spotted the fleeing police officers with their charge, dragged himself out from beneath the carriage, gathered a handful of stones, and jumped to his feet. He immediately started to bombard the bandits. It was enough to draw their attention, but only one of the bandits on horseback came after him as he scrambled away, running for the edge of the embankment. Then, a thunderous bang filled the crisp morning air and Trench felt a sudden sting in his thigh. His legs buckled underneath him and he fell, tumbling through the banked snow and down the embankment into the ditch below. He had been shot.

***

Sir Arthur and the Edinburgh officers had not got far with their prisoner, who was now gagged as well as handcuffed. They had managed to manhandle the woman out of the door and drop her down to the tracks, but she fought against them, kicking and striking out with manacled fists. Sandy and the boys did what they could to help, grabbing her legs and holding them tight. Together, they managed to carry her along the tracks for a short distance, but they were soon spotted by one of the bandits who shouted, "There!"

A gunshot sounded and Sir Arthur released his grip on the woman, pulling out his own revolver in response. Two more armed bandits came at a shambling run through the snowy fields towards them. Sir Arthur fired a couple of shots at them but missed. He was a rotten shot. Miss Birrell began to wriggle again, trying to free herself of her captors' hold. But the constables, boys, and Sandy held her fast. One of the bandits in the field below - a tall fellow in a large hat with a grey scarf wound around his face - pointed his gun and fired a shot at the policemen. An officer hollered in pain as the bullet entered his shoulder and let go of the woman, who kicked furiously at the boys, striking Jamie square in the jaw. The boys and Sandy lost their grip on her legs and Miss Birrell scrambled away from them, plunging down the steep embankment to the two bandits below. Still holding their guns on the gang, they grabbed her roughly and pulled her to her feet. Sir Arthur pointed his gun at them, and they pointed theirs straight back at him.

"Don't even think about it," said the taller bandit. "One move and you're dead. Now put your hands up! All of you!"

The gang did as they were bid, all except the injured officer who was still yelling with pain.

The mounted bandits trotted out from behind the train and along the edge of the embankment towards them. "Stay where you are if you value your life," the one in front demanded, firing his gun in the air as a warning, which made both horses bray. The bandit behind him guided his horse down the slope to join the two bandits below and swiftly manhandled Miss Birrell up onto his horse, placing her across the front of his saddle. He pocketed his gun and held her fast with a leather-gloved hand. With his right hand he pulled the reigns and swung his horse around, riding off into the field beyond, the captive woman screaming as they went. The two bandits on foot followed and, a few moments later, so did the other mounted bandit, who fired another shot in the air and whooped "yeeha!" as he jumped his horse down the embankment and galloped off. Sir Arthur sprang into action a few seconds later and chased after them.

"Look for Detective Trench. He may be injured," he called as he clambered down the embankment and into the fields. The constable - waving his truncheon - Sandy, Jimmy, Andrew, and Jamie followed close behind, while the other boys searched the embankment and ditches for the missing detective.

By now, everyone on the train was at a window watching the drama unfold. Some of the men, witnessing the hold-up, had jumped down from their carriages to help the pursuit of the escaped criminals.

The bandits and Miss Birrell had fled across a field and into some woods. The group of pursuers entered the tree line not far behind them. Sir Arthur was in front, brandishing his revolver with the truncheon-wielding policeman beside him. The boys and Sandy followed closely behind, carrying sticks they had managed to find on the woodland floor. The snow was thin here, but the tree cover was dense. The bandits and their tracks were lost among the thick shrub, but broken bracken and trampled undergrowth led the way deeper into the woods.

"Over there," Jamie mouthed, and pointed when he spotted something through the trees. Sir Arthur looked in the direction he was pointing and saw the bandit and Miss Birrell, still captive on horseback. But the man had seen them too and fired another shot in their direction. Sir Arthur returned fire. The horse reared, then galloped further into the copse. Sir Arthur and the gang pursued, but they lost sight of him almost instantly. As they continued to search the forest floor for any sign of the bandits, the gang heard the sudden click of a gun cocking, and Sir Arthur found himself with a weapon pointed straight at his head. The second mounted bandit had found them.

"Give it up, Doyle," he said in a deep, muffled voice.

Sir Arthur looked to his left and up to the bandit on horseback. There was something so familiar about him, even though his eyes were hidden in the shadow of a large hat and the rest of his face was obscured by a scarf.

"No, you give it up," he bravely responded.

The man fired his gun and Sir Arthur fell.

"No!" shouted Sandy as she and the boys ran to his side and dropped down next to him. The gunman galloped off deeper into the woods. Sir Arthur groaned.

"You're alive!" Sandy cried with relief.

"I'm fine, I'm fine! He shot past me. My ears are ringing, that's all. I fell with the shock of it, I suppose," he said, sounding a little embarrassed as Jimmy and Jamie helped him up.

Then they heard more gun shots and a man yelled in pain. Moments later, Miss Birrell, brandishing a pistol in her manacled hands, came running and stumbling out of the thicket. She fired the gun again, but it was empty. She tripped, badly twisting her ankle, and the boys and Sandy were on her in seconds, wrestling the gun from her fingers and pinning her to the ground.

The Edinburgh officer hit her over the head with his truncheon and knocked her out.

"That should put an end to her escapes," noted the officer. He grabbed an arm and leg, slung her over his shoulder in a fireman's lift, and began trudging back out of the woods and wading through the snowy meadow towards the train.

"Why do you think she ran away from them?" Jimmy asked as they tramped back to the train.

"I have no idea," replied Sir Arthur. "But something definitely isn't right."

They got back to the train as quickly as they could, convinced that at any moment the bandits would follow, shooting as they came, but they didn't. A few minutes later, they were back at the train, this time all together in one carriage. It was a bit of a squeeze, but Sir Arthur thought it best they all travel together, what with Detective Trench and one of the policemen having been shot. As the train built up a head of steam again he inspected their wounds.

"Nothing to worry about. Thankfully, both shots were very superficial. The bullets have grazed the flesh only. You should be fine in a couple of days," Sir Arthur announced.

"Still hurts like hell," Trench said as Sir Arthur tied a bit of cloth he had got from the guard as a temporary bandage around the top of Trench's leg.

"Well, it could have been worse. Should have been worse. None of this hold-up makes any sense," he said.

"What do you mean, sir?" asked the Edinburgh officer, still holding on to the unconscious Miss Birrell, who was propped up between himself and his injured colleague.

"Well, they could have killed us; instead they only injured. I could have been shot in the head, but instead he shot the air next to my ear. It's still ringing. And why didn't they come after Miss Birrell when she escaped them? And why did Miss Birrell run away from her rescuers in the first place?" Sir Arthur answered the question with more questions.

"Ask her yourself," the officer replied, as Miss Birrell began to stir. She opened her eyes and stared blearily around. Realising she was back on the train and with her police escort, she groaned.

"Miss Birrell, did you know your rescuers?" Sir Arthur asked.

But Miss Birrell just gave him a glare before putting her head back down and closing her eyes. She didn't wake up again until they got to Glasgow. The rest of the journey was spent in silence as the travellers gazed out of the windows and watched the countryside pass by, each deep in their own thoughts.

Chapter Thirty-One

Back in Glasgow

When the train arrived in Glasgow, the platform at Queen Street Station was thronged with police, press, and people. Word of Miss Gilchrist's murderer being captured in Edinburgh had spread through the city like plague. It was the story of the century, and the city was buzzing with the news that the Gilchrist murder had been solved; and not by just anyone, but by the famous author Sir Arthur Conan Doyle, the Glasgow detective John Thomason Trench, and a gang of Glasgow urchins. By the time they arrived with their quarry, the news had also made it to the press that the train had been held up by a gang of bandits. They had failed to liberate the villain - thanks to the brave intervention of Trench and the Edinburgh police officers escorting the murderer, two of whom had been shot in the ensuing chaos.

When the crowd saw that the person in police custody was a woman it erupted at the scandal. Newspaper men jostled to get close to her and the heroes of the day, shouting questions above the noise of the mob. A limping Trench and the Edinburgh constables escorted Miss Birrell to the waiting Black Maria as a squad of Glasgow constables held back the excitable crowd.

Sir Arthur and his little gang did not escape the crowd so easily. Sir Arthur Conan Doyle was a familiar face to many, his Sherlock Holmes stories were not only printed in The Strand, but were further popularised as dramas on the theatre stage and parodies in the music halls. Journalists clambered for statements and fans jostled for autographs until the station guards and a dozen or so policemen managed to forge an escape route through the melee.

The world beyond the dirty, smoky, densely-crowded station looked like it had been whitewashed. The murky sky was thick with huge, swirling white snowflakes. Buildings, people, horses, and vehicles were nothing more than indistinct charcoal shapes. The station guards helped the little group into two waiting hackney carriages, which clip-clopped through the snowy streets back to the Panopticon, where they hoped to track down the time-travelling man in the pale-coloured overcoat.

Somehow, returning to the Panopticon brought them all back to reality. Back from the foreign streets of Edinburgh, safe from attack by gun-wielding bandits and the thrill of the chase, away from the excitement of the Queen Street crowds, they were suddenly back to their own lives and, for Jamie and Bobby, their own grief. Sir Arthur paid their admission to the music hall and they went silently up the stairs with the rest of the lunchtime mob. They made their way into their usual balcony spot, but they were too late. Another group of boys had beaten them to it. Normally they would have fought for their favourite forms, but somehow it didn't seem important anymore. Instead they made their way back through the crowd, back down the stairs, and stood near the rear of the stalls.

Sir Arthur felt a pang of sadness for the boys.

"It's not over yet," he shouted brightly over the noise of the band that had just struck up the opening overture. "And when it is, when we have captured the man in the pale-coloured overcoat, and handed over the items," he said, patting his pocket to indicate the letter and brooch within, "safely into the hands of Detective Inspector Ord, then we will celebrate with a special party complete with every cake of your hearts' desires."

The gang cheered up a little at this promise and sat through the bill of dancers, comedians, singers, magicians, silent films, and novelty acts in a daze, barely taking any of it in. As the audience left, jostling past them at the end of the show, they stood still and waited, gazing at the empty stage. Minutes later, they were the only ones left in the cavernous auditorium. The sounds of the attic carnival above drifted down like dust. But they were not on their own. As Sir Arthur was about to suggest that they go and get something to eat, the man in the pale-coloured overcoat entered. He didn't see them standing in the shadows but, as they glimpsed him, the gang withdrew deeper into the darkness of the back of the stalls. They watched as he walked over to the magic lantern that stood on a platform only a few feet to their left. They held their breaths as he switched it on and walked down the centre aisle to the front of the stage. The light of the magic lantern flared brightly for a second, bathing the man in white light. Then he was gone.

The boys, Sandy, and Sir Arthur looked at each other, stunned.

"Well, that proves it without a shadow of a doubt. He did indeed travel here through the magic lantern," Sir Arthur said, turning the 18th-century French coin around in his fingers.

"But where's he gone?" asked Jimmy.

"Aye, Sandy didnae disappear when she went back to her own time. It was like she hadn't left at all," said George.

"That's because she wanted the magic lantern to bring her back to the exact moment that she left us. Assuming, of course, that I am correct about how it works. Obviously, this man has gone somewhere else in time. I doubt he would come back to the here and now, so to speak, as he would run right back into us. I fear we may have lost him," said Sir Arthur.

"We'll see about that," declared Sandy, determined that she was going to find out who he was and drag him back to face justice beside Miss Birrell. She jumped into the beam. Follow that man, follow that man, follow that man, she thought, over and over again in her head, eyes tight shut, visualising the skeleton man in the pale-coloured overcoat. Hoping that it would work and concentrating as hard as she could, she felt herself floating upwards.

She was travelling forwards in time.

Chapter Thirty-Two

A Chase Through Time

She had no idea where she would end up in time and really no time to think about it. When Sandy opened her eyes she was very surprised; it wasn't what she had expected at all. She thought she would suddenly find herself in some kind of futuristic place, but instead she was in what appeared to be an old-fashioned study. Large, green velvet curtains were drawn over the tall windows and a large oak desk was illuminated in a pool of golden light cast by an electric desk lamp.

The man in the pale-coloured overcoat stood next to the desk, his skeletal face hidden in the shadow of his cloth cap. "Who are you?" he whispered as he stepped forward.

Sandy instinctively moved backwards and knocked against a plant stand, toppling a potted plant which went crashing to the floor.

"Who's there?" a man's voice called from somewhere outside the room. It sounded like Arthur Conan Doyle.

The man bolted at the sound of the voice and jumped back through the beam. Sandy followed. She was sure that had been Sir Arthur's voice, but she had no time to stop. She had to catch the man in the pale-coloured overcoat.

She concentrated again and this time felt herself begin falling back through time, hurtling to the floor of what looked like a dark stone vault. Wherever they were, it wasn't the Panopticon. Silent, shadowy figures loomed around the edges of the darkness beyond the magic lantern beam's reach.

Sandy called out, "Have you seen a man in a pale-coloured overcoat and cloth cap?"

The response was stone cold silence. She pulled her phone out of her pocket and, using the torch function, washed the dark shadows with its light. She gasped as each ghostly figure appeared. A skeleton in a narrow cage stared blindly ahead with empty eye-sockets; the tortured, bloody face of a man grimaced at her.; gruesome severed heads, stuck on metal spikes, tongues lolling from their open mouths, glared at her; men and women manacled and mangled with death and terror seemed to lurch towards her as she moved the light from left to right. Fear gripped Sandy in the pit of her stomach. Her phone made a descending sound and the torch blinked off as it ran out of charge. She screamed. She felt something move behind her and spun around just in time to see the dim silhouette of the man in the pale-coloured overcoat disappear into the beam again.

A door opened and a figure entered, carrying a candle. "Qui est là?" a woman's voice cautiously called into the darkness. Sandy turned and ran, darting back through the beam, her heart racing.

Sandy dropped again, but only for a moment. She almost instantly hit the stone floor of another dark room, lit by flaming torches. Or was it a room? In her brief glimpse it looked like an underground dungeon or cellar with low arched ceilings. Around the edges were shelved recesses. It smelt of dirt and damp. There were screams in the distance - horrible, terrifying cries of someone being tortured. Where was she now? Where was he? Had he jumped again? There was a shrill, piercing shriek of agony from the other side of the dank stone wall to her left. She covered her ears and ran back through the beam, plummeting through time, spinning and tumbling further than before.

This time she was in an oil-lit attic filled with strange-looking mechanical devices and a long bench covered with tools, cogs, springs, and all manner of strange things. Why had he come here? There was nothing here but junk.

She stepped out of the beam and towards a machine that looked like some kind of strange mechanical clock. As she did so, the man stepped out of the shadows and back through it. Sandy felt him behind her and spun on her heel. What was the point of running away every time when she could just keep following him? Did he intend to keep jumping through time until they were back at the beginning of the world? Could they go back that far?

She jumped.

Sandy landed on a stage in a grand theatre. She had never seen anything quite like it. For a moment, she was transfixed by the small amount she could see in the gloom beyond the candle-powered footlights. Golden pillars supported ornate carved balconies which swept around her in a golden semi-circle. An audience of men and women sat watching agog. The man in the pale-coloured overcoat was nowhere to be seen. She stared down at the seated group of curious and bewildered people in large white wigs and colourful, elaborate clothes. Their upturned faces caked with white make-up - even the men. The air was filled with cloying perfume. Her stomach turned. She wasn't sure if it was the smell or the time travelling, but she felt like she was going to throw up.

She closed her eyes and willed the beam to take her away - take her to where the man in the pale-coloured overcoat was. But the instant jump didn't happen. Perhaps the time between them had become too long. Or perhaps she was becoming tired. One more attempt, she thought to herself, just one more try. Please, she begged the magic lantern, please help me find him. She felt herself rise for the briefest moment, and then there was a sensation like she was floating. She opened her eyes and found herself at the edge of the lens looking out into a dark, cavernous room. She tried to step out into the room, but she was trapped behind the glass. She peered out. It was hard to see anything through the lens; it was like peering through a dirty window with the sun shining in. All she could see was vague shadows. The man in the pale-coloured overcoat was standing just in front of the lens with his back to her. He didn't seem to be aware that she was there. He began to step back towards the magic lantern. Sandy tried again to push herself out of the lens and into the room, but no matter how hard she tried she couldn't push past the glass. She felt like a goldfish suspended in a bowl. Then she heard someone shouting, but she couldn't hear what they were saying. It was as if she were underwater; sounds were muffled and indistinct. She heard a bang, and the man in the pale-coloured overcoat fell forward. Sandy was sucked back by the magic lantern.

She felt herself pulled up like a marionette on strings, lifted up and away from this scene at breathtaking speed. A muffled shout echoing through time behind her, just one word; "Dead!" Had the man in the pale-coloured overcoat been shot? Was he dead? And why wouldn't the magic lantern let her into the room? Why had it kept her captive behind the lens?

The magic lantern sucked the bewildered Sandy up through time and spat her out into the first room with the green drapes and the large wooden desk. She had been sure she had heard Sir Arthur Conan Doyle's voice earlier in the chase. Was this his house? She was curious. What did it have to do with the man in the pale-coloured overcoat? Had the future Sir Arthur discovered something? Why was she back here now? She stepped out of the beam. The potted plant she had knocked over had spilled soil over the patterned rug. The door burst open and in strode Sir Arthur Conan Doyle. He was older, more care worn. He stopped in the doorway and stared at her with a startled expression.

Chapter Thirty-Three

7th July 1916

Sir Arthur walked into the room and headed for the desk and asked. "Who the devil are you?"

"It's me. Sandy. Don't you recognise me?" asked Sandy. "Sandy. You know, from the future?" she said, pulling the now dead mobile phone out of her pocket and waggling it at him.

Sir Arthur obviously thought she had pulled out a weapon as he ducked behind his desk.

"I have never seen you before in my life, boy!" He said as he reappeared, staring curiously at the black slate in her hand.

This struck Sandy as very odd. *How could he have forgotten her? He had the magic lantern, so how did he not know who she was? Maybe something had happened to him and he had lost his memory.*

Sir Arthur stood at his desk, staring at the small stranger who had magically appeared in his study. The light cast by the electric bulb of his desk lamp glowed beneath a green, glass shade and a fire smouldered in the large fireplace. The curtains were closed, blocking out the miserable, wet July evening outside, but Sandy could still hear the patter of wind-driven rain on the window panes.

When he had left the room only a minute earlier, the magic lantern had been switched on. He had been checking to see if it worked when the doorbell rang. It had been a messenger boy delivering a telegram, which he still held in his hand. He had been about to open it when he'd heard something crash in his study. Now, he was staring at a smashed potted plant and a strange little boy who claimed to be from the future and the magic lantern had mysteriously turned itself off. Though he supposed the boy could have done that.

The magic lantern sat on a table on the opposite side of the room, its lens glaring darkly back at him. He had recently bought the magic lantern from an old music hall in Glasgow. The owner, a Mr. Pickard, had been auctioning off some old exhibits from his museum and amongst the moth-eaten Egyptian Mummies; pickled oddities in jars; broken bits of wax work; automatons; and weird taxidermy, was the magic lantern.

He had received an invitation to the auction through the post along with a small catalogue. The magic lantern had been highlighted as an item that 'must be seen.' It was described as having once belonged to Marie Tussaud and possibly Paul Philidor. Sir Arthur was sceptical, but Paul Philidor had been a great magician and the magic lantern had been his most famous trick. He had used it in his ghost shows, and it was believed that he could actually communicate with the dead through it. After his death, the magic lantern was said to have mysteriously disappeared. Some believed that Marie Tussaud, who had been a close friend of the great magician, had hidden the magic lantern to ensure Philador's secrets remained safe. The magic lantern was legendary among magicians and occultists around the world. It was the holy grail of spiritualism and it seemed unlikely that it would turn up in an old, run-down music hall in Glasgow. But, for the price of a few shillings, Sir Arthur felt it was worth the risk. If nothing else, he could use it to entertain his family with a few old magic lantern slides.

"Where did you come from, boy?" he asked the stranger.

The child pointed at the magic lantern. "Where do you think," Sandy replied rather cheekily.

"Do you expect me to believe that you are some sort of ghost boy brought here by the magic lantern?" Sir Arthur quipped.

"I'm not a ghost. I am from the future. Surely you remember me? Sandy? Sandy McMillan? We met in the Panopticon Zoo after you received a mysterious letter. Don't you remember? You have to remember," Sandy pleaded, feeling herself at the edge of tears. She was tired and this wasn't funny. The beam had switched off and all she wanted to do was get back and tell the others that the man in the pale-coloured overcoat was dead. Why had the magic lantern brought her here?

Sir Arthur suddenly felt sorry for the child. This poor boy looked on the verge of sobbing. He was sure he had never met this lad before, but something about him was indeed familiar. When he had first seen him, he would have sworn he had never met the boy before, but now, as he studied the child more closely, he was sure he had.

"Did you turn off the magic lantern?" he asked.

"No, it turned itself off. I don't know why, but it obviously wanted to send me here," Sandy said.

"You seem to think I should know you, and I have to admit something about you is familiar. Tell me truthfully, now, how do you know me and how did you get in here," Sir Arthur asked.

Sandy sat down and explained the whole story, from the time she left the 21st century until the chase through time which had led her to Sir Arthur Conan Doyle's study. She told him about the murder of Marion Gilchrist and how they had just captured the murderer. She told him about the boys, Detective Trench, the diamond brooch, the letter from the king, and the man in the pale-coloured overcoat who had also come from some other time. When she had finished, Sir Arthur sat back in his chair and mulled over the story, his chin resting on steepled fingers.

"I have to say that, bizarre as it all sounds, for some reason I believe you," he said at length. "But why don't I remember any of it? I vaguely remember the case of Marion Gilchrist, but I don't remember being involved in solving it. This really is quite fascinating."

"You really don't remember? But you must. The stolen diamond brooch. The letter. The chase through the snow on sledges. Miss Birrell. The man in the pale-coloured overcoat," Sandy began again.

"Yes, yes, so you say. But repeating yourself is not going to make me remember something I was never involved with," Sir Arthur got up and walked over to his bookcase. "When did you say you were from?" he asked

"December 1908," Sandy responded. "But I'm really from 2016."

He ran his index finger along a row of large scrapbooks. "Ah, 1900-1910," he said as he pulled out one of the large black books and placed it with a thud on his desk. He turned the cover, licked his thumb and index fingers on his right hand and began to search quickly through the pages, repeating, "Marion Gilchrist, Marion Gilchrist, Marion Gilchrist…" under his breath as he did so. "Aha!" he finally announced as he stabbed his index finger down on a page "There you are!"

"What's that?" asked Sandy.

Sir Arthur, who was now lowering himself into his seat whilst his eyes read the page, his lips moving slightly beneath his bushy moustache, lifted his hand to silence her. Sandy waited for him to finish reading.

"This, my dear young man–" Sir Arthur began.

"I'm a girl," Sandy corrected.

Sir Arthur looked at her with annoyance at being corrected. "Well, missy, this is one of many volumes I have collected of murder cases. I found your Marion Gilchrist, a brutal crime by all accounts. A man called Oscar Slater was identified as the man in the pale-coloured overcoat and accused and found guilty of the murder. And I can't see any mention of myself whatsoever in the case," Sir Arthur Conan Doyle said, a hint of disappointment in his voice. "The man in the pale-coloured overcoat. Mmm, quite a good title for a book, that," he mused.

"I don't understand. It wasn't Oscar Slater. He was innocent. I chased the man in the pale-coloured overcoat here earlier. That's when I knocked over your plant," Sandy replied, indicating the mess on the carpet from the spilled soil and broken pot. "Then I saw him shot."

"And you're sure you are not dead?" Sir Arthur asked.

"No! I'm not dead," Sandy replied, almost laughing. "I'm from the past. Well, I'm actually from the future, but I travelled to the past through the magic lantern beam," she indicated to the projector. "And now I'm here."

Sir Arthur suddenly shot up out of his seat again and marched over to the magic lantern, which he now viewed with awe. He pulled a small magnifying glass out of his pocket and inspected every inch of it in close detail.

"This amazing machine! I would never have dreamed that it could transport you through time and space. So, you are originally from…?" Sir Arthur paused, waiting for Sandy's answer.

"2016," Sandy offered.

"One hundred years into the future! Tell me, who wins this damned war? No, no, don't tell me. I probably shouldn't know that. No, no, I need to know. Who wins?" Sir Arthur begged.

"We do," Sandy answered simply.

Sir Arthur glanced at the unopened telegram on his desk. He had forgotten about it in the unusual turn of events. He dreaded what its contents held. His son Kingsley was fighting at the front in France and a telegram could mean only one thing; something awful had happened to him. He opened it and read it. Sandy watched the colour drain from his face.

"Is everything ok?" Sandy asked at length.

"My son Kingsley is at the war front. He has been injured. He is on his way home," Sir Arthur replied, the words choked with emotion.

Sandy didn't know what to say for a moment. "Did you say this is 1916?"

"Yes, it's the 7th of July, 1916." Sir Arthur replied.

"Then, believe me, he's had a lucky escape. We just did the Battle of the Somme at school, and it was the most brutal battle ever in war history. Literally thousands of soldiers were killed," Sandy explained. "If he is on his way home, then he'll be safe."

"Thank you." Sir Arthur replied, his eyes glistening. "Perhaps he is one of the lucky ones, then." He carefully put the telegram back on his desk and stared at it.

Sandy stood silently watching and waiting. She didn't know what else she could say. Then, Sir Arthur suddenly seemed to brighten.

"Yes, I am sure you are right. You would know because you are from the future," he said, then returned his attention back to the exciting matter at hand. "You say that your adventure started at your school?" he asked.

"Not at my school. We went on a ghost hunt to the old theatre," said Sandy.

"Ah, yes. The old theatre."

"Yeah, and you must remember because you started all of this!"

"I started all of this?" Sir Arthur Conan Doyle was mystified by the girl's insistence.

Sandy stared at the author. "You left the magic lantern to the Panopticon in your will. You said it was to be kept in a vault until 2nd November 2016, when it was to be delivered to the Panopticon in time for my school's sponsored ghost hunt. You even mentioned my school's name."

Arthur Conan Doyle's eyebrows shot up. "Why, this is extraordinary! Pickard's Panopticon in Glasgow?"

"Yes," said Sandy.

"I don't understand. Why would I leave the magic lantern to the Panopticon? I just bought it from there..."

"You just bought it from there?" asked Sandy.

"Yes, from an auction. I was sent the auction catalogue anonymously and the magic lantern was indicated as a highlight. I would like to know why I was sent it, and by whom," he smiled, "I expect I will find out in the fullness of time."

"I don't know who sent it to you, but I know why, it was so I could use it to travel to 1908 and help you catch Miss Gilchrist's murderer and stop the King's secret from coming out," said Sandy.

"I see your point," acknowledged Sir Arthur, who was now finding the revelations of the last hour more than even his imaginative mind could process. Here was a girl from 2016, dressed as a boy from 1908, chasing a man in a pale-coloured overcoat, who had been involved in the murder of an old lady and was shot dead in some other time, and all to keep a King's secret? Or was it because he wanted the valuable diamond brooch? Whatever the case, it was apparently all because of this magic lantern - all because of him! It was damned exciting! The game was afoot!

"Well, then, I suppose I had better write my will, hadn't I?" he said. "It seems to be, by what you have told me, the only sensible thing to do."

He closed the large black folio of newspaper cuttings that still lay open and pushed it away to the side, then pulled a sheet of paper out of the desk drawer. He sat down, dipped a pen in the inkwell and began to write.

7th July 1916. The Last Will and Testament of Sir Arthur Ignatius Conan Doyle. His pen raced across the page. He paused. "What school is it that you are attending when you visit the Panopticon?"

"Thornliebank High," she replied. "And it's the 2nd of November 2016."

When he had finished writing his will, he folded it and placed it in an envelope which he addressed to his lawyers. He then pulled a second piece of paper out and wrote another letter, which he blotted and read back to Sandy.

July 7th, 1916
Dear Sir,

You will think this an odd sort of bequest, but I can assure you that this is no ordinary projector. It is imperative that this magic lantern be used on the night of the 2nd of November 2016, when children from Thornliebank High School will be carrying out a ghost hunt in the Panopticon music hall. I cannot explain why, but it is vital that this wish be fulfilled. The future of us all depends upon it. I beg you not to take this request as a hoax and leave it in your trust to ensure that my final wish is granted.

Yours Sincerely,
Sir Arthur Conan Doyle

"Does that sound right to you?" he asked.

"Yep," she nodded.

Sir Arthur folded the letter and put it in an envelope which he addressed, 'To the Curator of the Panopticon, Trongate, Glasgow. Not to be opened before the evening of the 2nd November, 2016.'

"Done," he said. "One letter to the Panopticon curator of 2016 and another to my lawyers instructing them that the magic lantern is to be kept in a bank vault from the time of my death, which I hope is still far in the future," he looked at Sandy for confirmation. Sandy shrugged.

"I dunno when you die," she answered.

"Well, from the time of my death, whenever that will be, until the night of your ghost hunt." He looked at Sandy for verification and Sandy smiled back. "Tell me, Sandy, how do we meet in 1908?"

"You received an anonymous letter which told you to go to the Panopticon and look for a gang of boys in the zoo. You came and found us," Sandy replied.

"When did I receive this letter?" Sir Arthur asked.

"Well, you arrived on the second day I was there, so I guess you must have got the note on the 22nd of December or maybe the 23rd." Sandy answered.

Sir Arthur's eyes lit up. "You say it was anonymous?"

"Yeah. But you said it wasn't the fact that it was anonymous that interested you, but that the handwriting was identical to your own... as if someone had cleverly forged it," answered Sandy.

"Then perhaps it was I who wrote it," he said, as he pulled out another sheet of paper from his drawer and refilled his pen.

After he had finished writing, he placed the new note in another envelope, which he addressed to himself and handed to Sandy.

"Now, I want you to go back to the 21st of December 1908 and send this letter to me. Try and catch the last post - then you had better get back to where you left me in 1908," Sir Arthur instructed.

"I will, and, yes, I had better get back," Sandy replied. "See ya later - or should that be earlier?" she said with a little salute as she switched the magic lantern back on. It flared instantly into brilliance, and she jumped through the beam that swallowed her up.

Sir Arthur was suddenly alone again. He returned to his desk and stared across the room at the magic lantern that still blazed away. Then, suddenly, his mind began to fill with new memories. He remembered receiving a mysterious letter in a hand identical to his own, he remembered finding the boys in the basement zoo, encountering the magic lantern for the first time, discovering a diamond brooch wrapped in a handkerchief at the back of a monkey cage - and he remembered that Sandy is a girl.

It seems the plan had worked.

Chapter Thirty-Four

Mack Millan, the Boy Comic

When Sandy stepped into the beam in 1916 she had squeezed her eyes tight shut and concentrated as hard as she could on the time destination she wanted. She wanted to go back to December 21st, 1908, arriving no later than 4 o'clock between the afternoon and evening shows. She focused her thoughts by chanting, "21st of December, 1908, at 4 o'clock, don't be late," over and over - and then suddenly she felt the familiar floor-dropping, stomach-jolting plummet through time.

She fell for less than a minute before landing heavily on a concrete floor. Where were the wooden planks of the stage? She opened her eyes and looked around her. She wasn't on the stage of the Panopticon, but in what appeared to be a small workshop. It was in shadowy darkness, except for the light from the magic lantern, but the shrieks and yowls from beyond the walls told her she was in the basement zoo. Probably in old Mr Hill's workshop. The magic lantern blared away on a work bench covered in tools. The electric bulb sat next to it, lifeless and dark, still to be installed. Sandy wondered for a moment how the magic lantern was still illuminated, without any kind of lamp or bulb, but then thought to herself that a ghostpowered magic lantern probably didn't need them. The light it gave off when it was sending a person through time and space was not the same as that emitted by any light bulb, candle, or lamp.

The radiant light suddenly flared brighter, filling the whole room with a wash of white brilliance that made her squint as if staring into the sun. A figure appeared in the centre of the wash and Sandy instantly dived beneath the workbench on which the magic lantern rested. She could see filthy feet and ragged trouser hems. She could smell dirt and the high, rank odour of stale sweat. Before the lantern light went out, Sandy caught a glimpse of a skeletal man. Was it the man in the pale-coloured overcoat? Now, plunged into darkness, the man felt around and cautiously trod the three steps to the door. He opened it, briefly filling the little room with the sounds and smells of the zoo beyond, as he stepped across the threshold. The door closed behind him and Sandy, crouched beneath the workbench, wondered where he had come from to be in such a stinking and dishevelled state. She waited a few moments before emerging from her hiding place and then, carefully, feeling in front of her, she stepped through the darkness and across the small room to the door. She slowly opened it an inch and peered out. The zoo was full of the usual crowd and the skeleton man was nowhere to be seen. She took in a deep breath and stepped out into the maelstrom of noise and people, disappearing into the crowd just as Tam and old Mr. Hill were approaching the workshop to finish fixing up the magic lantern for that evening's show.

* * *

The tollbooth bell struck four times as she left the Panopticon and made her way along the Trongate to the post office. She knew she had plenty of time as long as it was the 21st of December. She spotted a newsboy standing on the corner of King Street. When he looked up, Sandy saw it was Jamie, but he didn't recognise her. How could he? They hadn't met yet and wouldn't for another few hours.

"What day is it?" she asked.

He looked at her as though she were simple and curtly replied that it was Monday the 21st of December. Sandy felt a deep sense of relief. The time and date were exactly right.

"Thanks. See ya later," she called to the boy, as she briskly strode up the street to the post office.

She waited in the short queue and bought a stamp with her last penny, which she stuck on the letter to Sir Arthur. The gnarled old man that served her gave her a questioning look when he saw the addressee. "Sir Arthur Conan Doyle, is it, wee man?"

"Yes, sir," Sandy replied.

The old man tutted as he placed it into a mail sack for the Edinburgh post.

"It'll not get there 'til tomorrow morning, now," he said.

"That's okay, thanks," Sandy replied and left the post office to set about her next task. To do that, she needed to get back into the Panopticon. The question was how. She didn't have any money left to pay for a ticket and because she wouldn't meet Harry the zookeeper until tomorrow, she had no hope of sneaking in through the zoo. She had to get back in as soon as possible, back to where she had left her friends on December 29th, and she had to do it before she arrived from her ghost hunt in 2016. She didn't think her 2016 self would cope with coming face to face with her 1908 self. She would freak.

She sneaked around the corner and up the New Wynd towards the stage door with the slim hope that it had been left ajar. As she approached it, the door banged open and a young man with a look of pure panic on his face came rushing out, nearly knocking her off her feet. As he ran past her, George, the stage manager, stepped out and into the lane.

"Never mind running, Tam. You'd better start flappin' yer arms and flying. If you don't get they films back here by the 7:30 p.m. show, Mr. P will have your guts for garters!" he shouted after the boy.

Sandy stared after him as he ran up the lane. *That was Tam*, she thought to herself. "Tam!" she called after him. He didn't hear her and he quickly disappeared around the corner into the dense crowd of the Trongate. She thought for a moment that she should run after him, stop him from going to the west end somehow, but she knew she couldn't. She had to get into the Panopticon and back to the magic lantern as soon as she could. George, the stage manager, was standing in the doorway and lighting the stub of a cigarette which poked through his wiry moustache. He was staring at her.

"What do you want?" he asked when Sandy approached.

"I was, I mean, I, I…" Sandy stuttered.

"Front doors are on the Trongate. Pay yer ticket at the front desk," he said as he shook out his match and turned to go back in.

Sandy knew she had to get in, whatever it took, and so she said the only thing she could think of that would get her through the door for free. "But I'm one of the turns," she said, hoping she had said the right thing.

"Oh, you're a turn, are you? And who are you on the bill?" he asked, looking at what he thought was a small boy up and down.

"I'm not actually on the bill. I was, well, I was hoping that Mr. Pickard would let me perform," Sandy said hopefully.

"I suppose that young fool Tam encouraged you, eh?"

"Tam?" Sandy asked, bewildered.

"Don't play the idiot with me. I heard you shout after him," spat the stage manager.

"Well, I don't technically know Tam. I know his brothers,"

"Oh, ya dae, do ya? Well, amateur night's Friday and auditions are at 11:00 a.m., every morning. Come back then," he said, clearly annoyed by Sandy's persistence.

"But I can't. I won't be here in the morning. Oh, please, please let me have a go. I've been told this is the best place to start your stage career. I've heard Mr. Pickard encourages young acts. Oh, please, Mr. Saprini."

"So, you know me, dae ya, laddie? That Jamie and his daft wee brother been telling you about me, eh? That I'm a bit of a soft touch?" he said, and grabbed Sandy roughly by the ear.

"No, sir!" she squealed through the pain. "They just told me that you're the boss really and that no one gets a job unless seeing you first," Sandy appeased, hoping this plea would work. It did. George seemed to be relenting.

"All right, lad," he said. "What dae ya do?"

Sandy hadn't thought about that. She didn't really have any theatrical talents whatsoever, but she did know a couple of jokes.

"I'm a comic," she said confidently.

"A comic, eh? What's your bill banter?"

"My what?"

"What do you call yourself?"

"Oh, um," she thought for a moment. "Mack Millan?" she gingerly offered.

"Well, Mack Millan, boy comic, you wait here and I will ask Mr. Pickard. He does like to encourage young talent - and you're lucky, we're short an act. The acrobats are a man down after the matinee - a well-aimed rivet from the balcony," George said, chuckling slightly as he pushed Sandy back out of the door and into the lane.

She stood in the cold and drizzly dark, hugging herself to keep warm and jumping from foot to foot. Had he really gone to ask Mr. Pickard? As the minutes lengthened, she began to doubt it. Finally, the door opened, and George reappeared.

"You, lad. Mr. Pickard has agreed to let you perform tonight. Two minutes and no more. Be back here for 7:00

p.m., and don't expect to get paid," he called, shutting the door behind him again.

Sandy had nowhere else to go. She huddled against the stage door, slightly sheltered from the wind, though lashed by the rain, and waited.

About fifty minutes later, just as Sandy was losing the last of the feeling in her fingers and toes, a flurry of performers arrived, rushing up the lane in costume and grease paint, carrying bags and props. George let them in, and Sandy snuck through the door with them. George noticed. "See you're still here then?"

"Yes," she replied.

"Two minutes and no more. Wait in the band room 'til I call for ya," George instructed.

Sandy followed the other turns through the music hall and waited with them in the band room at the back of the stalls. She chatted with the dancers, who fawned over her, telling her what a cute boy she was and what a heartbreaker she would grow up to be. She listened to the comic as he complained about the audience. "Cor, I tell you, if I have another audience like that one earlier, I'm giving up and going back to coal mining."

"I hear that poor acrobat's head got split open when that rivet hit him earlier," a woman in a red gown was saying.

"Never lost his balance, though. I'll give him that," replied the comic. "I'm giving them a comedy song at the next show. It worked a charm in the Metropole earlier."

This was going to be hard. Sandy hated being the centre of attention. She never volunteered for school plays, not after the horror of forgetting her one line in Oliver, and, right now, as the full reality of what she was about to do dawned on her, she was terrified. She began rehearsing her jokes over and over in her head. They were rotten and she was useless at telling them, but it was the only way she could get on stage and in front of the magic lantern in time. Hopefully, Mr. Hill had finished fixing it, and it would be standing at the back of the stalls. It had to be there.

The first two acts had already gone on and the dancing girls were next. Sandy squeezed out into the stalls to watch them but she couldn't see anything except the backs of the people in the crowd, so she returned to the band room to wait. When the dancers came back, one of them - a red-headed girl called Elsie - told Sandy that after the magic lantern show it would be the comic, and Sandy would be on after him. Good, the magic lantern is out there. Hopefully, as soon as I walk on stage, the magic beam will zap me off again before anyone gets a chance to lob anything, she thought. Or worse, pee on me.

Sandy fought her way out of the band room and began the battle across the auditorium to the stage. She squeezed between the closely-packed bodies and, as she was elbowing and shoving her way through the dirty, smelly crowd, she suddenly became aware of a sweet, sickly perfume. It pervaded her nostrils. She looked up and straight into the face of Miss Anne Birrell, dressed in a man's cloak with a hat drawn low over her eyes. For the briefest moment, Sandy stared straight into her eyes. Then the woman was swallowed up by the crowd. The skeleton man in the pale-coloured overcoat followed close behind. She wanted to go after them or warn Tam, somehow push him out of the way or run to the street and call for the police. She had to do something; She knew they were obviously after Tam. This must be when they murdered him, she thought. She began to push her way back through the horde towards where Tam stood - but a hand suddenly grabbed her shoulder and moustachioed lips brushed her left ear as a familiar voice said, "Leave it, Sandy, it's too dangerous. You have to get back to the future."

Sandy looked up and into the face of the 1916 Arthur Conan Doyle. His eyes were gleaming. "Go - now!" he commanded, and then - like Miss Birrell - he disappeared into the crowd and smoke.

By the time she got to the stage, she felt bruised and battered from battling through the crush of people. The comic was just finishing his act and the stage manager was standing at the side of the stage with his arms folded, scowling into the audience.

"There you are, at last! Talk about cutting it fine. Now get up there," he urged as he hustled Sandy into the narrow wings. Before she knew it, her act was being announced.

"Go on, you'll be fine, son," encouraged George, the stage manager, as he shoved her on.

The footlights were too bright and the tobacco smoke too thick for Sandy to see anything of the audience. She stood there frozen for a moment, waiting for the welcome sense of travelling through time. It didn't come and the audience began a slow, rhythmic stamping of impatience.

"Go on," George shouted from the wings. "Before they turn on you."

Thump-thump-thump-thump went the feet of the audience, and Sandy felt terrified. Thump-thump-thump. She had to do something, say something. Taking a deep breath, she bellowed as loud as she could, "What did the stamp say to the envelope?" The thumping stopped and a more terrifying, expectant silence replaced it. Sandy felt every eye in the house staring at her, waiting. "Stick with me and we'll go places," she announced, rather apologetically.

A cacophony of boos and jeers rang around the music hall and Sandy stood still, willing the magic lantern to switch on and zap her out of there. With her eyes tight shut, she fixed on that thought and visualised her friends' faces as she had left them on 29th of December. She visualised each face behind her closed eyes as if they stood before her. She crossed her fingers and wished as hard as she could that the magic lantern would zap her away to those few days in the future. So much had happened since she had last seen her friends. She had so much she had to tell them. Then she felt something whistle past her face. She opened her eyes just as the magic lantern beam flared into life and suddenly the music hall and its vicious audience faded away through a darkening tunnel as she felt herself being pulled quickly upwards and away.

Chapter Thirty-Five

Arrival in Hell

Sandy was pulled up with such force and at such speed that she felt sick. She looked down. Far below in the fading distance she could see herself in her puffer coat and fluffy boots land heavily on the wooden, debris-covered stage of the Panopticon. She braced herself for the sudden drop she knew would happen - should happen - any moment when she landed back in the music hall a split second after she had left friends on the 29th of December. But the feeling didn't come. Instead, she continued to rise. Something was wrong. She knew this was taking too long. She began to shake, then she felt herself jolt, first to the left, and then to the right, and then up again.

"Take me back to them. Take me to the 29th of December 1908!" she shouted into the darkness.

Suddenly, it felt like the whole of time had slowed down. She moved her arms and legs as if she was swimming through the dense liquid of time, and she tried to move herself in the darkness to where she thought she should be, to where she thought her friends were. The air around her was thick and her movements were in slow motion. At last, she plummeted down, landing in mud - wet, sticky mud. Torrential rain lashed down on her, soaking her instantly.

She could tell it was night, but the darkness was illuminated by bright flashes and loud, booming bangs. Bombs and gunshots penetrated the world around her and made her eardrums vibrate as the ground beneath her shook. Where were her friends? Where was the music hall? Where was she?

As the explosions blasted in every direction, and the freezing rain soaked her, she couldn't see where she could run to safety. Feeling utterly hopeless and desperately lost, Sandy squatted down in the puddled mud, placed her hands over her ears, and screamed into the night.

A new and terrifying journey had begun.

Follow the next story in…

Part Two

The Lantern of Terror

Releasing 2025

About the Author

Judith Bowers has been writing since she could hold a pen. She has had several works published including *The Best of Edinburgh and Glasgow*, a pamphlet called *The Obscure History of the Merchant, Stan Laurel and Other Stars of the Panopticon,* and *Glasgow's Lost Theatre*. Researched and written over thirty history segments for various programmes and walking tours. History has been her life, especially the quirky, strange and gruesome, but she has always wanted to write fiction, and with *The Magic Lantern*, Judith blends her passion for history and the love of a certain music hall to weave a mystery told in three parts, and this is part one *The Magic Lantern.*

Other Works By this Author

The Best of Edinburgh and Glasgow

Stan Laurel and Other Stars of the Panopticon

Glasgow's Lost Theatre

Judith Bowers